LIVES
WITHOUT
END

ANNE M. McLOUGHLIN

POOLBEG

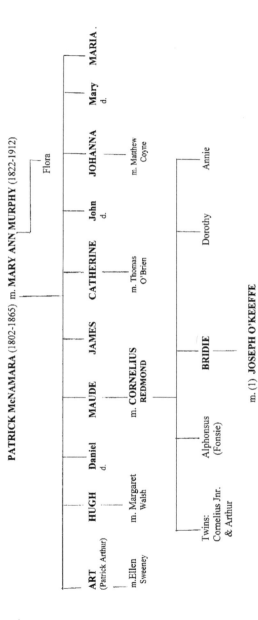

PATRICK McNAMARA (1802-1865) m. **MARY ANN MURPHY** (1822-1912)

Flora

ART
(Patrick Arthur)

m.Ellen
Sweeney

HUGH

m. Margaret
Walsh

Daniel
d.

MAUDE

m. **CORNELIUS
REDMOND**

JAMES

CATHERINE

m. Thomas
O'Brien

John
d.

JOHANNA

m. Matthew
Coyne

Mary
d.

MARIA.

Twins:
Cornelius Jnr.
& Arthur

Alphonsus
(Fonsie)

BRIDIE

Dorothy

Annie

m. (1) **JOSEPH O'KEEFFE**

m. (2) **SEAN RYAN**

Mary Josephine

m. (3) **MICKIE JOE DOYLE**

Published 2021
by Poolbeg Press Ltd.
123 Grange Hill, Baldoyle,
Dublin 13, Ireland
Email: poolbeg@poolbeg.com

A catalogue record for this book is available from the British Library.

ISBN 978178199-425-2

www.poolbeg.com

About the Author

Anne McLoughlin was born in Dublin, Ireland, and now divides her time between there and her home in rural Wexford.

She has written stories for the RTÉ children's programme *Anything Goes*, has published a series of local social-history books and written articles for newspapers and magazines.

Highly commended in the Colm Tóibín International Short Story Competition in the Wexford Literary Festival, this gave her the encouragement to begin working on the novels that have been niggling at the back of her brain for years.

Her debut novel *Lives Apart* was also published by Poolbeg.

Acknowledgements

I owe a deep debt of gratitude to the following:

The extended O'Keeffe family from County Clare and the USA, who provided lots of raw material from which I plucked ideas for development in my fictional novels.

Patricia O'Reilly, my former tutor in UCD and the other members of the class for their constructive comments at a very early stage in Bridie's life.

When it came to the next level, my rough-draft readers – Gemma McCrohan, Margaret Martin, Mary Doyle and Jenny Burns Duffy – were brave enough to give me their constructive criticism.

Psychiatrist Ivor Browne who cast his expert eye over the chapters relating to Bridie's brush with the psychiatric system. Any historical errors that may have crept in are mine and mine alone.

My neighbours and friends in Ballygarrett, County Wexford, from whom I've learned so much about rural life. In particular, I'd like to thank the extended Casey family who took me to their bosom and made me one of their family over forty years ago. Their friendship and love have been such an enormous bonus to my life in Peppardscastle, County Wexford, and the number of unfortunate situations they've rescued me from over the years are too numerous to admit.

My extended family, friends and former RTÉ colleagues

for their endless patience in listening to me going on about the books I've been writing. They've waited so long to see the fruits of that labour, I'm not sure how much longer they could have sustained their enthusiasm. I imagine they are well pleased that I have reached the publishing stage so they can now have a bit of peace.

My pal Alice Walsh who once again managed to make me look presentable with her photography skills.

As for Poolbeg Press – publisher Paula Campbell, editor Gaye Shortland and the production/design team David Prendergast and Lee Devlin – huge thanks for their expertise and encouragement at all stages of the process. They're a great team to work with.

To all the readers of *Lives Apart*, my first book in the 'Lives' series, many of whom gave feedback and complimentary comments – many thanks. Your enthusiasm for a good book keeps me going – where would we writers be without you? I hope you enjoy *Lives Without End* as much as you enjoyed the first book.

If there's another world she lives in bliss.
If there's none she made the best of this.

Adapted from Robert Burns

Prologue

When they found her, both the nieces were surprised by the expression on her face, although at first neither said anything. That came later. Only barely there, a mere trace, but it was most definitely recognisable as a smile.

The morning sun was well up in the sky. A pale beam lit her face, slanting in through the gap where the curtains didn't quite meet. To those who first came upon her, what they saw was a woman enjoying basking in its rays. She was still warm, her face smooth with the peace that descends upon one who has slipped away without a struggle.

Neighbours arrived to the house in their ones and twos as if signalled. Like a well-oiled machine primed for the ritual, it was the women who took charge while the men were dispatched to organise gravediggers, undertaker and priest. Candlesticks, lace cloths and holy water, on standby for such occasions, appeared from nowhere as if by a miracle.

"Has anyone a match?"

No answer. Just a shuffle in the tweed pockets of the men, matches handed over and the candles were lit. A decade of the rosary started. No-one minded by whom.

"The First Glorious Mystery . . . the Resurrection . . ."

They were glad that someone else had taken the

1

initiative, each picking up the chant, joining in one by one, until the end of one "Hail Mary" overlapped the start of the next. Almost imperceptible, but it was there, the increase in the pace as it galloped towards the *"Glory be to the Father, and to the Son, and to the Holy Ghost . . ."*

A brief pause followed the *"Amen"*, before the leader, comfortable now in his uncontested role, led them into the next decade. "The Second Glorious Mystery – The Ascension into Heaven . . ."

Those kneeling felt the hardness of the floorboards. The shuffling began as they shifted their weight from one arthritic joint to the other. Some of the men knelt on one knee and used the other as a prop for their elbow, hoping they didn't look like they were on the side-lines of a hurling match. They envied those old or crippled enough to have been offered one of the two chairs in the room, as they rested their heads on their hands and droned on in muffled tones.

It was with a new wind that they all joined in the *"Eternal rest grant unto her, O Lord . . ."* Those who had faded out joined back in when the chant arrived at the *"and may she rest in peace"*, and by the final *"Amen"* half of them were already on their feet.

Large teapots had appeared from neighbouring houses, loaves of bread and scones and jams arrived. Everyone was fed whether or not they had just stood up from the table in their own house. No-one refused the hospitality for fear of giving offence.

They took turns sitting with her, never leaving her alone. There were always at least two. Some were content to stay around for hours. To leave would mean they might miss some important insight into Bridie's past life, a little nugget hitherto unknown to them. And, sure, they'd nothing important to do at home anyway. Others might sit

2

with her, a flicker of guilt at their straying thoughts which slipped over to all the jobs that needed doing in their own homes, children to be fed, cattle to be milked. They sat there hoping for someone to enter the room so that they could stand up and offer their chair to them and depart quietly to get on with their own business.

The sepia photograph sat on the top of the chest of drawers. They glanced from the smiling woman standing beside Mickey Joe in the wedding picture to the woman lying peacefully on the pillow. Each gazed at her face in the silence, at the wonder of her smooth complexion that had always attracted comments. They marvelled that for these few short hours Bridie had lost over fifty years from her face. Had travelled back, shedding all time and transformed into that younger woman again.

"Some beauty in her day, wasn't she?" The comment was barely more than a whisper.

"Still is. Would you look at her. Not a wrinkle and she nearing the hundred."

Silence fell again.

That she'd not had an easy life had earlier been the subject of much discussion. Looking at the expression that rested so comfortably on her face not a soul would have guessed it.

"Poor Bridie. Didn't have much to smile about." The pronouncement was made with the certitude of one who considered herself more than just a neighbour. No-one contradicted her, all unaware that they knew but the half of it.

"She was a survivor alright, our Bridie. You'd have to hand that to her. Have to admire her."

Each mourner departed reassured by the evidence before them, that in her final hours she was at last at peace with herself and the world.

3

BRIDIE

Chapter 1

Knocknageeha, County Clare, Ireland
1895

Bridie often wished she'd known Pops McNamara. Mary Ann loved telling her stories about him.

"I really wish you'd met him, Bridie. He'd have loved you." Mary Ann passed the bundle of bed linen to her granddaughter.

"I wish I had too, Gran." Bridie took the pile and sat down.

"You can leave them up on the bed. I'll put them away later." Mary Ann laid the iron on the stand to cool.

"The way everyone talks about Pops, it sounds like he was great fun."

"He was that alright." Mary Ann smiled. "A hard worker though, but he never took life too seriously. A good mixture. And he died far too young." She sighed. "The two of you would have got on well. I know it."

"Did any of the others know him, Granny?" She tried to do the sums.

"No, Bridie. Unfortunately not. Patrick was gone before any of you grandchildren were born." Mary Anne sighed. "I really missed him then. No-one to share the joy of all your births. He'd have loved watching you all grow up."

PATRICK

Chapter 2

Knocknageeha, County Clare, Ireland
1844

Patrick sat by the fire. He threw a handful of kindling on the glowing embers and watched as the twigs blazed, making it spring into life again. He then laid a couple of sods of turf on the flames and carefully added one of the logs he had earlier left to dry on the hearth. Reaching into the basket he took out three more logs. They felt slightly damp, so he placed them close to the fire to dry for later.

He lay back and relaxed against the headrest of the armchair, listening to the hiss and sizzle of the flames. The patter of rain outside beat a tune on the window, the two sounds mingling in a companionable rhythm in the quiet of the kitchen.

It was too early to be nodding off, so he picked up the newspaper but the fading light of the dark evening made reading a strain. A hard labouring in the yard earlier had left him satisfied with his day's work. Lucky he'd got it done before the weather broke. He'd put a finish on the cleaning out of the barn, a job he'd been working on for days, slotted in between the other daily chores. It had left him too tired to make the effort at battling the fading light, so folding the newspaper he laid it on the stool beside him and rested his head back again.

Gazing into the fire, as the minutes passed he enjoyed the looseness of his mind wandering backwards and forwards. It swung hither and thither until he arrived at contemplation of the future. It was here the pendulum slowed and seemed to get stuck, despite his best efforts to swing it back to less worrying thoughts.

The notion of spending the next thirty or forty winters sitting at home alone on a wet evening, listening to the howling wind rattle the windowpanes did not fill him with joy. A lot of old farmers around did it and on the surface appeared contented enough, but it was not what he wanted for his own future. And so it was at the age of forty-two that Patrick decided it was time to survey his life and come up with a plan.

None of the facts had changed. He'd waited a long time for it to happen, to fall into place like it seemed to do for others, but for him it hadn't. A large farm, no children, a spinster sister who was always going to be that way, and advancing age. What he needed now was a wife and with a bit of luck a family. With the simplicity of these basic mathematics he had no difficulty making a decision and working out his strategy.

The waiting was over.

One crisp sunny Sunday in March he took extra care washing himself.

"Not bad. Not bad at all, Paddy, me lad." He admired his reflection in the cracked mirror as he shaved.

He rinsed the razor and dried his hands.

"Any woman's fancy, wouldn't you think?" He ran the comb through his thinning brown hair one final time, patting a wayward strand down.

Selecting his best shirt and tie and dressing in the suit reserved for funerals and special occasions he set out for

Mass, after which he would proceed to the door of Mary Ann Murphy on his mission.

Patrick Joseph McNamara was the only son born after six daughters to what were described locally as 'big farmers' in the middle of County Clare. By the time he hit forty his parents were dead and five of his six sisters married, leaving him in the homeplace.

He ran the farm single-handed except for the help of his sister Agnes. Aggie was going to be there for life. That was a certainty, just because that was the way of things. She was born deaf and dumb. On top of that she was a bit slow. As a child, her being unable to speak was attributed to her deafness but, growing up, the way she turned at the sound of the dog barking or someone yelling her name suggested that she had some hearing. Short sharp sounds emitted at a certain level seemed to penetrate.

She went along to school with the other children in the family. The teachers never worried if Aggie didn't attend and, on the days she did, they weren't concerned which of the two classrooms she went to, as she just sat there quietly at her desk, looking around her, not bothering anyone.

At break time in the school yard she rarely joined in the games, just sat on the wooden bench and watched, eating the jam sandwich one of her sisters had given her.

"You alright there, Aggie?"

They knew that their smiling over at her was enough to confirm that she was part of them, one of the gang, part of their lives. They'd never worked it out, never thought about it, but they knew she was confident that when there was something she could do they would include her. Like when she was needed to hold one end of a rope for a game of skipping. Aggie knew she had to clutch the knot of the rope firmly in both her hands. Hunching her shoulders, she looked across at her sister who turned the rope from the other end, a tense importance imprinted on her little face as she held the rope rigid.

"Good girl, Aggie, that's the way."

There was always something that Aggie was useful for.

At home it was the same. She was given little jobs to occupy her. Washing windows or collecting kindling for the fire. Nothing that needed doing in a hurry. Aggie had her own pace. No concept of urgency. A picture of contentment as she went about her tasks. Completely engrossed.

Even though there was a barn full of fire logs and twigs she was often sent out to the field with an old sack to fill. On her return she would empty the sack in the middle of the yard and take out the wicker basket. With a face set in determined concentration she brushed it out, removing the cobwebs and dust. Only when she started to fill the basket twig by twig in a pattern, visible only to herself, would her face relax, a beatific expression radiating serenity. On the top she would lay her treasures, the pretty sprigs of cones from the larch trees and the large single ones from the pines.

But she never spoke much. Just the occasional little sounds. That was Aggie and she just slotted in.

Chapter 3

1845

The Irish Potato Famine was just about to strike when Patrick McNamara and Mary Ann Murphy were married early in 1845. The celebrations were not marred in any way as nobody who danced to the music of the local musicians that evening was to know what was winging its way towards them.

The failure of the potato crop that year, disastrous for many, went over the heads of the pair of lovers with eyes only for each other. They took it as a once-in-a-lifetime misfortune, that saw some families struggling more than others.

Patrick and Mary Ann had pigs, sheep and cattle and the kitchen rafters were never without a big ham hanging from them, slowly smoking to a rich brown by the open fire. The vegetable garden, apart from the potatoes, was still productive with turnips and cabbages and carrots. The orchard, their inheritance from previous generations of McNamaras, gave a plentiful supply of apples, pears and plums. Patrick, gifted with green fingers, took pride in propagating fruit bushes. Over the years, whenever he visited an orchard with gooseberries or blackcurrants, especially when they were of a different variety to his own, he had taken cuttings and nursed them to maturity, lovingly feeding them with rotted cow and horse manure twice a year.

The potato harvest failed a second year.

For the small farmers and cottagers, with their dependence on a sole crop for survival, the effects were devastating. For the McNamaras and their like, things were different. Mary Ann rose to the challenge and became creative in the kitchen in order to eke out the alternative provisions and make up for the loss of the potatoes.

The talk of the hardships for many headlined the chat around the country. Mary Ann went to bed, thankful that it was on a full stomach. But as tales that earlier had seemed far-fetched began to move closer to her locality, the reality and scale of the problem began to come between her and her sleep.

While she could do little to help, the situation became more difficult to ignore. She gave something to each caller to the farm. A couple of eggs here, a turnip or a few carrots there. Not much, but with the numbers increasing each week she had to stretch the meagre rations so that everyone got a little something.

"You can't save the country single-handed, love," Patrick reminded her gently when he saw their stocks depleting. "Everyone has to help out."

"You try telling that to the cadavers that call to this door!" It came out with an anger she knew was unfairly directed at him. "How could I refuse a drop of milk for the baby when that woman called this morning?"

"I know, I know." He could see the tears forming. "That's not what I meant. But we're just going to have to pace ourselves. We've no idea how long this situation is going to go on."

There was sense in what he said. That, she had to acknowledge. But more importantly in what he didn't say.

11

It was the Kelly family with their twelve children living at the end of the lane that provided her with a focus. Something to take her mind off what might lie in the future for all of them. She could only deal with the present and it wasn't a problem to find excuses to call to the cottage.

"Patrick was wondering if one of the young lads might be free to come up to the farm today. There's a cattle byre that needs cleaning out?" She needed something to dispel the feeling of helplessness.

Patrick was leaning against the wall of the byre taking a breather.

"Will you go in there to Mary Ann and bring me out a mug of tae and a slice of bread and jam?"

He sent the young fellow in to the kitchen, knowing she would feed the lad before she attended to himself. He could afford to wait.

He would finish up the work and send the youngster home early. He had seen the energy drain out of him. Just kept him long enough so the lad would feel he had earned his wage and allow the family to hold their heads up. Paying him partially with a box of food to take home ensured the family could get through the week.

They were nearly finished anyway. Patrick had just shovelled the remainder of the rotted manure into the barrow and was having a break before he took this last load around the back to the vegetable garden when he saw the boy coming out of the house with the box.

"Hey, where's me tae? I've a mouth on me too, yeh know?"

"She's bringing it out to yeh in a minute." The boy grinned back at him. His hands were fully occupied carrying the box but he managed to waggle his fingers, an effort at a wave, before heading down the avenue.

12

More jobs followed. One or two a week when the need was there. He knew they made a difference to the family. So long as they managed to stay afloat themselves.

He watched as Mary Ann came out the door, carrying a basket covered with a cloth. Her bump, recently more noticeable, gave him a quiver of pride. A son would be nice, to give him a hand with the farm, but a daughter would be fine too, so long as she was like Mary Ann.

Aggie followed behind her, carrying a jug. He guessed by the care she was taking that it was full. From the distance he could only guess at their conversation. He watched as Mary Ann put her basket on the ground and showed Aggie the best way to place her hands to keep the jug upright. They walked together across the yard, Mary Ann strolling slowly while Aggie, a broad beam on her face, shuffled along beside her.

As they reached the piers that once supported gates leading down the tree-lined avenue to the roadway he saw Aggie stumble, the toe of her black lace-up boot catching on an egg-shaped stone. Even though it was a long time since gates had hung there he hadn't removed it. The smooth granite stone with the bolt-hole, half buried in the gravel in the centre between the two piers remained, just in case he ever got around to replacing the gates.

The buttermilk slopped over the top of the jug. He watched Aggie's face crumple as the liquid deposited a creamy stain down the front of her navy wrap-around apron.

Mary Ann laid her basket on top of the pier and taking the cloth from it made a fuss of mopping Aggie's front. Patrick could see her lips moving and could almost hear the comforting "There, there, no harm done, Aggie" coming from her lips. Just like he'd seen her quell Aggie's storms so many times before.

13

Replacing the cloth, she handed Aggie the basket, swapping it for the jug. A watery smile returned to Aggie's face and, as the two headed off again, a bounce entered Aggie's step, one born of a confidence that the basket's contents were secure. It amused him how Mary Ann, head bobbing, always chatted away to his sister even though he suspected that Aggie hadn't any idea what she was talking about.

"Yeah, I got a good one there."

He pushed himself away from the wall with the boot which had been resting on the ledge and taking the handles of the barrow began pushing his load.

Chapter 4

1848

The grass growing from the thatch was one of the first signs that all was not well in the little cottage. It wasn't the fact that it was growing there – grass would often seed in the rich bed of a thatch. No, it was because it had been left there to expand and thrive over time with no effort made to dislodge its roots. Neddie always kept things shipshape in his own simple way. He would normally have been up on his ladder, fixing and patching the weak spots on the roof, but now that he was gone the place had a neglected air about it.

It was unusual to find the door closed. At this hour the top half of the door would usually be open to let the day in.

Mary Ann knocked on the door and waited. She rapped again and tried to quash the niggle of worry that had entered the silence as she and Aggie stood waiting.

"Hello, anybody home?" She put her ear to the door and listened. A reassuring shuffling came from inside.

"Coming, coming!" The weak voice of someone disturbed from their slumbers answered.

She could hear slow footsteps dragging their way across the floor, followed by the heavy bolt clunking as it was drawn back. The wood of the door scraped on the floor and jammed. Jane Kelly appeared in the narrow opening, almost indistinguishable in the dim interior but for the whiteness of her face.

"Ah, Mary Ann, come in, come on in, and Aggie." She struggled to free the door to allow access.

"Have we called at a bad time, Jane?"

"Sure every time's a bad time now. But I'm glad to see the pair of you." Her face had the red-eyed weariness of defeated spirit.

Inside the cottage signs of neglect were starting to show. The ashes from the fire had built up, spilling over onto the mud floor, no longer gathered and swept out.

Jane took a bundle of rags from a chair, patting the seat of it.

"Sit down, sit down there, won't you?"

"Have you a jug there, Jane, for Aggie to pour the buttermilk into it?"

"You could pour it into that one on the table, Aggie, it's empty. The children will love that for their tea."

"And here's a square of bread to go with it. It's still hot. And a drop of vegetable soup I had left over."

"What would we do without you, Mary Ann? I just don't know. We'd be all dead. Even the yellow meal has run out."

"Sure it's nothing much. And aren't we lucky to have it to share?" Mary Ann dismissed the thanks with a wave of her hand. "Anyway, what I really called for was to see if some of the children might be able to help out with the apple harvest?"

"They'd love it." A faint light lit Jane's pale face. "When do you want them?"

"Well, tomorrow morning would be good. They'd be better at shinning up those trees than myself." Mary Ann laughed. "Especially in my present state. And Patrick hasn't the time."

As they chatted at the table, the face of a young child appeared from the gloom of an upstairs loft. She slowly climbed down the ladder and, like a silent ghost, walked over and leant her head against her mother. Three smaller children, on hearing voices, had come out from the back room and stood in the doorway watching.

"Come over and say thank you to Mary Ann. She brought you something nice for your tea." Jane took the bread and cut a slice each for the children.

"Bring me over the jam here, Daisy, and I'll put a bit on it for you."

The older child, with a new energy, walked over to the cupboard. She took out the container of jam that Mary Ann had delivered on an earlier visit and brought it to the table.

A wail came from the back room.

"Oh, Daisy, will you go in to see to the baby before he wakes up the other two?" Jane sounded weary as she beckoned to the younger ones who were slowly making their way across the room. As they passed Aggie stroked their heads but, oblivious to her affectionate pat, their eyes never left the loaf of bread. Their backs to her, Mary Ann spotted the bones of their shoulders coming through their thin cotton dresses. Disturbing in their prominence. She thanked God for her two healthy children at home, watched over for an hour by Patrick while she made this visit. She knew her offerings weren't enough to save Jane's children from the pangs of hunger, but it might help prevent them starving to death and keep the threat of the workhouse at bay.

Days passed before she had a chance to call again after the apple-picking session. She'd sent the children home with a

17

few boxes and bags of windfalls. She'd divided them up to make them lighter to carry, happy there was enough to keep them going for a few days.

"Tell your mam they're lovely stewed."

The clouds had been heavy all morning but the threatened rain never came. When a watery sun came out early in the afternoon, she decided to take a chance on a walk down the lane.

She passed the garden at the side of the cottage with only a brief glance. The silence was such that it might well have been empty, a stark contrast to earlier times when the ringing voices could be heard drifting up the lane long before she'd arrive at the cottage.

"Hello, Mary Ann."

The light voice surprised her. She turned to see the smiling face of Daisy holding the hand of her little brother who, taking his cue from her, raised his hand in a shy wave. Of the other children sent out to play in the sunshine, two were leaning against the stone wall while three others lolled around on the grass, sunk in a lethargy so deep that it drained the childhood from their pale bodies.

"Hello, children. Is your mother here?"

"Inside."

The drooping children just watched as the Daisy pointed towards the cottage.

Inside two small bodies lay huddled together on the settle bed, dull eyes sunk deep into the navy shadows of their faces. The skin of their dehydrated limbs looked dry and sore. Their arms, no more than abandoned sticks, lay awkwardly across their bodies.

"How are they today, Jane? One of the lads told me some of them weren't too well – when they came over to pick the apples. If I'd realised it was more serious, I'd have come sooner."

"Worse. They haven't managed to keep even a glass of water down." Jane turned away, beckoning Mary Ann over towards the fire. "They're going the same way as poor little Tommy and Seán went last year." She whispered her fear, her pallid face crumpling. "And Neddie. You know, Mary Ann, I'm lost without him. For all his faults he was a great husband."

"I know, Jane, he was a great worker. You must be lost. All gone in the space of a year." Mary Ann put an arm around her shoulders to comfort her. She could feel the bones like twigs under the thin shawl. "I don't know what I'd do if anything happened to my Patrick." She paused. "You're doing very well under the circumstances – this can't last forever. Don't give up now, the children need you more than ever, with their father gone."

"But they've had the diarrhoea for days now. I can't stop it. I'm only afraid the others will catch the cholera."

"We can only hope and pray that doesn't happen. Look, I'll send Aggie down later with a little something for the supper. You have to keep yourself well. We don't want you getting sick too."

Stepping out from the gloom of the cottage, the brilliance of the sunshine almost blinded her.

"Look, Mary Ann!" Daisy had followed her to the gate. "They're for you."

She held up a posy of daisies and buttercups, thrusting them towards Mary Ann.

"Oh, aren't they lovely, Daisy! Just like you. Thank you. I'll put them in water when I get home."

"Can I walk to the top of the lane with you, Mary Ann?"

"You can. I'd like that. But just to the bend. In case your mother is looking for you." You might as well come, child, for as long as you can, was the unspoken thought as she smiled down at the little girl.

Chapter 5

In 1865 Mary Ann McNamara gave birth to her youngest child Maria in the bedroom she shared with her husband. He died shortly after the event at the age of sixty-three, leaving her devastated. It was many, many years later before she was able to joke that he was worn out from having fathered ten children.

Mary Ann, twenty years his junior, was a fine build of a woman. She outlived him by what for many would seem a lifetime, spilling herself over as she did into the next century. She managed to reach the age of ninety, before turning up her toes, having harboured a secret. A very big secret. That she had actually given birth to eleven children not ten, the first of whom was not fathered by her husband Patrick Joseph. He never knew about that one. As far as he was concerned she had given birth to their first child on Christmas Day 1845 – his handsome son. True. Their first. But not her first.

"Patrick McNamara, will you not be standing there in the doorway? Come in here and meet your son," the big comfortable midwife chided him as she bustled around the room. She picked up the basin of water and waited for him to step out of her way.

Mary Ann, her chestnut curls now damp and plastered to her head from her exertions, smiled across at him from where she lay resting in the soft well of the pillows, a bundle in her arms.

He stepped into the room and waited until the nurse had started her journey down the stairs before closing the door and taking a few steps closer. He sat down on the side of the bed and, leaning over, he pulled the towel back and exposed the wrinkled face. A chubby red fist flailed out almost hitting him in the eye, giving him a slight start.

"I think we've got a boxer here." He smiled at her.

Mary Ann noted the wonder written all over his face and studied him as he watched his first-born nuzzling in the towel. Enjoying the quiet silence, she realised that this was possibly the first time her husband had had any close contact with an infant. The youngest of his family, he had grown up being the baby himself.

"D'ye know, I've never seen a new-born child before. It's only now I realise that."

She heard the note of awe in his voice as if he had read her thoughts.

"Well, not one as young as this little lad."

Touching his son's cheek in a way that suggested he was fearful of marking the delicate pink skin with his rough farmer's hand, he glanced shyly at Mary Ann.

"Handsome little devil, isn't he? But then sure how else could he be with a father like me?"

"What are we going to call him?" Mary Ann asked.

She watched as he gazed down at his child. The besotted expression on his face gave no indication that he was even listening. She waited awhile, not wanting to break the spell between them before re-introducing the subject.

21

"I was thinking maybe 'Arthur'?"

"I thought it was to be Patrick?" He looked up at her.

"So, you were listening then?" She laughed. "I thought you were so in love with the little man that I was forgotten."

And so it was. He was christened Patrick Arthur McNamara – Patrick after his father and grandfather and Arthur just because his mother thought he looked like an Arthur.

Mary Ann was happy to go along with the old naming custom but didn't want any confusion. She was determined he was going to be himself and not a copy of anyone else. So from the day of his birth she took to calling him Art.

Despite opposition she persisted in her mission, responding to all enquiries about Patrick with a wave of her hand, pretending she thought it was her husband they wanted. She informed all such enquirers that he was "out in the fields somewhere tending the cattle" or "out and about around the yard".

"It's not that Patrick I mean. Just wondering how the little fellow is."

"Oh, you mean Art?"

Eventually her son Patrick Arthur became Art. Years later no-one ever remembered that he was once a Patrick.

After that Mary Ann popped them out more or less every two or three years. Patrick loved the sight of her bump and coming up to each birth was more excited about the event than herself. For him it never lost its novelty.

"Isn't it a great miracle of nature?" The wonder of it all never ceased to amaze him. He couldn't explain it nor discuss it. But he knew she knew the pleasure it gave him.

"It is surely. And do you know what? The greatest miracle of all is how it gets out, but you'd never want to know anything about that, Patrick Joseph McNamara, sure you wouldn't?"

He smiled at her as he ran his great big calloused hand over her stretched skin, enjoying the shared mystery.

Most of the babies lived. Mary Ann grieved for the ones who didn't, but it being a difficult topic of conversation to bring up, she never knew if she grieved alone. Patrick looked after her, more attentive than usual, but otherwise just appeared to get on with the farming, so while they could discuss most things, this was something they didn't seem to be able to share.

Well-meaning members of the family and female neighbours advised her to put it behind her – sure hadn't she been blessed with lots of other healthy children? As if it was that easy. She wanted to snap at them when they offered their unwanted opinions but she held back. It wasn't their fault. And so she did just as they suggested. Got on with it, that is. But not before insisting that the lost child's name be added to the limestone slab that marked the family burial plot at the Abbey.

There was another burial place. A seldom mentioned one. It was located at the bottom of what was known as the Long Acre on McNamara land.

A low dry-stone wall separated the small triangular area from the rest of the field where the cattle grazed. There was a right of way, but no well-worn path led to this almost forgotten lonely place. Faint traces existed on the approach to the stile which formed part of the wall. The grass here didn't grow as abundantly, suggesting that occasional visits were made. Anyone not knowing about it would likely miss it. The two steps, made from large flat stones, wedged in place by the chunkier rocks, had large chips out of them and the bottom step was almost hidden by the long grass.

Apart from those with a reason, the only time it was

remembered was when a few locals gathered there each year on the first day of May and recited the rosary. The creamy May flowers clothing the normally scrubby hawthorn trees that surrounded it softened the edges of memory. The tiny bodies of infants who never drew breath in this world were laid to rest there in the unconsecrated ground. Unbaptised. Unnamed. Unmarked. And most of them unloved.

Growing up nearby, Mary Ann had always been aware of the significance of this lonesome place even though it was seldom spoken of. Mounds of freshly dug clay would appear every so often and a whispered mention made as to who had lost a child before its time. Occasionally an uneven bit of ground with a carefully placed sod of grass was the only clue that an attempt had been made to conceal a recent burial. The barely visible imprint of a boot on the surface hid a secret, the owner of the boot hoping that the sod of grass would have knitted in seamlessly before anyone came. A few whispered about that poor little scrap of a child.

And one of these secrets was Mary Ann's.

BRIDIE

Chapter 6

The farm in County Clare was a haze of soft pink and purple memories when, years later, she lifted the blanket covering that corner of her mind and peeped under it. Not something that happened often but when it did a strange mixture of feelings wafted out.

To start at the beginning was no problem, but she was wary. To wander about in those long-ago dreams was a temptation. But there was a danger. The risk of stumbling carelessly across the border into the territory where it all ended sometimes made her afraid to embark on her journey. One false footing would be enough to release the pain of those days. The temptation to replace the blanket came from a half-fearful sense that the current peacefulness could so easily be destroyed by a wrong move.

County Clare, 1895

The year she turned seventeen, Bridie arrived for a two-week holiday at her grandmother's farmhouse – an annual occurrence throughout her childhood that, up until now, blended into one long summer, each one pleasantly melting into the next with few outstanding incidents.

Bridie lay a few minutes in the bed, listening to the sound of doves cooing. There was movement downstairs. The familiar *"Here, chuck, chuck, chuck!"* of her grandmother's voice was comforting. She could picture Mary Ann wiping the table, catching the breakfast crumbs in her hand, before throwing them over the half-door to the hens pecking about outside. She could now hear the increased sounds of the clucking as the excited birds scrabbled around in the gravel. Throwing back the eiderdown, she stretched and, taking a deep breath, rose from the bed. Her reflection in the oval mirror on the dressing table caught her eye as she stood up. She'd better run a brush through the mane of auburn curls before she went downstairs. They seemed to have taken on a wild life of their own overnight.

Mary Ann must have heard her moving about. By the time she'd dressed and had arrived down to the kitchen her grandmother was already stoking the still-bright embers and moving the kettle, hanging on its crane, to a position over the fire.

"There's still some tea in the pot there, child – see if it's hot enough for you. You can have it while I'm making a fresh drop."

"Thanks, Gran."

Bridie cut herself a chunk of oaten bread from the loaf standing on the board in the middle of the table and buttered it. She spread some of the raspberry jam she'd made the previous day on the slice and took a bite.

"Oh, that's gorgeous!"

"What? My bread or your jam?"

"Both." Bridie grinned over at her grandmother and reached for the teapot.

"I've a job for you, Bridie, when you've finished your breakfast."

"What's that, Granny?" She was pleased when Mary Ann had tasks for her.

"Will you take the basket there and go down to the potato field and collect spuds for the dinner?" Mary Ann had a plan to delegate a few of her own tasks to ward off any possibility that boredom might set in with nothing much happening around the house.

"I will."

Bridie was easy to entertain. Perfectly happy sitting chatting long after the breakfast was over and this morning was no exception. Not an idea in her head that her grandmother might have her own schedule to stick to.

"Well, what about those potatoes?" Her grandmother recognised the signs – the contentment to sit there until dinnertime had she a listener. "How about today?"

"Oh, I forgot."

"Already? You'll find a basket in the scullery." Mary Ann stood up. "Shoo! Off with you!"

Walking along the laneway, the pink and white of the wild roses in the hedgerow caught her eye. She picked a spray and stuck them in her hair, where they sat bunched above her ear in a nest of curls.

Not aware that she was humming to herself until the childhood hymn burst forth at full volume into the sunlight.

"Bring flowers of the rarest,
Bring blossoms the fairest,
From garden and woodland
And hillside and dale
Our full hearts are swelling
Our glad voices telling
The praise of the loveliest flower of the May!"

Twirling in circles swinging her empty basket, Bridie danced along the lane in time to the tune, face held up to the sun. Breathless, she stopped at the gate into the potato field.

The bolt was firmly stuck in the wooden post as she tried to slide it open.

"*Oh, open, yeh divil!* You have to come." She rattled it before standing back to consider climbing over. "No, you're not going to best me." Muttering to herself, she put down her basket and tried dislodging it from its hole with both hands but it was stuck fast. She placed her shoulder under the top wooden bar of the gate and, struggling, managed to lift the weight, raising the gate slightly, enough to release the bolt from its captor. As she did so, a movement down the field close to the hedge caught her eye. A man already working along the drills was standing, looking in her direction.

She blushed at the thought that with nothing but birdsong in the air he couldn't have failed to hear her talking to the gate and probably had heard her wild singing. Her only consolation was that she had a good voice, but not good enough to douse the embarrassment of her foolishness. Wishing her grandmother hadn't omitted to tell her that she might not be alone in the field, she tossed her head and walked towards him and the cart that stood nearby in the shade of a hedge. Nothing to do but brazen it out..

"Well, that brings me back a bit. My First Communion, wasn't it?"

"I didn't know there was anyone listening."

"Obviously." He grinned at her red face. "Suits you though. I always thought it was a bit of a girl's hymn."

He wiped his clay-covered hand in his trousers before extending it. "Joseph O'Keeffe." The muscles in his forearm rippled as he gave her a firm handshake. "Sorry about the dirty paw, but if you've come to pick potatoes it won't be long before yours are the same."

"I suppose you're right." She laughed, relieved at the change of subject.

"I take it you're Bridie from Wexford?"

"Yes, I'm that Bridie." She smiled. "How did you know?"

"Mary Ann told me you were coming."

As he pulled the spade from where it was wedged in the earth, she noticed the tanned skin exposed by the rolled-up sleeves of his shirt. Clearly a man used to spending his life outdoors if his bleached hair and dark skin were anything to go by.

"Yes. I'm her granddaughter."

"I know. She told me that too."

"What else did she tell you then?"

"Not a lot. I think she must have been leaving that to you."

"Was she now?" Bridie laid her basket down on the crumbly earth he'd just cleared. "I've been sent down to get a few for the dinner."

"I guessed as much." He grinned with a nod towards where she had laid it. "The basket's a bit of a giveaway. But there was I hoping you'd come to help me."

He followed her look as she glanced across at the half-full cart.

"You can take them from there if you want."

She hesitated. It was tempting. But if she did so their encounter would be brief. Barely started before it was over. He seemed interesting. Maybe a mistake to take the easy way with the spuds. She mightn't have another excuse. Not a lot happened in these parts and he mightn't be around here again.

"Well, what's it to be?"

"Ah no. It's alright. I'll pick my own. To be honest, I think Granny has had enough of me for the morning." She looked around her. "Where's the best place to start?"

"I've loosened up that ridge. They'll be easy enough for you to collect and sure there'll be enough for a few dinners out of that."

She picked up the basket and moved across as he returned to work. She straddled the ridge and stood there watching his back as he continued along the drill he'd been working on. Afraid he would look behind and see her studying him, she bent down and began filling her basket. Slowly.

They worked in silence for a while. She watched as he emptied the full buckets into the wooden cart that stood in the shade of the hedge. Each time he returned from emptying them she kept her head down but was aware of him glancing at her. The lack of conversation, under more familiar circumstances, might have been companionable. In the current situation it merely created a space for the embarrassment of her previous performance to return, niggling away at the corner of her mind. Although she pushed it aside, every time it came back it seemed to have increased in size. She considered asking if he thought she was some sort of lunatic, but no, that mightn't be wise. As the silence began to shout at her she tried humming quietly to herself, in a vain attempt to make her earlier madness appear half normal.

The basket filled up too quickly. Unable to eke it out further, she stood up.

"Here, give me one of those buckets and I'll do a few."

"What?" Eyebrow raised, he looked back at her. "There's a spare one at the end of the cart." He stood watching as she put the basket in the shade of the cart and fetched the bucket. "Thanks. I don't often get an offer like that."

Working the ridge two away from his, she stood up to stretch her back. He continued his steady pace ahead of her. As she bent down again she trailed a few steps behind.

She needed a longer gap in order to get a good look without raising his awareness of being studied.

A dark stain showed on his shirt where it was stuck to a patch of sweat in the centre of his back. Her eyes wandered upwards to where his fair hair curled damply. Had she been closer she would have been tempted to reach out her cool hand and soothe the pink tinge that radiated under the mahogany of the skin of his neck.

Something about his smile had caught her fancy. Despite his confident handling of the situation, his smile bordered on shy, even though he'd had the upper hand.

He picked up his full buckets and turned towards the cart. Her back was beginning to ache. She adjusted her method, assuming a squatting position beside the drill, watching from the corner of her eye the way he tipped the potatoes onto the pile, as if careful not to bruise them.

"How long are you here for?" It was he who began chatting first as he walked back to his drill, swinging his empty buckets.

"As long as they can put up with me." Bridie laughed. "A few weeks, I suppose, just to give Granny a hand. I think it gets a bit lonely for her here now that most of them are scattered all over the world."

"Yeah. She lives for the letters. She often reads bits of them out to me over the tea."

"I haven't seen you before – have you been working here long?"

"Oh, I just do the bit of casual work during the harvesting season when an extra pair of hands are needed. I'm actually a fisherman."

"Are you living nearby?"

"I live over in Gortnamara, a few miles over the road. Well, a good few miles over the road. Do you know it?"

"Ah, no. I'm not familiar with the townlands around here."

"Over that direction." He pointed westwards. "Our families go back a long way. D'yeh know, I think we're related by marriage to Mary Ann someway, generations back."

"Everyone around here seems to be related one way or another. A bit like over in Wexford." She laughed. "You'd have to be careful what you say."

By the time her back gave out she knew that he was building a cottage on a plot of land given to him by his parents. It was nearly finished so he was taking any farm labouring he could get for the extra money to progress the work and bring the build to an end. She also knew, as she headed back along the lane to the farmhouse, that he was the one for her.

MARY ANN

Chapter 7

By the time Bridie decided to extend her holiday, Mary Ann was happy to have her round the farm and she'd got used to the company.

"Are you sure they don't need you at home?" As soon as Mary Ann had said it she realised how it sounded. Glancing at her granddaughter, she was relieved to see it hadn't been taken up the wrong way. "It's not that I don't want you here – you know you're welcome to stay as long as you like," she added. Just in case.

"Oh, I think my mother is glad to be rid of me." Bridie gazed out the window. "She thinks I mope around the place doing nothing."

"I don't see too much of that around here then." Mary Ann smiled. "I wonder why that is now?" She paused. "You can stay so long as you write to her . . . and she agrees. Alright?"

"Thanks, Gran." Bridie stood up from the table. "I'll do that right now."

"Before I change my mind." Mary Ann laughed. "And don't forget to tell her why you're staying on."

"To help you of course, Granny. Why else?"

They'd settled into a companionable existence together

and, like a breath of fresh air, she gave a lift to her grandmother's life. With only Art and Ellen next door and the grandchildren all scattered it was nice to have the company in her own home. No matter how ordinary an errand Bridie was sent on, she managed to make an adventure of it, even if only meeting some elderly person on her travels. She'd offer to carry their shopping for them and it would start there. She never came home without an interesting twist to her encounter.

Mary Ann often found herself watching from the window as Bridie set off on an errand and the wonder of her beauty never ceased to amaze her. None of the family were exactly ugly, but none had the elegance of her granddaughter. Maude was fairly good-looking but had nothing of the height or the ethereal quality that her daughter seemed to radiate.

Watching Bridie stepping from the shade of the house into the sunlight, Mary Ann could see that more care had been taken today. No doubting where she was headed for.

When the seasonal work ran out for Joseph, he continued to come to the farm. It was with a flicker of envy that Mary Ann watched the young couple light up at the sight of each other. Her envy was tinged with a sadness born of the knowledge that such a flame is reserved only for the young. Life's responsibilities would see to that. Would cause its gradual dimming. Just as well they didn't know. Could enjoy it while it lasted.

Maybe she had been lucky. In a way. Losing Patrick young. Well, youngish. The little let-downs had happened. Occasionally. Probably the same for most. For others it was worse. She had witnessed that. Yes, lucky. Patrick had been a good man, even if he forgot the birthdays of the children sometimes. Well, once. She hadn't allowed it to happen again after she saw the disappointment on young Hugh's face when his father came in for breakfast and didn't mention it. Such small disagreements or disappointments had never caused bitterness between them. She wondered what might have been, had he lived?

She'd seen it happen around her. Might they have gone down the same road too? The couples who never had a good word to say to each other. Or about each other. They surely didn't start out like that. It can't always have been that hostile tone used to ask a simple question. Not the words but the tone that revealed so much of the resentment. How long had it lain there before it had risen to the surface? No longer hidden, no longer caring what others would think. What must it be like for those, gone beyond disguising that the love between them was extinguished forever. The only flame left was anger. Or for others, silence. No, she hadn't had that. She'd been lucky.

BRIDIE

Chapter 8

Their courtship was short – a round of soft and gentle balmy evenings as one week rolled into the next. Everything Bridie had ever dreamed of. Something that might happen to others but never had she imagined that she would experience the same exhilaration. Or more surprisingly that someone would feel the same about her.

It was while riding on the crest of this particular wave that the letter arrived from home, bursting her bubble.

"Your father and I think it is about time you thought of returning home. The others miss you and we will soon be needing help around the place here now that the autumn is almost upon us. Give our regards to your grandmother and be sure and thank her for having you stay for so long. Tell her I will write soon. Let us know what train you will be arriving on and we will arrange for you to be collected from the station in Gorey . . ."

The letter put a halt to her gallop. She could rely on her mother to bring her down to earth. Trust her to remind her that the summer was ending, a realisation that she hadn't allowed enter her mind, living on a cloud of love as she had been.

On her last full day Joseph borrowed a pony and trap to take her on an outing. The rug he'd put on the plank seat provided very little cushioning from the jolts of the potholed roads. The trap pitched to the side as its left wheel sank into a deep crater.

"Hang on there, Bridie. Looks like we're in for a bumpy ride."

The pony strained to pull the trap forward before giving up. Joseph stepped down and saw that Bridie was about to follow.

"No, you stay there, just move over a bit to the other side and I'll be able to sort it." He went behind the trap and with a bit of jiggling and a few shouts to the pony he managed to dislodge the wheel and push it forward to firmer ground.

"That was a deep one. Let's hope there are no more like that. *Giddy-up there, boy!*"

After their picnic in a field emptied of cows gone for their evening milking, they headed westwards. Bridie was surprised that the setting sun was not leaving a red-and pink-stained sky as she expected. Maybe too early yet. Instead a creamy brightness lit the sky, making it difficult to look at. She averted her eyes from the burning sharpness – a hangover from childhood, a memory of being told never to look straight into the sun for fear of burning her retinas.

Joseph took a turn to the left, down a narrow roadway as if he had only just decided at the last moment. In the suddenness of the movement her hand shot out to grab his arm.

"Where are we going?" She clutched the wooden rim of the trap on the other side, her spine tensing to a rigid pole between the two props.

"A surprise. Somewhere you've never been before."

"Take your time or I'll never get the chance to go there again."

He reduced the speed as the road narrowed into a

laneway, wide enough for only one vehicle to pass along.

"Let's hope we don't meet anyone on this or we'll have to back up."

"Doesn't look like that'll be much of a problem." Bridie released her grip on his arm. "I doubt that many travel down here. Where are we anyway? Looks like we're going to the end of the world."

"Well, here we are. The very edge." Joseph pulled up the pony just as the lane ended and the pebble beach opened up before them. "We've arrived." He hopped down from the trap and reached up to help her.

"It's beautiful."

"Ballard Bay."

"It's just beautiful." It was all she could say as she shaded her eyes and stood looking at the two rocks out in the sea. They stood there stark, darkly silhouetted against the creamy sunset. White foaming waves caressed their base where they disappeared down into the depths of the sea. The cliff to the left cutting down, like a sharp black knife, into the ocean.

"Isn't it just Heaven?" She didn't want him to answer.

Her hushed voice told him that as he stood in silence beside her.

Bridie had no idea how long they'd been sitting on the grass mound, nor how long they had been listening to the hypnotic shush and whoosh of the sea washing the pebbles. A lullaby to the setting sun as it disappeared below the horizon. It was only when Joseph put his jacket over her shoulders and took her hand to go home that she felt the chill that had drifted into the air.

The busy chatter of starlings filled their world as they headed back up the laneway, away from the shore. They couldn't see where the sound was coming from in the dusky light as they walked, Joseph leading the pony alongside, both reluctant for the evening to finish.

A dark diamond patch in the corner of the field suddenly rose up with a rushing sound. In perfect formation the flock of starlings circled the air, specks of black spreading out against the dimming sky.

Joseph brought the pony to a halt and they watched the thrilling spectacle of the flock swooping hither and thither across the heavens, never losing a member. The dark gliders came to rest in a line along the fences and atop the few hayricks that still remained, dotted around the field.

"You know there are a million of them?" Joseph leaned on the fence watching as the birds regrouped.

"You've counted, I expect?" Bridie's laugh was almost drowned out by the starlings' chatter.

"Oh, believe me I've tried." He chuckled. "But no, there was a wildlife man here one time and he said there would be up to a million on the lake. He was doing some sort of a survey."

They watched as the flock rose up again.

"Did you know it's called a 'murmuration'?"

"Aren't you some fount of knowledge. But yes, I did. My father told me that. We have them in Wexford too, you know." Bridie, head thrown back, watched them skating and weaving about the sky before the flock drifted downwards to blacken the corner of the field again, their moment of glory suspended. "But why a 'murmuration'? Sure they're as noisy as hell."

"Well, that I can't tell you. It's what the survey man told me." Reluctant to leave, Joseph took her arm and kissed her lightly. "I think we better move. Before it gets too dark."

He helped her up into the trap. As he climbed in beside her she took one last look at the dark field.

"All the same, isn't nature wonderful?" Her words floated into the air. She knew that if she were to breathe her last breath at this very moment she would die a happy woman. She was surprised at the foolishness of the thought that had drifted across it. She glanced at him, glad he couldn't read her mind and he smiled back at her before flicking the reins and the pony took off.

FLORA

Chapter 9

Country Clare

1838

John O'Sullivan was the love of Mary Ann Murphy's life. At least her sixteen-year-old self thought so at the time. The dizzying whirl of romance danced her through the first year of their courtship but it was at the start of the second that he became impatient for progress.

By the time they left the sun-dappled laneway that Sunday afternoon and headed into the cool leafy shade of the forest, he had worn her down with the pressure of his urgency. Despite her niggling doubts, his charm had lowered her resistance and led to her making a bad error of judgement.

That first painful woodland coupling resulted in a missed period. By the second month she had to tell him. And within the week he had disappeared. To work on the farm of his uncle in County Mayo. That's what he told her anyway and she had no reason to doubt that she was part of the plan. There had been mention of this bachelor uncle and his requests for John to come and work with him. That if he did, the farm would be his in the future. So her trust wasn't entirely without foundation. And convinced he was putting the initial steps of their long-term plan into place Mary Ann was confident that John would send for her when he got established.

"I'll write to you when I get there," he assured her. "Let me just take the first step. There's no point in making plans too far ahead. Trust me. It'll all just fall into place after that."

She waited for the letter. By the second week she worried that it had got lost in the postal system. The third week told her she could fool herself no longer. And once a month had passed she knew there would be no discussion about the future. Whatever agreement she thought she had, it was clear there was no future with him. No happy-ever-after for her. The few short weeks left her with no alternative but to realise her dreams were shattered and accept the truth of the situation. She was on her own. Their problem was her problem now. Unsolved.

The cold winter that year was a blessing. It enabled her to cover up her ever-expanding waistline without any awkward questions. She confided only in her older sister Maggie.

"What are you going to do?" She paused. "How did that happen?"

"How do you think it happened?" She was sorry about the edge to her voice. It was a legitimate question and her sister was her only hope of assistance.

But Maggie's shocked face now had her doubting if she should have chosen someone else to tell her secret to. Always the holy one in the family, the nunnish one, who had the younger siblings on their knees before bedtime teaching them how to say their Rosary. Too late now to reconsider.

"Have you even thought what you might do?" Maggie stared at her. The miserable look on her sister's face confirmed what she already suspected. That there was no plan.

Thoughts of what to do when the baby was born tormented every waking moment of Mary Ann's life. They came between her and her chores, poking at her brain until her head swam. She couldn't let them settle. If she batted them away often enough maybe it would never happen. Would turn out to have been a false alarm. What nonsense, well past that stage. All her efforts for the moment had to be focussed on keeping the situation hidden.

The memory of the hot tearing agony of that wet slippery day had all but disappeared into the darkness, never to be revisited.

Mary Ann directed her pain into the scrunched-up pillow. Maggie hoped the muffling would be enough to stop her sister's groans travelling along the narrow corridor of the landing and down the stairs to where the busyness of the kitchen was in full flow.

With all sense of time having dissolved, the waves of agony seemed to have lasted days but Maggie assured her it was only hours. Eventually, at long last, with one last gut-wrenching push the baby girl slid into the world in deathly silence. It would have been hard to disguise the mewling cry of an infant – their earlier worry of someone hearing no longer a problem, as they looked at the floppy red-streaked scrap that Maggie had caught in the towel. It had been much too early, of course. Far too soon.

Mary Ann slumped back on the pillow, exhausted. Maggie cut the cord with the old blunt kitchen scissors and put the afterbirth in an old bucket which she hid in the alcove beside the wardrobe. That could be dealt with later. The least of the problems.

"What do you want me to do?"

"I don't care." Mary Ann turned her face away towards the wall, numb with shock. "Just go downstairs and act normal."

"I don't mean that." Maggie paused. "I mean with the baby."

43

"She'll have to be buried." Mary Ann swung around. "Will you bury her for me? Please, Maggie."

"I don't suppose I've a choice."

"You know where."

Maggie sat on the side of the bed looking down at the doll-like infant in her arms, still wrapped in the bloodied towel.

"Here, hold her while I get fresh water. I'll have to clean her up first and get something to put her in." She gently passed the bundle over.

Mary Ann looked down at the closed eyes of her daughter. A tear rolled down her cheek, falling with a splash onto the infant's face. She rubbed it away with her thumb, surprised at the softness of the baby's still warm skin. She was glad she hadn't used the towel to wipe some of the blood. It might have been too rough.

Maggie returned, placing the emptied basin on the bedside locker. She unfolded a piece of white linen and laid it on the back of the chair before pouring the fresh water.

"Here, give me the cloth and I'll do it." Mary Ann gently wiped all traces of the bloody slime from the baby's head and face.

"You'll need to do her body as well." Maggie began opening the towel. "Here, I'll help you. I'll rinse the cloth. We don't want the foxes getting the scent later."

She handed the cloth back to Mary Ann whose outstretched hand left no doubt but that she wanted to do the job herself.

"I've a clean towel here. It's an old one so it won't be missed. We'll dry her off and wrap her in this one. Then put her into this white pillowcase." Maggie lifted the linen from the back of the chair and held it up. "It's one I made myself. For my bottom drawer. It's special. Look at the embroidery."

"It's lovely, Maggie. Thanks."

"Better than taking one of mother's. She'd be sure to notice." She helped Mary Ann put the swaddled infant into the pillowcase. "I'll have to leave her here with you for the moment. I'll do the rest in the evening."

"Alright. Go down now before anyone gets suspicious. Tell them I'm not feeling well and don't let any of them come up here. Only you."

"I'll do my best. But you know how hard it is to stop them." Maggie looked around. She pulled out a drawer and shifting the contents to one side she made a space. She picked up the pillowcase and gently laid the little body into the nest of socks. She glanced across at Mary Ann watching her from the bed before slowly pressing the drawer closed.

All in the house was quiet that evening when Maggie crept off to the field at dusk to prepare the ground.

It was too soon but she had been insistent. They had walked down the field slowly. Mary Ann stopped every few yards, wincing as her foot stubbed the uneven ground. Maggie worried that her mother would see them and wonder at the hesitant pace and start asking questions. Relieved that they had arrived unnoticed, she helped her sister over the stone wall.

"I put one of the rocks there to mark the spot so you'll know."

"Oh, thanks, that's good but will you dig it into the ground a bit more, Maggie?" Mary Ann sat down on a boulder. "Wedge it in more so no-one will take it up and put it back on the wall."

Maggie searched around until she found a sharp-edged stone and removing the rock cut into the grass, lifting a few clods of the turf. Once she had them removed she gouged deeper into the soil, testing the depth every now and then until she was satisfied the slab of rock would be securely wedged. She turned it in the hole and stood back to check the angle.

"I think it might be better the other way, the flat side to the back. What do you think?" She checked with Mary Ann.

"Yeah. I'd be happy with that."

Maggie knelt down. She placed her two hands on the rock and, leaning forward, used her full weight to press it hard into the clay. She stood up and, replacing the turves of grass, heeled them into place with her boot.

"I think that'll be alright." She bent down and tested the slab to see if she could rock it. "What do you think?"

Mary Ann nodded.

"Well, what do you want to do now?" Maggie looked across at her.

"Will you say a prayer?"

"I don't know one. Well, not for this situation."

"Well, make one up. I can't . . . You're good at that sort of thing."

Maggie closed her eyes while Mary Ann waited.

"Bless this little innocent baby who was born sleeping. Please God look after her. She did nothing wrong. Amen."

Not the time to comment on the slight reprimand Mary Ann thought she detected. Maggie wouldn't have meant it.

"Will we go home or what?" Maggie glanced at her sister.

"Give me a few minutes on my own, will you?" She stood up stiffly and moved forward.

"Alright. I'll go for a walk and rinse my hands and I'll come back for you."

"Thanks. Thanks, Maggie." It came out in a whisper.

"For everything." Not sure if Maggie heard, she
her back as she walked away, heading towards t'

Letting out a deep sigh, she dropped to her n..
ran her hand lightly over the grassy turves before sitting
back on her hunkers to gaze at the little grave and what
might have been.

It was a few minutes before she noticed the sound of
the birds chattering from their hiding places in the trees.
Nice for her baby to have company when she went home
and nobody was nearby to watch over her.

She looked around. She had never really thought much
about it. This lonesome place. It had always been here.
Now it meant something. Always would.

She wondered if there was such a secret burial ground
in every parish. A strange place to choose. Between the
two townlands. Whoever thought it up, it created a resting
place for the unbaptised in this sort of no-man's-land.

Sharing such a secret might have created a special bond
between the sisters. But for reasons that remained unclear
to Maggie, apart from two efforts on her part, it resulted in
neither girl mentioning the event again.

"Do you want to talk about it?"

"No."

There was no need to ask what the talk was to be about.

The second occasion a week later drew a similar response.

"No. But thanks."

"Thanks for what?"

"For helping me."

Mary Ann's slight expansion encouraged her sister to
pursue the matter.

"You shouldn't bottle it up, you know. It'd be better to
talk about it. I won't tell anyone if that's what you're
worried about."

47

I know that. I just can't. I just want to forget the whole ing."

"You'll never do that."

Maggie kept her eyes trained on her sister, but the lack of response forced her to drop the subject. Maybe Mary Ann wasn't ready to talk yet.

What she didn't know then was that Mary Ann was never going to be ready to talk about it. So great was her fear that someday in the future it could just slip out unintentionally. Or if they argued, she couldn't be absolutely sure, unlikely though it might be, that Maggie mightn't blurt it out. Their parents' rigid attitude towards 'girls in trouble' was unambiguous. No doubting what would happen. She would be shown the road.

Whether the event itself was the reason, or the fact that Mary Ann refused to talk about it, the experience changed their relationship forever. It hung like a grey leaden sky over them both, its drizzle falling between the two sisters, a misty barrier that gently pushed them apart.

Mary Ann often went walking in the fields alone, a magnet drawing her to the same corner of the same field. Fearing someone would someday move the rock, she planted a clump of wild primroses on the spot. As she firmed the plant into the damp soil with the heel of her shoe, she decided it was time to give her child a name.

Flora.

Chapter 10

Knocknageeha, County Clare
1851

It was this secret that had strengthened Mary Ann. Not the secret itself but the route it travelled as it tangled its way in and out and around her thoughts as she lay in bed at night. Not just for nine months but for many years after.

The panic of the situation and the possibility of her secret being found out came between her and her sleep in the early days. That was before she had accepted that she had been left on her own to deal with the problem. As time progressed the worry changed. Perhaps someone had begun to notice her bump and was biding their time, waiting to ask the relevant question?

The fears came in waves. Time and the progress of the pregnancy saw to that. As one was eradicated it was soon replaced by another. In between were brief pauses when the wonder of it all managed to penetrate. But these breaks were short-lived.

Even after the event the worries continued. What if someone had seen them burying the baby, perhaps watching from behind the hawthorn hedgerow?

It didn't happen with any speed but, as the months and years passed, a calmness gradually descended on her nightly anxieties. Despite the circumstances, the very fact that she had managed to give birth, to bring another human being into the world amazed her, fortifying her as the worries receded. She allowed it to seep its way into her brain even though the fear of being found out still occasionally punctured it.

The dimensions of the miracle eventually pushed everything else aside. She felt her worries shrink to miniscule proportions, leaving an airy space in her head. With a glistening clarity she could see what was and what was not important in the overall scheme of things. To understand fully that she had lived through such an incredible occurrence. The wonder of birth – life and death. And no-one in the world, apart from Maggie, would ever know her secret.

The fact that she had managed to keep it hidden, had to keep it concealed, now and always, would forever sadden her. Had Flora lived she'd have faced a different dilemma. But that was not the case. Not something she needed to dwell on.

Her secret. It provided her with a confidence and the power of that gave her the strength to lie about her other 'lost' children with Patrick Joseph. A white lie to ensure that they too would not end up in the unconsecrated field at the end of the Long Acre.

"I feel a faint heartbeat. The baby is alive."

The firmness in Mary Ann's voice struck Gráinne as strange.

"I don't think so, love, but if you felt it, you felt it." She had assisted at the delivery of both Art and Hugh but this time it was different. She was aware how Mary Ann was avoiding her eyes, how determinedly her eyes were firmly fixed on the baby that she kept facing away from her, as if anxious that the midwife might give voice to her lie.

"I think he mightn't be long for this world. I can feel him getting weaker."

The firmness was still there in her voice. None of the sobbing or disbelief that usually went with a stillbirth.

"Maybe we should baptise him." Gráinne sat on the side of the bed, aware of Mary Ann's adjusting of the towel that swaddled the baby, pulling it up further over his head to shield his face from her view. "What do you think?"

Mary Ann nodded. "Will you do it, Gráinne?"

"Leave it to me."

Relieved at her acceptance of her dead child and reluctant to cause further pain, Gráinne stood up and went to get the basin from the washstand. Placing it on the bed, she watched Mary Ann's flushed face as she pulled back the towel and gently cupped the baby's head, edging him over the rim of the bowl.

"Will you pour the water, Gráinne? We need to do this quickly."

The midwife trickled a few drops over the baby's blood-streaked head as Mary Ann said the words.

"*Daniel James, I baptise thee in the name of the Father and of the Son and of the Holy Ghost.*" She made the sign of the cross on her son's forehead with her thumb.

Neither spoke as Mary Ann wiped away the water from the baby's face and kissed him. The balm of the silence was broken by the sound of a chair-leg scraping the tiled floor below.

"I think we were just in time." Gráinne removed the basin. "I think he's gone, love."

She took the child gently from Mary Ann and wrapped him in a fresh towel before holding him out to his mother.

"Here, take him. Time for a last goodbye and a little cuddle."

"Is it safe to come in?" A light tap on the door.

Gráinne opened it. Patrick stood there, hesitant, concern showing on his face. She knew he'd have been listening for the usual new-born cry. But before she could say a word his eyes caught sight of his wife brushing away a tear, confirmation that his worry was justified.

And it was thus that Mary Ann made certain that Daniel was buried in the graveyard at the Abbey where her parents and grandparents already rested. What she didn't know then was that she would be repeating the procedure twice more during her childbearing years. Important to ensure her silent babies would rest with their family. Something she hadn't been able to do for Flora.

Mary Ann hated unfinished business.

Like an itch that she couldn't scratch it had been there for the last few weeks. The anniversary Mass for baby Daniel and the family get-together planned for afterwards was something she looked forward to. A chance to talk about her lost child. What troubled her was not related to Daniel. At least not directly. But it was strange that an infant who hadn't drawn breath had a reason for being. Could still have a function. She loved her baby boy for that, for giving her this chance. It was Daniel who had awoken something in her and set her on a determined path to put the niggle to sleep.

Patrick was reluctant. "I think maybe we should just do it quietly, Mary Ann." He lifted his cap and scratched his head slowly. "Maybe just you and me."

"Why? I want people to remember that we had a baby, even if Daniel isn't here. I don't want him to be forgotten." Mary Ann added more flour to the bread mix. "Nobody mentions him now."

"They're afraid they'll upset you. That's why they don't mention him. It's not that they've forgotten."

"Even you don't mention him." She paused, looking him straight in the eye before tipping the bread out onto the table.

The comment stung. "I may not talk about him. But it's not that I don't think of him."

"Well, the tea back here after the Mass will give us a chance to talk about him again." She kneaded the bread with an unnecessary force. "They won't be able to avoid it."

"And do you think that's a good thing?" Patrick glanced at her. "I mean, now that there's another child on the way?"

"That's exactly why I want to do it this year." She pushed a lock of hair off her face with the back of her floury hand. "By Daniel's next anniversary no-one will remember he ever existed. He'll just be history. Well . . . to everyone but ourselves."

"Maybe you're right." Patrick put on his cap and headed for the door.

"I am." Mary Ann turned her attention to the final kneading of the bread. "It's the least he's entitled to."

"You are right."

It was only as he disappeared out of sight that she heard the "as usual" tagged on to the end of his sentence. She smiled as she set the bread to bake.

Taking the kettle from the crane, she wet the tea and sat back to enjoy a rest. As she sipped her tea, content now that she was doing her best by Daniel, the urge to put something else right preyed on her mind. Now was the time. If she couldn't put it right, at least put it half right, which was probably as close as she could get to fixing it.

The afternoon was sunny and remarkably mild for April. Patrick had already left for a sports fixture before she'd finished clearing the dinner dishes. Leaving them on the drainer to dry, she wiped her hands on the towel and reached across to open the window.

"Art." She could see him kicking a stone around the yard. "Will you tell Aggie to come here for a minute."

The opportunity to get away alone with no questions asked. Aggie was perfect. Very good with the children was Aggie. Allowed them to do whatever they liked, while all the time never leaving them out of her sight. Only one of the reasons they all loved her.

"You boys be good for Aggie now. Do as she tells you."

"That'll be easy, Ma." Art chuckled at his own joke.

"Less of your lip now or maybe I won't go at all."

"Ah, go, Ma. Only joking. We'll be good."

"Be sure you do now. And don't let Hugh get up to any mischief." Mary Ann slipped a trowel wrapped in a sheet of newspaper into her pocket and headed off.

She visited the Long Acre first before walking the mile and a half to the Abbey. The heat on her back as she walked the grassy pathway that led to the graveyard could have been mistaken for a summer sun, except for the unfurling of the lime-green buds of a young spring, on the trees along the route.

She smiled and bade the time of day to an elderly couple as they passed her at the entrance gate. The man nodded and mumbled a greeting. The woman, in her long black coat, too hot for the day, gave a sorrowful glance in her direction. Her red-rimmed eyes discouraged Mary Ann from engaging in further conversation.

Wanting the place to herself she watched until the pair were out of sight. Removing the wilted flowers from the grave she set aside the glass jar, careful not to spill the remaining green slimy water. The soil was surprisingly soft. It crumbled away easily as she dug the hole. Taking the parcel of newspaper from her pocket she unwrapped the bundle, careful not to disturb the clay which clung to the roots of the plant. A few tight, yellow primrose buds nestled in the fresh young leaves, waiting to open.

"I've brought you a present for your birthday, Danny. A playmate. Make room for your sister Flora."

Once she'd planted the clump in front of the limestone slab she reached for the jar. Pouring the slimy water over the primroses she hoped the liquid would be enough to give them a good start in life. It was the best she could do for her daughter whose flowers had seeded freely over the years spreading themselves wide, covering the little mound of earth at the bottom of the Long Acre. With time they would spread here too, all over the grave. A reminder forever of her first-born. And no-one else need ever know. She was a part of the family too.

Once she had completed her task she lay back on the grass. The springy softness of the ground beneath her felt good. The soil had not yet compacted into the unyielding hardness of summer. For a few minutes she watched an image of two cherubs at play in the white puffs that floated across the blue sky, before her eyes, heavy with peace, began to close as she felt herself drift off.

Chapter 11

James was sitting at the table munching on his bread and jam, his head slightly sideways, propped on his left hand. His forehead was knitted in thought, bringing his eyebrows almost to a peak in the middle above his nose.

"Who's going to give Maude away, Ma?" He took another bite of his bread and looked across at his mother.

With the booking of the church, the making of dresses, the planning of guest lists and everything that went with wedding preparations, all women's work, the subject of who would walk Maude up the aisle had never arisen. They hadn't got that far yet.

The question gave her a jolt. She set down her teacup. The enquiring look on his face indicated a complete lack of awareness that his question was anything other than ordinary. If anyone else had thought about it they had kept it to themselves in the hope that it might just fall into place. What James had unwittingly done was to stir up a deep dull ache that had lain dormant for years.

Mary Ann looked at the cap, lying upside down beside her son on the wooden table. An old one of Patrick's, the grease of years discolouring the brim. James had recently taken to wearing it when he helped milk the cows. He had asked and she had let him.

"Don't lose it though or I'll kill you." She had watched him that day remove it from its lonely peg on the back of the door and put it on his head. She had expected him to turn around and ask how he looked but he didn't. He just smiled to himself and went out the door. The feel of it might bring him closer. Enough to fill the gap for him as he went about the chores of his father.

She remembered having stood up from the table and moving to the door to watch him. He resembled Patrick, everyone said it. Only ten when his father died. She had willed him to turn around so that she could get another look at him in the cap. Just to get a flash of what Patrick might have looked at James' age. She hadn't known him then.

She was surprised that after so many years, the pain could still be resurrected by a chance remark or question. Hugh had married in America but it had been lonely in the front seat of the local church when Art got married. Even though she'd had James and a row of daughters beside her she had missed Patrick's presence, his reassuring nudge at her elbow.

"Well, Ma?"

"Well, what?" She looked across at James expectant face.

"Maude. Who's giving her away?"

"Oh, I don't know son, I hadn't even thought of that." She wondered if Maude had considered it and maybe was afraid to bring up the conversation with her. "I suppose it'll have to be Art."

Mary Ann leaned her chin on her hand and turned her head to look out the window, her thoughts no longer at the breakfast table.

"I suppose so." James fingered his father's cap, disappointed. A man now that he'd started wearing it, but maybe that wasn't yet obvious to others.

"I'll get on with the work in the yard then." The chair scraped on the stone floor as he stood up and footed it away from the table.

"What?" The grating sound brought Mary Ann's attention back to the table, a slightly dazed look in her eyes. "Oh, yes, you do that and I'll have a word with Maude. She's still in the bed."

After James left the kitchen Mary Ann poured herself another cup of tea. His question had taken her back on a journey through a time she hadn't visited in quite a while. Her tea grew cold as she pondered the love and loss she had endured and wondered what it had all been about.

MAUDE

Chapter 12

Cornelius Redmond was a good man. Maude knew her mother had to acknowledge that even though she had a feeling that Mary Ann might be harbouring a little resentment that he was taking her daughter away.

It wasn't his fault. Not even his choice. He was forced to do so by the rule. The same rule for all the members of the police force. They were not allowed to serve in their own counties. That was how he came to be stationed in Clare in the first place.

"You'll find the Royal Irish Constabulary Barracks on the right-hand side of the road." The bit of pomposity in him slightly irritated her. Everyone else called it the R.I.C. station or the Barracks, but not Cornelius. He felt obliged to give it its full name if anyone enquired.

Now that he was married, a further restriction that he could not serve in the county of his wife was imposed. This had forced the move to a police station in County Wexford. He simply had to go where he was sent.

"Don't worry, Mrs. McNamara, I'll bring Maude home to see you every summer and you'll be most welcome in our home whenever you wish to visit."

She knew her mother felt uncomfortable with his

formality but, having tried many times and failed to get him to call her Mary Ann, she had abandoned the effort. His rigidity annoyed her but, as she watched him shake hands with her mother as they left the farmhouse, she knew he would be true to his word and that her mother would be reassured.

"Goodbye, Maude. Don't forget what he said. You're to come back and see us before the summer is out."

"I will, Mama, I will."

Cornelius placed the luggage into the trap, stashing it securely, ensuring the weight was evenly distributed.

Maude stood a moment in the doorway, unsure what to do while Cornelius shuffled about beside the trap, waiting.

"I'm going to miss you all." She leaned forward and kissed her mother, their tears mingling as their cheeks met.

"Go on, will you, he's waiting. You don't want to miss your transport."

"I'm going to be so lonely in Wexford."

"You'll be grand, Maude. It won't be long before you make friends. Off with you now." Giving her daughter a slight shove, she raised her arm in a wave. "Goodbye now, Cornelius. Look after her, won't you?"

"I will indeed, Mrs. McNamara." And, raising his hat to her, he turned to help his wife up into the trap.

As they reached the end of the lane Maude looked back. The forlorn figure against the doorway of the house tore at her heart. She glanced at Cornelius as he sat silently beside her in the trap, his expression telling her that his thoughts were already on the journey ahead of them. Envying his facility to let go and look to the future, she gave a last wave and, sitting back, set her eyes on the road in front.

As the distance lengthened behind them a loneliness engulfed her. The sudden realisation that unlike herself, her mother didn't have far to go to find company. Family members, farm hands, neighbours . . . all familiar. Even the dogs. Maybe Mary Ann had already put her out of her mind and she no more than a mile down the road? Her turn now to feel abandoned.

The clacking of the hooves filled the silence between them but she wished he would talk to her. Comfort her in some way. Unable to speak her anxiety, she wished he would give her some sign, a glance, a smile, a reference to indicate that he understood what she was leaving behind. She waited. But nothing.

A small shadow of resentment began to cloud the sunny morning. His lack of empathy was something she couldn't have put words on at that moment.

MARY ANN

Chapter 13

County Wexford
1896

Catherine had taken her shopping in Ennis for the occasion. Had insisted that the navy dress and brimmed hat were the most suitable for a woman her age.

"Do you not think it's a bit dull, Catherine?" Mary Ann was doubtful as she looked in the long mirror in the shop. "I feel a bit dowdy."

"You won't when I've finished with you, mother." Catherine went off to the far end of the shop as Mary Ann twisted and turned, not impressed with what she saw before her.

"Here, I've got just the thing that will give it a lift. Take the hat off."

Mary Ann watched as her daughter attached a large peony-type cream flower to the side of the hat.

"Put that back on now and see how it looks." Catherine placed the hat on her mother's head. "Now, you can't but admit that gives it a lift."

"But the dress is still a bit dull."

"That'll be sorted. Just look at the hat for the moment."

The assistant arrived back with a bundle of cream lace pieces in her hand.

"Now, how about we put a cream lace collar and cuffs

on the dress and there you are all sorted?" Catherine took a piece of lace from the assistant and placed it around the collar of the dress. "Doesn't she look good now?" She addressed the assistant.

"Perfect." The assistant smiled at Mary Ann. "You'll be the most elegant grandmother there."

"Well, don't say that to Stasia O'Keeffe when she comes in to get her outfit. She won't be best pleased." Mary Ann chuckled. She should have trusted her daughter. Always had a good eye.

Mary Ann sat in the top pew of the little red-bricked church in Riverchapel, wondering why she didn't come more often to County Wexford. The only time she made the journey across the country from County Clare was when there were major family events like births, deaths and marriages. Mostly births. She knew Maude had appreciated her usefulness when she'd stayed a few weeks after each child had been born to keep things ticking over while her daughter concentrated on the new-born.

She felt more of a guest this time. Less effort on her part was expected. She'd already been here a week, observing the wedding preparations from her seat beside the fire. She knew her daughter well enough to read between the lines of the letter. "*Please come a week or two before the wedding. As her grandmother you always seem to have a calming influence on Bridie. Being her mother I just seem to fuss her even more than she is already fussed and we end up arguing over silly little things. It really would be a great help if you were here and Cornelius will pick you up from the station when you let us know the date . . .*"

She was well aware that mother and daughter were indeed inclined to rub each other up the wrong way, but as the only adult family member who knew him well, Mary

63

Ann knew what her real function was. To reassure Cornelius and Maude that, yes, Joseph was the perfect man for Bridie. They had met him and his parents fleetingly on their summer visit but Cornelius appeared to be having last-minute jitters. He'd taken her aside on the evening she arrived.

"Just tell me, Mrs. McNamara. I know we've met them briefly, but in your opinion are they a good family?"

"The salt of the earth, Mr. Redmond."

Her joking formality did nothing to loosen him up. The tension on his face drew furrows above the bridge of his nose.

"I've known them all my life, Cornelius." She patted his arm. "You couldn't meet better if you searched the whole of County Clare." She paused and smiled. "Or even County Wexford."

"Hmmh." He didn't look convinced.

"Now, Cornelius, you're surely not worried that the family are small farmers? Sure aren't you yourself a small farmer? And only a part-timer at that?"

"Well, it's not just that ..."

"So, he's just a fisherman. Is that's what's bothering you? He's not in the higher echelons." She shook her head. "I'm disappointed in you, Cornelius. I never realised you were such a snob."

"You're right, Mrs. McNamara." He looked uncomfortable. "I'm being ridiculous. So long as he makes her happy." He paused. "This Joseph, would you be sure he'll look after Bridie well? She's very young and her head is easily turned."

Mary Ann could understand his worry.

"He's a very decent young man, Cornelius. I know she has an impulsive streak but this time it is well directed. I don't think you or Maude have anything to worry about on that score."

"I hope you're right. I wouldn't like to think he's some fly-by-night."

"He's as solid as they come and a hard worker."

"I'll just have to trust your judgement, Mrs. McNamara."

"Have I ever been wrong, Mr. Redmond?" She cocked her eyebrow and watched the half smile smooth his frown.

As the days progressed she watched her daughter. Poor Maude's impending loss was evident in the way she hung about Bridie, involving herself in every arrangement, much to her daughter's annoyance.

"I know we squabble a lot but I'm really going to miss her."

"You will, of course, but you'll get used to it." Mary Ann reassured her, careful to suppress her own pleasure. She couldn't allow her daughter to see her delight that Bridie would be coming to live in Clare. "You will, Maude. You have to get used to letting them go. She's only the first, well, apart from two of the lads. Cornelius Junior and Arthur may be married, but they're still living down the road from you. Sure, wasn't it the same for me when you got married, so I understand completely how you're feeling." Mary Ann looked at the sad face before her. "It is a wrench, but haven't you got your husband? Remember, I didn't even have your father for company."

"I suppose."

Mary Ann leaned back in the armchair. There was nothing more to be said.

They sat in silence as her mind went back to the lonely days and evenings that, years ago, had followed Maude's wedding and her move to Wexford. She had the postman plagued. Watching out for him. Waiting at the end of the lane so he wouldn't have to come all the way up to the house. At least that's what she told herself.

65

Initially the weekly letters were her only comfort. All she'd had to fill the absence. She loved to read them again in the evenings when she was alone. She had well got used to the lack of daily contact by the time the letters became less frequent, children taking up more of her daughter's time. Her one consolation had been that Cornelius, with a reliability that never missed a summer, had brought Maude and the grandchildren over to visit her in Clare.

She wasn't sure if Joseph would be in a position to make a similar promise to Maude.

The roadside hedges foamed with creamy hawthorn blossom. The soft fuzz of the May bush against the blue of a cloudless sky as they arrived at the church. They stood in groups outside enjoying the perfect day. There was a scurry inside when word filtered through that the bride was arriving.

Mary Ann couldn't resist turning around at the sound of a rustle from the back of the chapel. Her breath caught in her chest as she saw the vision. She reached out for Maude's hand and gave it a squeeze. She hoped her daughter had turned in time to see the moment when the sun filtering through the church window caught the auburn of Bridie's curls, creating a halo of light.

As Bridie walked up the aisle on her father's arm, Mary Ann glanced at Maude and the tears in her eyes gave her the answer. They watched Cornelius's proud straight back turn as he gave his daughter's hand a pat before parting with her at the altar. With a quick smile at him, Bridie turned to Joseph as he stepped out from the front pew. The pair faced the altar where the priest was waiting and took their first steps into the next phase of their lives.

BRIDIE

Chapter 14

Gortnamara, County Clare

There was no honeymoon but Bridie didn't mind. She just wanted to get back to Clare and start life with her handsome fisherman.

He'd spent the previous winter finishing the work on the little cottage overlooking the wild Atlantic. It was now ready and waiting for her when she arrived. While the building work was finished it was still rough. She was glad of that. That he'd left enough room for a woman's touch. The decorating chores inside would give her a chance to put her own stamp on their home.

His parents farmed a smallholding nearby with the help of Joseph's older brother. This arrangement worked out very well for everyone as it left Joseph independent. He hadn't much interest in farming other than making himself useful helping out during the busy time and still being free to answer the call of the sea.

Always content on the ocean, he now went off in his fishing boat each day a happier man, knowing that Bridie was at home creating a nest for them both. After the supper most nights he would take out the old melodeon passed on to him by his grandfather and play a few tunes for her at the fireside before they went to bed.

Bridie hated the night fishing but it went with the job and the seasons.

"I wish you didn't have to go out, Joseph."

Hugging her on the doorstep, he had to unpeel her arms to unfree himself.

"You're strangling me." He laughed. "I know you don't like it, Bridie, but someone has to do it. Sure you won't feel it 'til I get back."

"Literally." She grinned at him to dispel her neediness. It was something she'd just have to get used to. "Off with you. The sooner you go the sooner you'll be back."

As soon as she tidied up she slipped her shawl around her shoulders and took herself up the dusky lane to visit her in-laws. She had the habit of dropping in on Stasia and Dan on the evenings Joseph went night fishing. It made the wait shorter. A sudden sound in the ditch as she passed made her jump. She laughed at herself when she saw the rabbit halted in the middle of the road staring at her, his fright equalling hers.

She knew every sound and every bush in the ditches near her home in Wexford but the lack of familiarity with these roads made her nervous once night fell. Dan would always walk her back to the cottage on such evenings after supper.

"There's no need, Dan. I'll be grand on my own." She hated disturbing him from his seat at the fire.

"Can't have you wandering the roads at this hour, alannah. Sure I need to stretch my legs anyway before they seize up altogether."

Being glad of the company she didn't protest too much, his kindly presence taking the anxiety out of the walk. At her cottage door he'd never leave without a reassuring pat on her shoulder.

"You'll be alright now, Bridie, you're home."

"Thanks, Dan. See you tomorrow."

She'd watch his back disappearing into the dark night, reluctant to close the cottage door. Only when she could no longer see him would she close it.

Hating the thought of going alone to the cold bed, she would stoke up the dying embers and get the fire started again. Just for the company.

Chapter 15

It was a wild evening. She had stepped out earlier at twilight to check the strength of the storm. Shards of sleet stung her face as the wind whipped the woollen shawl from her head, releasing her hair. She held the edges of the wrap firmly as it threatened to part company from her shoulders. Her eyes watered as her hair lashed hither and thither, cutting across them like a lance.

With her visibility further reduced with the descending gloom, there was no point in staying outside to get soaked. She turned to open the cottage door. The force of the wind almost wrenched it from her hand as she turned the knob. She released her grip on the shawl as she struggled to hold the door. The shawl was saved by the prickly hawthorn that snagged it before it managed to float away, and she was forced to let the doorknob go to rescue it. She could hear the door hit the wall when it swung back into the hallway as she unpicked the shawl from the thorns. She rushed inside. Throwing the shawl in the direction of the armchair, she used all her strength to push the door shut, her muscles straining, leaving the wind outside.

She turned and leaned her back against it and listened. Even from behind the closed door she could hear the waves crashing on the rocks below. She tried to quash the anxiety that stirred inside as she busied herself setting the table for supper. This wasn't the first time he was late back from fishing. That wind would surely slow anyone down.

"You shouldn't be worrying!" he would scold her, cupping her face in his hands. But she knew he was pleased that she did. "Am I not always telling you that anything can delay us? The winds might be blowing in the wrong direction and we can't burst a gut trying to get home on time just because the tae might be getting cold." He would smile at her. "It's all part of the job and you're going to have to get used to it. You can't spend your life fretting every time I'm a bit late."

But tonight was important. She hadn't said anything so he mightn't realise it but tonight's fish dish was to celebrate their first month's anniversary. She hadn't said anything because it might sound foolish. Didn't want him to think he'd married an excitable child. The fish might not be special to him but it was to her. He had caught them and she had got a recipe from his mother and made a fish pie for the supper. Adding her own creative touch she had cut out a series of kisses in the shape of X's from the pastry and laid them along the top of the pie.

They sat her in the armchair when her legs melted. Everything started to fade. Lots of people in the room. All far away. They hadn't mentioned Joseph's name. This must be for someone else. They couldn't have been speaking to her. She pushed the thought away, pushed the people away.

"What are you talking about? Who are you talking about?" Not even aware she was screaming at them. Not her Joseph. It couldn't be.

Gasping for breath, pushing and pulling away as arms went around her. She tore at them trying to get away, but

71

all the while drowning in terror. Seconds, minutes, hours, she never knew how long it took before the searing ball of pain engulfed her completely as the truth sank in.

DAN & STASIA

Chapter 16

"What do you want to do about the funeral?" Dan was aware his question was unnecessary.

"I don't know. I don't know." Her voice wobbled as she looked up at him. "I don't know what to do."

"Would you like us to organise it for you, alannah?" He was just giving her the opportunity to make the decisions, knowing there was no possibility of her being capable of carrying out any of the necessary functions. But he didn't want her blaming them in the future for the way things were done. She had to be given the chance to decide for herself. It didn't matter that in the end he knew it would be himself and Stasia sorting out the priest and the coffin and the gravediggers.

The one thing he didn't ask her was about the burial. The grave. His son would be laid to rest in the nearby cemetery which overlooked the sea. He would be buried there alongside all his people before him. Of that there would be no question.

He told no-one where he was going as he left the house.

"I'll be back in an hour!" he called back to his wife.

"Where are you going?" Stasia rushed out from the back kitchen to see him disappearing out the door. The house

was filling with callers, neighbours coming from miles around. She knew her daughter-in-law was going to be no help. Bridie had gone way beyond that. She needed looking after and Dan was needed here to talk to the people

"I've to check out a few things for tomorrow. I won't be long."

She saw him leave. Watched him walk towards the gate and lift the latch, not bothering to close it behind him. There was no point. There would be many more callers to the house. She saw his shoulders as they gradually leaned over in the stoop of a much older man the further he got away from the house. A broken man, unaware that she was watching him.

Leaning against the stone wall that surrounded the cemetery, he looked around at the location of the vacant plots. A series of juddering sobs escaped. He pulled a crumpled handkerchief from his pocket. No tears came, just the hiccupping gasps. The order was all wrong. It should be him. The first one to go into the new grave. And even he wasn't ready for that.

He stood for a few minutes, waiting until the spasms subsided. He could feel the sharp edges of a stone on the wall as he placed his hand on it to push himself upright.

Focusing on the job in hand was like a fresh start. He surveyed the cemetery, marking a few vacant plots in his head in case his first choice was already taken.

He then went along to the house. The priest was expecting him.

"I'll look after that, Dan. As far as I know that one on the south side is free but I'll check it out for you and get it organised."

"Thanks, Father, I'd appreciate that."

"'Tis very sad, Dan. Poor Joseph. Long, long before his time. And he just married and starting out. A tragedy."

BRIDIE

Chapter 17

Knocknageeha

For months, consumed by an agony that stretched from wall to wall, nothing that happened around her registered in her brain. Aware of activity going on but trapped in a prison she couldn't break free from. Detached from all around her.

Her parents had stayed on for a few days after the funeral.

"Would you not come back home to Wexford with us, love?" Maude had held her arm, trying to force her to look at her. She caught her glancing at her father, willing him to intervene.

"Listen to your mother, Bridie. Maybe it would be a good idea. Might do you good."

She saw his anxious face looking down at her and hoped her hesitation wouldn't let him think that she was ready to decide anything.

"Just for a little while?" He spoke softly giving a final push.

"I don't know what I want to do." Her eyes blank as she looked at her parents. "I just can't think." She didn't want to stay but had no wish to leave.

"You don't have to decide anything yet, love." Her

grandmother glanced at her daughter and son-in-law.
"You can stay with me if you want. If you find it too lonely
at the cottage."

She saw Mary Ann shake her head at Maude and
Cornelius, willing them to leave it in her hands and she
was glad that they took the hint.

Later Bridie had no recollection of their efforts. It was
all wiped from her brain by the overwhelming enormity of
her situation. Surely she'd wake up from this nightmare.

Gortnamara

Every day she walked to the shore to look out for his boat.

She went in the mornings and the evenings and several
times during the day. The grass wore thin from her ghostly
walking. The same place she had always gone to look out
for him coming home in the evenings. The evenings when
he did come home. She couldn't give up. If she stopped
now he might never return.

She thought about him all the time. Even when the
conversation around her drifted to other topics she thought
of nothing but Joseph. The hum of talk just swam over her
head only touching her if his name was mentioned.

In the beginning she never spoke when others joined
them at the fireplace in Dan and Stasia's house. The
neighbours dropped in more frequently than normal,
reluctant to leave them to grieve alone. When it was just the
three of them she sometimes opened up and when she did,
Joseph was the sole topic of conversation. Pleased that she
was talking at all Stasia and Dan allowed her to ramble on
as much as she liked. They too wanted to talk about him
but when she spoke neither interrupted her flow. When
they sensed an ending, they talked about the little
happenings of his childhood and Bridie's eyes shone with

a hunger that broke their hearts. It was as if she was willing them to go on forever talking about him, revealing little snippets that she had never known about him.

The first evening she joined in the conversation in the presence of two neighbours, Stasia was bringing the teacups over to them seated at the fire.

"Joseph always loved your brack, Stasia. Always said it was the best brack in Ireland. I tried making it but could never get it the same." The way all heads jerked towards her, Bridie realised that her initiating of the conversation had taken them all by surprise.

"I'm sure yours was every bit as good, Bridie. A brack is a brack. Sure he only used to say that to keep me happy or maybe to keep you on your toes."

Bridie smiled at her. "I don't know about that, Stasia."

"You must give me your recipe, Stasia, my husband is always talking about it too!" the high squeaky voice of the neighbour grated like a rusty hinge through the kitchen. "How do you make it?"

Bridie retreated into her teacup but not before she caught the look on Stasia's face. As if she was fighting the urge to pour the scalding tea over the neighbour. Could she not have waited a few seconds before wading in and sending the conversation down another road. In that moment she realised how hard this was on her mother-in-law. She'd have to make a better attempt to share the pain and engage with people. But it was too soon.

Bridie raised the cup to her lips, unaware that she had forgotten to add milk.

It didn't happen suddenly. Nor did it cease completely.

At first, she only dropped one or two of the walks to the shore and that was only when the rain and wind was too fierce to make the journey inviting. It took weeks

77

before she finally stopped her constant walking to the strand and changed her route.

The extra few miles' walk to her grandmother's farm began to fill her days and a new pattern emerged. One that offered a small element of comfort to her sundered soul.

She strolled down the lane to the potato field where she'd first met Joseph. She wanted to be alone so she headed straight for the field. She avoided the house, wanting to have time alone before she called in to say hello to Mary Ann. Hoping she hadn't been seen, she sat there for an hour thinking about her loss. The loss of his life. Of hers. The loss of their life together. Their children's lives. The children that would never be. The sheer emptiness of it all filled her entire being.

On her approach to the house, Mary Ann didn't ask where she had been. Bridie knew that her grandmother knew. Art had seen her in the distance as he worked in another field. She was thankful he'd had the wit to leave her alone. She had to work it out of her system her own way. Whatever way that might be.

By midsummer both her grandmother and mother-in-law could see Bridie take on the hollow-eyed gauntness of the famine women. She'd overheard them discussing her. Her aimless wandering of the roads, a pattern developing that they'd seen before.

She picked at the meals they set before her, not aware she was willing herself to die. They coaxed some food into her and she knew they worried that she didn't eat at all when she was home alone.

Throughout the harvesting season the two women took matters into their own hands. Through her despondency she knew what they were at. Seeing to it that she ate by asking her to come and help prepare the dinner for the workmen at whichever farm had most activity going on. A bit of responsibility that might help focus her and keep her occupied. To keep them happy she went through the motions of the chores they set her in silence. It helped to have something to do as the talk and banter went on around her. Detached from it all, she pondered on how they could take life so lightly. She didn't resent their good humour. It didn't irritate her. She just wondered at how they didn't notice the pain oozing out through her pores.

The only peace for her was in the first ten seconds on awakening. Her sleep was light. Not the deep slumber of a tired body and relaxed mind, rather the half-awake doze of someone not at peace with life. Drifting into the day, not quite sure where she was, but relieved that she was coming out of a bad dream.

The value of those few early moments was short-lived. As she allowed a slit of morning grey to enter under her eyelids reality began filtering through. Her mind struggled to draw down the blind on it before it happened.

Sleep had just been an interval, a pause in the blackness. Like a swimmer walking to the tip of a diving board, ready to plunge into the day, only to find herself betrayed as she dived into the pit of darkness that waited below.

Chapter 18

The walk to the chapel took an hour. She didn't care how far it was. There was something positive in the pounding of the road. A force from underneath the gravel and dust that propelled her along, sending an energy through the soles of her leather shoes. She could feel it travel through the bones of her ankles and up her legs. Other than the physical pumping that kept her on track she was so far inside her own head that she registered nothing of the landscape.

It was a relief that she met no-one on the road throughout her journey. She didn't want anyone or anything to distract her from her mission. The occasional farmer could be seen in distant fields, far enough away not to have to wave. Aware she had interrupted their grazing she ignored the pair of curious cows who had raised their heads to look over the stone wall. She avoided looking at them. There was no way she wanted to be softened to tears by the liquid brown eyes surveying her.

By the time she arrived the anger inside had boiled up a head of steam. The gate squeaked as she opened it. Even the usual grating on her teeth that resulted from the sound was eradicated by the focus on her task. She had already reached the chapel entrance before it had time to swing closed.

The heavy wooden door gave a loud bang as it hit the stone wall inside the porch as it swung back. She immediately regretted the force with which she had shoved it open, hoping there was nobody in the church. It was not her intention to disturb any innocent person who had come there for a few peaceful moments. She had no issue with them. It was God she was angry at.

She stood a moment at the bottom of the aisle, waiting for her eyes to adjust to the gloom. She was alone. The empty echo of silence rang in her ears.

She fixed her eyes on the golden tabernacle adorning the centre of the altar. Taking a deep breath she strode forward, her face hardening with each step. She was going to have it out with Him.

It took fifteen strides to reach the brass gates of the altar rail. As usual they were closed, barring her from going any further. She didn't need to. From where she stood she had a perfect view. Any closer would have put her at a disadvantage. Too far below the crucifix that hung above the altar. No, she needed to be able to eyeball him. Here was perfect.

The agonised face of Christ had droplets of blood oozing from his crown of thorns, his eyes raised to Heaven. He couldn't even look her in the eye. She felt no sympathy. Her Catholic instinct to genuflect in his presence was smothered by her anger.

Standing there she threw out her arms and shouted at the figure.

"Why? Why did you do it?" She waited for an answer. "Look at me." She paused. "I said look at me. Don't just hang there silent, feeling sorry for yourself. Tell me. Go on, tell me. I need to know why."

She wanted a reply. A reason. Something she could make sense of. The least she was entitled to was that.

"What did I ever do to you that was so bad you thought I deserved such a punishment as this?" She dropped her arms and listened to the silence. Some of the fire had already left her, but reluctant to let him off so easily she drew in a breath and gave one last loud lash.

"*I hate you! I hate you!*" Something burst inside her and she began to slip to her knees. "*I hate you! I hate you! I hate you . . .*"

With each sobbing reprimand subsiding, each repeat fading and spilling onto the tiles of the church floor, she dissolved in a heap in front of the altar.

She lay there for ten minutes before the cold of the tiles began to seep into her bones. Her anger spent, she gathered herself together and sat up. Rubbing the heat back into her arms, she looked around to check that no-one had entered the church unnoticed. The confession box. She had forgotten that the priest might be sitting in there in the dark saying his prayers while waiting for stragglers to whisper their sins into his ear. Well, if he was, she didn't need to go in to him. He'd already heard hers. Blasphemy or what, she didn't know, nor did she care. If he had been sitting in there throughout, he'd surely have made himself known by now. Even if it had been to throw her out of the chapel.

Her legs, stiff from the cold as she stood up, were slow as she walked to the back of the church. She limped into the last pew and massaged her knees until she felt the blood starting to flow again.

She sat back and looked up at the crucifix in the distance. Maybe it was no harm to have let Him know how she felt. Nothing had changed, she was still alone, but she felt the better for having vented her spleen. Emptied herself. She wasn't sorry. It would be hypocrisy to pretend

she was. All that nonsense she had learned at sc..
These things are sent to test us rubbish. It had to be do.
and now it was. But she didn't want to look Him in the eye
anymore. She couldn't forgive Him but at least now He
knew and could be in no doubt as to why.

She dropped her gaze to the bench in front and traced
the grain in the wood with her eyes, backwards and
forwards around the loops and knots until she began to
feel dizzy. Blinking she averted her eyes to a spot further
along the wooden bench and noticed fish scales on the
seat. Kneeling down she moved along the pew until she
drew alongside them. She reached out and ran her finger
across their silver transparency. Firmly dried into the
wood, it was impossible to say how long they'd been there.
Probably for years. Glancing along the bench she saw more
small clusters of scales stuck here and there along its
length. She'd never noticed them before. She reached out
and began to scratch at them. They didn't come away
easily but she managed to prise a few off with her nails,
each silver sequin springing up before shooting in different
directions, as if not wanting to be caught. She persisted
until she dislodged a clump, easing it up with her
thumbnail, and caught it in her palm. She put it on the tip of
her finger and bringing it to her nose she sniffed, closing
her eyes as she inhaled the faint salty smell of the sea.

It came back to her, something Mary Ann had said. A
comment long forgotten. From a childhood holiday. Her
grandmother ushering her up the church one Sunday
when she went to sit in one of the back pews.

"Go on up further, Bridie, unless you want to smell all
fishy. Never go into the last two benches. That's where the
fishermen sit when they come in after a haul."

With all the holidays to Clare over the years she had
never recalled it until now. With her nail she began to pick

n. Some of them might have been Joseph's.

n her intention that day to make her visit

egular trip. It was the fish scales that did

ack again and again to the chapel. A link

between them to replace the walks to the seashore. Maybe her tantrum hadn't been in vain.

Knocknageeha

With the harvest in, the produce pickled and the jams made, new ways of keeping her occupied were introduced. She knew the signs.

"Come out to the garden with me and we'll see if there are a few flowers for the grave."

She followed as Mary Ann led the way, knowing that her grandmother wasn't leaving any possibility that she might disappear again and not come back for hours. The last time it had happened Mary Ann had gone out looking for her, had got into a bit of a panic only to find her crying into the flowerbed.

As they walked along the track to the cemetery, she watched her grandmother hold her face up to the weak sun.

"Oh, that's lovely. There's still a bit of heat left in it. Nothing like nature to ease the soul."

Envying her this simple pleasure in the afternoon light of autumn, Bridie wished she could share it. "How long did it take, Granny?"

"For what, Bridie?"

"For you to be able to come here to the grave in peace."

"A while, alannah, a while. And not a short while either. In fact it took a very long time. It's not something you can rush, child."

"I don't think it'll ever happen for me."

"I thought the same when I lost your grandfather. But it will."

"I doubt it."

"Well, look at me now. I wasn't always as good as this. I know what you're suffering but believe me when I tell you it gets easier. I know that's hard to believe but it will happen for you too, love. Eventually. Just give it a bit more time."

And so she followed passively whenever they took her to visit Joseph's grave. She didn't resent any of this, quite the opposite. She was happy to be led, relieved that others were taking control. It wasn't always Mary Ann – sometimes it was Joseph's mother and sometimes Dan came with them. That was often easier because it meant they could talk amongst themselves and she didn't have to make any effort. It left her free to trail behind. To wander the earth like a phantom. Nothing much expected of her, not even chat. She went along with them each week, biding her time in the vague hope that her grandmother might be proved right.

Chapter 19

Gortnamara

1897

One day a breach appeared. No more than a hairline crack in the wall of grief. It was so narrow that Bridie hardly noticed.

At first it was a momentary thing. She stopped thinking about Joseph for a few seconds. It was only when her mind returned to him that she realised there had been a gap, a pause in her constant obsession.

The first few times it happened she felt she had let him down. Torn between wanting relief but not wanting to tear herself from him. As it became a more regular occurrence she realised she was powerless to control it one way or the other but the guilt remained.

Then one day it happened. She thought she saw something in the distance. A chink of light coming through, penetrating that crack from some far off place. Not piercing like it hurt her eyes, weak enough that blinking would leave her in danger of losing it. If she held her gaze steady she could see it down a long dark tunnel. But it was there. Definitely there.

Then there was a grey day when that light, small as it was, disappeared. It happened on a Sunday in winter. One of those days where the daylight never quite breaks through the leaden clouds.

Bridie stirred at dawn after a fitful night's sleep. A call of nature had woken her. She knew it was a mistake to return to the bed but she was tired. Her body ached as she climbed back under the now cool covers for another hour's sleep before beginning her chores. Chores that didn't matter anymore. She turned over, pulling the blankets up over her head and waited for the heat to return to the covers.

She woke again at with a heavy dullness that had her turning over for yet another few minutes' rest. She didn't know how long had passed before she checked the clock again.

Lying there, her eyes open she looked up at the shadowy ceiling, barely focussing. Slow images drifted through her mind. Each one fading and mixing into the next before her concentration was able to catch hold of any. None of the thoughts made any sense. The sound of bees on the lavender bush being captured in a glass jar. Yellow pollen stuck to their legs. The clove scent of the pinks in the flowerbed as she rounded the end of house on her way home from school. The swish of the teacher's wooden *bata* as it stung her childish palm when she didn't know her times tables. Thoughts of no consequence, random incidents that had happened years ago, not important at the time and even less so now. So why were they revisiting her?

The dull ticking of the clock on the bedside table took over as the thoughts ebbed and flowed. She had no idea when it was she fell asleep again nor for how long.

She woke with a dart. Her eyes snapped open. Shooting upright in the bed with a suddenness that made her head swim, she wasn't sure what exactly had woken her. A sound outside perhaps. She listened but all was silent. Propping herself up, arms rigid behind her, she looked around the room disorientated.

Once she established her bearings she glanced at the

clock. It showed half past five. All sense of time had deserted her. The gloom of the room provided no clue. Five in the afternoon or five in the morning? With a mounting terror she jumped from the bed and ran to draw back the curtain. It was raining outside. A fine drizzle. It might have been a grey dawn or a dusky evening sky. She had no way of knowing.

At the basin she splashed her face with cold water in the hope that it would clear her head and help her make sense of the world. She dressed in the clothes she had thrown on the bedside chair the previous night. Putting on her coat she headed out the door and began walking in the direction of the farm. The misty drizzle dampened her hair, making her wish she had thought to put on a hat. No point in turning back now until she established if it was day or night.

She began to worry that if anyone saw her at that time of the morning, if it was morning, they would think she had lost her mind wandering the roads at such an early hour. But that was the least of her problems. The very thought that she had actually lost her mind kept her moving in the hope of finding some sign of life.

She slowed as she neared the farm. She could see no light in the house. The fire was kept going all night throughout the winter as well as during the day so the smoke from the chimney was no help. She needed some other clue. She walked towards the house, treading softly in case the dog started barking. As she approached the corner she thought she heard Stasia's voice. Waiting a moment to be sure before rounding the end of the house she was relieved to see Joseph's mother putting food into the dog's bowl outside the back door.

Evening.

Bridie sat with her elbows propped on the table, her hands

wrapped around the warm mug as she drank her tea. Things had begun to slide. Her experience the previous day had scared her. Made her question if she was losing her grip on reality. It wasn't something she could discuss. Not something she wished to reveal to anyone in case they confirmed that what she told them was the first sign of madness. She couldn't continue as she was going along this road unless she wanted to end up there. It frightened her enough into making a few of decisions.

Already she had achieved the first step. Day One. Step One. It was a start. She hadn't wanted to do it, but she did. Throwing off the covers as soon as she woke, swinging her legs over the side of the bed and getting herself upright. She had forced herself not to think, otherwise she wouldn't have achieved it. Forced herself not to allow a thought in. Just do it. Pleased now with herself. She had passed that first test.

Emptying the dregs from her mug she rinsed it. She gazed out the window, seeing nothing, the mug still in her hand. Five, ten, fifteen seconds. She didn't know how long.

"C'mon, Bridie. Move it. Shift it. Time to take the next step." She heard herself. Not sure if it was said out loud or if she'd heard it inside her head, she repeated it. This time aloud. "C'mon, Bridie. Move it. Shift it. Time to take the next step."

Talking to someone each day other than Joseph's parents was on the list. Or better still – as well as Stasia and Dan. They must be getting tired of her. Talking to herself didn't count. Mary Ann would be the easiest to start with. Yes, she'd be happy if she achieved a total of three today. Something to build on.

Realising the mug was still in her hand she shook the last drops of water out and placed it upside down on the drainer. Time now to take Step Two.

She hadn't walked to Knocknageeha for a while. Stasia had mentioned it. Dropped it into conversation, a bit too casually, that she'd met Mary Ann. It was the unasked question that had stirred the guilt.

Step Two. Her grandmother would be a good choice. She might be surprised by the visit, but she was possibly the only person who wouldn't question why she was calling. Nor would she wonder at the increase in the regularity of the visits, that was assuming she could keep going with her new regime.

On the walk to the farm she mulled over what to say. She couldn't remember how long it had been. A few weeks anyway. All she knew was that once winter had set in she had stopped visiting the grave. Couldn't bear the sight of the leafless trees, the skeleton shapes and the cold grey of the lake. She didn't know if Mary Ann still went there. Maybe she didn't go so often in the cold weather. Or maybe the visits had just been an excuse to get Bridie out.

She hesitated at the door. It was open. She could hear delph clattering in the kitchen. Leaning forward, she poked her head around the frame and could see Mary Ann washing the breakfast dishes. She deserved whatever sort of a reception she was going to get after her weeks of neglect of her grandmother?

MARY ANN

Chapter 20

"Hello, Gran."

"Who's that?" Mary Ann half turned from the basin, wet cloth in her hand.

"Ah, Bridie. Come in. Come in, alannah. I was wondering where you'd got to, child. I was beginning to get worried. We haven't seen you for ages." As soon as the words were out of her mouth Mary Ann regretted them.

She'd met Stasia at Mass. "How is she doing, Stasia?"

"Not good." Stasia had shook her head. "Not good at all, but I'm keeping a close eye on her."

"Do you think I should call over? She hasn't been over to see me for weeks."

"I think maybe we should leave her for the moment. I can't get her to talk much. Doesn't seem to want to talk to anyone. I tell her each time I meet you and I'm encouraging her to go out but it's not working. Well not for the minute anyway."

"I can't help but worry about her, Stasia. I've written to her mother but it's hard to know what to do for the best. You'll let me know if I can be of any help, won't you?"

"I will indeed. I don't want to force her to do anything at the moment. It has to come from her but I'll watch it a bit longer and if I have to force it then I will."

Now Mary Ann wondered if Stasia had had to use force or if this long-awaited visit had been Bridie herself taking the initiative. She wasn't going to ask but hoped now that the "We haven't seen you in ages" hadn't sounded like a reprimand.

"I've been busy, Granny."

The foolishness of the response showed on her granddaughter's face but was not something Mary Ann was going to pull her up on or question. It might be better to act as if it was normal.

"Keep your coat on and come out with me and we'll see if there are any eggs to collect." Mary Ann reached for the shawl hanging on the back of the door and shooed her out the door.

"Very chilly out there." Mary Ann blew on her hands and gave a shudder. "Now will you pass me over that basket of eggs and fill the kettle there like a good girl and, when I have these eggs all wiped, we'll have a cup of tea and a good chat."

Bridie seemed happy to make herself useful. The teamaking ritual helped get over any awkwardness as the women settled down at the table. Once the mugs were filled Mary Ann let the silence hang as Bridie traced a deep score in the wooden tabletop with her finger.

She sat back on the chair, content to look out the window.

Let her take her time, Mary Ann thought. If she wants to talk she'd let her start but if Bridie just wanted to sit for the companionship that was alright too.

BRIDIE

Chapter 21

She couldn't admit to the happening of the previous day. Couldn't tell Mary Ann it had been that event that had instigated the change. She knew the earlier "busy" lie was transparent but hoped her grandmother would allow it to pass. The realisation that if she was on the verge of losing her mind her only option was to join the world again to have any hope of recovering. She didn't want a debate about a little white lie to derail her.

Bridie glanced over towards the door as the white cat came in from the yard. He stopped in the doorway stretching his legs out before him, easing the stiffness of a good sleep. She watched him walk slowly towards the table disappearing under it, the downy fur soft against her legs as he rubbed himself, slithering in and out between her ankles. She didn't want him to stop but she felt him gliding away as his interest waned. In seconds he reappeared at her side, looking up at her, expectant. She felt Mary Ann watching her as she bent down to stroke his arched back before running the length of his snowy tail through her looped fingers and thumb. He looked up at her. Pushing back her chair, she made room for him. He jumped up onto her lap before mooching around, turning one way, then another until he found a position he deemed comfortable before settling down.

"I never realised it would be so hard, Granny." She could feel the purring as she rested her hand on his back.

"I'm sure you didn't, love. Sure you'd have had no business even thinking about it at all and you young and just married."

"How did you manage? When Grandad died. I don't remember him but you must have been young too."

"Not as young as you, Bridie, but it was very hard. Even still. And I had a whole lot of young children to look after and a farm to run."

As they sat in silence Bridie could see the wretched desolation of that first year of widowhood echoed on her grandmother's face.

"D'yeh know, even though I was surrounded by a load of children I was lonely. I thought no-one understood the isolation. I thought no-one had ever felt as much loss as I did when your grandad died."

"But maybe that's the difference, Granny. Even though it was hard for you, at least you had the children and you had a good few years with him. You had time with him. I didn't have any with Joseph."

The cat stood up and jumped softly to the ground, moving over to Mary Ann. Her chair scraped the tiles as she moved it back.

"You're right there, Bridie. It wasn't fair on you. So soon for it to have happened."

"I've been left with nothing so I really don't think anyone can understand what that's like."

"Ah, they do, Bridie. You mightn't think it or they mightn't tell you but a lot of people do." Mary Ann gazed out the window, idly stroking the cat on her knee. "But, d'yeh know, it's funny you should say that about the

94

children. I know you'd have liked to have Joseph's child, a little bit of him still here for you, but I was sometimes angry at Pat for leaving me like that, leaving me on my own to look after the children."

"But at least you had them."

"I know, child, and it was only later that I realised it was them that kept me going. I'd no choice but to keep going. And with a farm to run. And on top of that I was looking after his sister Aggie and sure poor Aggie wasn't quite right. I couldn't even talk to her. She wouldn't have understood. It just wasn't fair. That's what I thought too, at the time."

The two women fell into the silence of their own thoughts until the cat jumped down to the floor, rousing Mary Ann.

"I think we'll get on with the chores. They won't do themselves." She stood up and taking the teapot emptied it into the slops bucket.

Bridie picked up the mugs listlessly and went over to the basin.

"Life is never easy, child."

"What am I going to do, Granny? I don't know what to do?" She could feel Mary Ann's eyes on her as she leaned over the basin, aware that her shuddering would confirm that she was weeping into the dirty water. "Tell me what to do and I'll do it. Anything has to be better than this."

MARY ANN

Chapter 22

She was going to have to do something to help her. They'd tried everything. The gentle route. It had to be that way at the start but now the time for sympathy was over. Bridie was not pulling up.

"As you get older, child, you'll realise life is but a series of hard knocks." The words were cruel. But fully aware of their brutality once she'd started Mary Ann had to push on. "It's not the good things in life that you learn from, Bridie, it's the bad things." She spoke slowly in the hope she was making sense to this broken girl. "The only consolation I can give you, child, is that you get better able to deal with them as you get older. Each blow makes you stronger."

"I don't want to be stronger, I just want Joseph." Bridie flung the wet dishcloth into the tepid water.

Mary Ann was unsure if she'd done the right thing. Maybe the bleak reality of her words was too harsh. She was unsure if it was this or if it was the truth in the message that caused Bridie to slump. She watched her as she leant her head on her hands, elbows propped on the edge of the basin wailing like a child. She had to hold back, to stifle her instinct. She wanted to allow her granddaughter to cry herself out.

Ten endless seconds passed. Her own tears rolled down her cheeks as she watched. She could wait no longer. In two strides she took Bridie in her arms and, pulling her away from the basin, she rested the auburn head on her own shoulder, stroking the soft curls.

It took a few minutes for the outpouring to subside. As it reduced to jerky intakes of breath, she waited until her granddaughter had control of her breathing before catching her gently by the shoulders. She leaned back slightly so she could see her face.

"If we don't stop we'll have each other drowned." Mary Ann saw Bridie's eyes stray to the damp patch darkening the shoulder of her wrap-around apron. "Would you look at the state of us, covered in wet and slime."

"Sorry, Granny." She took the towel and with a watery smile she attempted to mop her grandmother's shoulder.

"Don't worry about that. Give your own face a wipe. There's a good girl." Mary Ann smiled. "That's more like it. But it's best to let it all out. Go over to that drawer and get yourself a handkerchief and give a good blow. I'll finish these few things and while you're sorting yourself out and I'll put aside a few eggs for you to take back with you. And I'll put in a couple of duck eggs too. Dan is partial to them."

BRIDIE

Chapter 23

When she looked back on that session with her grandmother, she could see it clearly as the turning point.

With each passing week the gaps when she didn't think of Joseph occurred more and more often. Sometimes she turned it into a game. Rationing her time, when she found herself thinking of him she allowed herself to indulge for periods of five minutes. She would then force herself to get up and do something. It varied, but some little chore like going out and clipping back a bit of the overgrown hedge on the lane, washing the outside of the windows to let the sunlight in or filling a vase with flowers. Something positive, where she had achieved some little thing or had done something to cheer up the place. She would reward herself with another five minutes of thinking if she needed it, but only if she had earned it.

It didn't always work but as the short spells of activity turned into longer ones she saw the little chink of light at the end of the tunnel, the one she thought she'd lost sight of, returning, as if it was Joseph himself beckoning her back to life.

MAUDE

Chapter 24

County Wexford
1897

The surfaces inside her chest wall grated against one another. Each sandpaper grazing an agony, like there was no lubrication between the layers. She lay there trying not to move or cough in an effort to reduce the friction. If she concentrated on working to increasing the saliva and swallowing hard it might help to stem the tickle in her throat. Maude lay still, trying to breathe her way through it. But it was no good. Starting like a feather stroking the insides of her neck she could feel it again. She turned on her side in an effort to avert it. She reached for the glass of water but two swallows failed to work. The cough erupted, engulfing her in a spasm that wracked her entire body, so fierce that it relegated the agony of the sandpapering to a mere background sensation. With a loud sigh she lay back on the pillows, spent, as it subsided.

All sense of time had disappeared. She thought she must have been about a week or ten days in the hospital. Cornelius came every evening to see her after he had finished work in the Barracks in Gorey, and before he cycled the few miles home to Riverchapel. She looked forward to these visits, not because she was particularly pleased to see him but she was hungry for news of the children.

He arrived, tall and lean, in his Head Constable's uniform, looking handsome and imposing. His handlebar moustache, while she had to admit suited him, gave a certain air, an impression of self-importance, something that annoyed her, although she knew he was unaware of how he came across. It further irritated her that he insisted on continuing to stand instead of accepting the chair offered by the nurse. She wished he would just sit but she didn't have the energy or the patience to coax him. It was like he didn't intend to stay.

"Well, Maude, and how are you feeling today?"

Always the same formal opening from a place above her. He reminded her of the doctor. The use of her name coming from his mouth even sounded like she was a stranger whose name he'd picked up from her chart. He might as well have called her Mrs. Redmond.

"A bit better."

Most days she gave the same answer. Other times she introduced a variation.

"I'm grand."

Not wanting to waste what little breath she had on empty answers about herself, she preferred to save it for the vital questions about the children.

He never volunteered the information. No understanding that it was not news of big startling events she was looking for, just the everyday goings-on with the children. Who did what, had the older ones helped out, who was feeding the dog? She always had to drag it from him.

Occasionally he had news.

"The funeral went off well. A big crowd. It was well attended."

"And how are they all?"

"Bearing up."

"Well, were you talking to anyone at it?"

"Yes, I sympathised with the family."

"Anyone else? Did you meet anyone else?"

"Yes. I met Bart."

"Well?"

"Yes, I was talking to Bart."

"And?"

"I just went over and shook hands and said 'Hello, Bart'." He seemed surprised at her persistence. "He'd no news really."

On these occasions Maude gave up and slumped back on the pillows.

CORNELIUS

Chapter 25

Spotting something dark lying in the ditch as he cycled along in the fading light posed a dilemma. This was the last thing Cornelius needed. Torn between the urgency of his journey and his duty to investigate anything suspicious, even though he had finished his day's work, he decided to stop. He didn't want to, but he knew if he didn't it would niggle him the whole evening.

Dismounting, he laid his bicycle down on the grass verge. His polished leather boot skidded on a muddy patch as he took a step down the slope into the ditch. He clicked his tongue when he discovered it was nothing more than a sack of rubbish, but thankful it wasn't a drunk, or worse still a dead body. Had it been either, he would have been obliged to do something about it. He didn't need anything to delay him further.

The drumming of his chest pounded in his ears. It had started as he pedalled uphill and he convinced himself it was due to the exertion. With it continuing now even though he was simply parking his bicycle he knew without doubt it had nothing to do with the cycling. The blood churned in his heart, boiling and bubbling as if its heat regulator had malfunctioned. He knew it was not a heart attack, although that might have been easier. Spared him what he had to do. His heart was already broken, and he was about to break another.

Pausing a moment before heading towards the door of the hospital, the pounding reached a pitch where he could no longer hear the outside world. Concentrating on his breathing, he tried to dim the sounds which were already creating pictures inside his head. Images of his heart tearing through the chest wall and bursting open to spew its red hot contents onto the wet cobbles. The basket on his bicycle would be spattered with blood and his hands would slip on the blood covering the handlebars. The very image of the explosion released something, stilling the inner hammering. He leaned back against the cold damp stone of the hospital wall, eyes closed. He had to pull himself together. He had a task to carry out and no-one else could do it for him.

He wiped his boots on the mat and pushed the heavy carved door. Stepping into the hospital corridor he could feel the cold air rush in behind him as he slowly closed the door. After the dusk outside, all soft edges seemed suddenly stripped away under the lighting. Dim as it was he couldn't escape the harsh reality. The sharp smell of disinfectant caught his breath. Two nurses passed, nodding to him, the rustling of their starched aprons loud in his ears. He slowed his pace as he walked the long corridor. The scar in the paintwork of the ward door caught his eye as he approached. The constant scraping of beds being wheeled in and out had gouged a deep wound in the wood. He paused and took a deep breath before pushing the door open, heading over to where she lay watching.

MAUDE

Chapter 26

The relief she felt when he didn't ask her how she was feeling was short-lived. The moment he pulled across the chair and sat down she knew something was amiss. It was his reaching across and taking her hand, a gesture so completely alien to him, that had the prickles tingle the nape of her neck.

"What's wrong?" Her heart thumped the soreness of her chest into oblivion.

He sat up straight, his eyes never leaving her face.

"Maude, I've something to tell you. You're going to have to be very brave."

In the withdrawal of his hand she recognised the Head Constable returning and was reassured. A momentary pang of guilt as she thought, hoped, it might be some bad news about a neighbour. In that pause a nurse appeared and asked him to go to the office with her.

"I'll be back shortly." As he stood up a wave of something resembling relief cross his face.

Seeing it, she reached out and caught his hand. *"Wait. Tell me first."*

"I'll be back in a minute, Maude." He patted the back of her hand before releasing his and turning he followed the

starched uniform. It was only when he was out of reach
that he glanced back to give his wife a nod. His serious
expression gave nothing away.

She stayed sitting, propped up in the bed, eyes watching
the office, impatient for him to return. A Riverchapel
woman, a visitor to another ward entering through the
open door at the end of the room, distracted her. The last
person she wished to see on this day was Maisie Brien. A
prisoner in her hospital bed, she was trapped. There was
something about the way Maisie managed to place herself
at the centre of every drama that Maude disliked. The
purposeful stride and woebegone facial expression told
her that she was about to do it again.

"Wasn't that an awful thing to happen your poor little
Annie, Maude?" Maisie began to pull the chair towards
her, about to sit down. "I'm so sorry. Poor little mite, not
much more than a toddler. And you in here so sick."

"What are you talking about, Maisie?" Maude forgot
her antipathy. "Is it my daughter? My little Annie you
mean?"

"Oh my God.?" Maisie paused, still standing, her eyes
widening in horror. "You don't know? Do you not know?"
Her hand flew to her mouth. "Oh God, what have I done?
I thought you knew, Maude."

Cornelius appeared from the office and seeing the
tableau before him knew he was too late.

"*Get away. Just get away, will you?*" Hot anger rose,
burning through his gut until it burst out in flames
through the pores of his face.

The way he barked, together with the look on his
flushed face made Maude think he might strike Maisie.
Always measured, his reaction increased her panic.

"Cornelius, just tell me, will you? Has something
happened to our Annie?"

He sat down on the side of the bed and laid his Head Constable's hat down. He looked over his shoulder to see Maisie rooted to the spot.

"I thought I told you to go."

"Sorry. I'm really sorry." It came out almost as a whisper and with a final glance at Maude the woman turned and slunk out of the ward.

As he turned back to face his wife his professional ability to impart bad news deserted him and she watched him shrink, his shoulders crumpling.

"Something terrible has happened, Maude. Poor little Annie. The boys were supposed to be keeping an eye on her but they went out to the field to kick football. She went with them, but they didn't notice she'd wandered off back to the house."

"Cornelius, is she alright? What happened her?"

"I can't make this easy, Maude. She fell into the fire. It was Dorothy who found her."

His wife's face, a white mask of horror, stared back at him.

"But is she alright? Tell me she's alright?"

"Maude, she got burnt. Poor Dorothy tried her best but she didn't make it."

Anxious she was clear, that she understood what he was saying, she recognised the signs. He was closing the door on any hope, not wanting to allow room for ambiguity.

"Maude, she's gone." His eyes filled. "There's no other way I can put it, Maude. Poor little Annie is dead." The last sentence choked out of him.

She knew what he was doing but she didn't want to hear the brutal words that were intended to crush any false hope. Crush it completely. She knew why he'd used them. Not wanting to have to repeat it. Didn't want to have to answer her pleading questions.

In that moment everything went grey. She couldn't see. The only sound was an animal wail coming from somewhere. She had no idea it was from herself. As the grey turned black she didn't see his hand outstretched towards her as she burrowed into the pillows, leaving her husband alone.

Chapter 27

Once Maude had made the decision, she got up early. Dreading having to face the sadness, the finality of it, but it was done now.

Taking her mug of tea, she went into the garden for a rest before starting on her next lot of chores. She was glad she'd put it first on her list. The activities of the remainder of the day might now serve as a distraction. Sorting little Annie's clothes had been hard. No more children to pass them on to. Nor would there be.

She sat on the window ledge, its granite sill beneath her warmed by the late May sunshine. Every now and then she sipped the hot tea before resting her head back against the window frame. The flowers of the tree had faded almost to white. It was only looking upwards against the blue sky that she could see traces of its former pink petals. She watched as the gentle breeze blew drifts of spent blossoms through the air, carrying them along until they settled as soft pink tears to cover the dewy grass.

Time to move forward.

CORNELIUS

Chapter 28

He often wondered, but he never quite knew what his wife thought about him.

Day-to-day existence was propelled along by his going to work and her looking after the domestic chores. Not much discussion emerged in relation to either of these roles apart from the children's goings-on. He always asked about them. Otherwise, the hens, the few cows and pigs, the dog and the vegetable garden probably provided more material for discussion. And so between them both they plodded on, engaging in the expected rituals with no major friction in the home.

Things seem to trundle along, with nothing more than an occasional undercurrent of low-level irritation on her part. This was diffused by an occasional burst of wildness. They seemed to come out of nowhere to surprise him. She had no idea what he thought about her either but she didn't much mind. On the occasions when the urge came upon her to jolt them both out of their rut, she would grab him by the arms and whirl him around the kitchen or the yard in a mad dance and try to shake some spontaneity into him. Such was the suddenness that he would have no option but to go along with it for a round or two, relieved when he felt the speed diminish.

"Enough of this foolishness Maude. I've work to be getting on with." He knew his half-suppressed smile did not go unnoticed by her, hoped that it hid his underlying embarrassment.

The islands were a series of small tussocks of grassy land in the middle of the channel which ran at the bottom of the Bog Field. The channel was little more than a small stream into which the excess water drained from the surrounding fields, with bulrushes poking up here and there along its route.

The islands couldn't be seen from the road, hidden as they were down in a sort of valley that formed a boundary dividing the farms. They could only be accessed by walking along the lane that split their smallholding into two separate sections. He knew it was her favourite place to bring a picnic when they were first married. Sometimes the pair of swans were there and sometimes they weren't. It was disappointing when they were missing. Watching them move effortlessly along followed by their fluffy cygnets was a sight they both loved. Then came the year when a lone swan spent the summer gliding up and down and Cornelius remembered Maude's tears the first time the companion was missing.

"I heard it said they mate for life," he remarked, handing her his handkerchief.

"I know. That's the worst part." She blew her nose and handed it back to him. "The lonesomeness of it."

One sunny Sunday afternoon she sat on the edge of the bed and watched him as he took off his uniform. He could see her in the mirror. She had on her best summer frock. Her brown hair had curled in the heat, loosely brushing

110

her tanned neck and a certain luminous quality radiated from her. An essence of something that had first attracted him to her. He couldn't quite put a word on it but it was there again, when he had feared it might have gone forever.

"Come on, Cornelius, let's go down to the islands to see if the swans are there."

"Sure we can't just go off just like that." He laughed at her.

"Why not?" It sounded like a challenge. "It's a lovely afternoon."

He knew she was trying to soften it.

"Well, there's the lads' tea to be seen to."

"Fonsie can see to that." She got up from the bed and went to the door. "*Fonsie?*"

He heard the shout and came to the bottom of the stairs. "Yes, Ma. Were you calling me?"

"I was. Will you give them their tea about five? There's a fresh loaf cooling on the windowsill."

"Are you off somewhere?"

"We are."

Having swiftly removed the obstacle, she turned back into the bedroom before her son could ask any more questions.

"That's sorted. Not like you to be worrying about them getting fed." She sat back down on the bed again and looked at him

Cornelius took his patched gardening trousers from the back of the chair and began stepping into them. He wanted to go with her but there were chores to attend to.

"We'll go another time." He cursed his sense of duty that he could feel suppressing the desire to indulge in a few hours' idleness. "There's logs to be split." He tried to lighten the refusal. "I'd love to have the time to be off gallivanting but I haven't."

111

"It's the middle of the summer. The logs can wait."

She was still sitting on the bed when his head appeared through the tight neck of his ragged jumper. It emerged just in time for him to see the light fade in her eyes.

"Ah, sure maybe you're right. I'll go with you." He knew it was too late – he'd crushed the joy out of her.

"Ah, don't bother yourself!" Standing up, she brushed past him shouting down the stairs. "I'll go on my own."

Cornelius watched them from the window. Dorothy had joined her. He could have kicked himself. No point in going after them, that would only annoy her further and he couldn't blame her. It was his fault for ruining the moment.

He wasn't sure how long he stood there but it was well after they had disappeared from sight. They were probably already feeding the swans. He could picture it – Maude doling out the crusts of bread to throw into the stream.

Intimacy was something that had eluded Cornelius all his life. The closeness of it terrified him, something he was aware of and envied those who could embrace it. Something he desired so much, but an unknown fear rendered him unable to make the breakthrough, no matter how close he got.

If anyone had asked him about his rage that day in the hospital, the rage directed at Maisie Brien, he would have said it was to do with the terrible death of his child and her clumsiness in jumping ahead with the news. But he knew this was only part of it.

On that occasion in the hospital he'd recognised an opportunity in the midst of disaster. The truth of his rage at the village woman had more to do with her depriving him of the intimacy of sharing the tragedy with his wife. It was their child. Their heartbreak. Instead of being able to

112

comfort her, soften the shock, he had got the backlash. So close, and yet another chance snatched from him and that time it wasn't his fault.

He remembered his wife then. Couldn't get the image out of his mind. Lost to him in that moment, curled up in a foetal ball with her back to him, leaving him sitting on the side of the bed. A thousand miles apart.

BRIDIE

Chapter 29

County Clare
1897

There was no sound of footsteps crossing the yard but the moment Bridie arrived into the kitchen Stasia knew this was no casual visit. The absence of a "Hello, Stasia" or "Morning, Stasia" was unusual. There was something on her mind. The air prickled with it and whatever it was had erased the normal niceties of a social call.

"Is Dan around?" Bridie looked around the room.

Stasia couldn't decide if the look was wary or anxious. It gave no indication if she wanted him specifically or if she sought to speak to Stasia alone.

"Did you not pass him on the way in? I think he's out in the yard somewhere. Should be in for the tea soon."

In the silence that followed, Stasia glanced at her as she moved to the window and stood there, running her finger along the sill. She watched her head turn from side to side as she looked out, the uneasy stance of someone searching for something outside.

"Did you want him for something?"

"No. I just wondered." She turned from the window, pulled out a chair and sat down.

Stasia continued drying the dishes, the silence between them heavy with the waiting.

"Well?" The word came out stark, sounding like a challenge. Not quite as Stasia might have intended.

"Well, what?" She sat up straight. The single word impaling her. Surely Stasia couldn't know what was coming. She couldn't have guessed.

"Any news?"

"Oh? Oh no, I've none." Relieved, she slumped down again. The pause was enough for her to decide it might be wise to fill the gap until Dan appeared. "Sure where would I get news? I haven't seen anyone since yesterday. Have you any?"

"Ne'er a bit. Other than the dog got his head stuck in the old kettle outside the door there. It was full of water and he dunked his head in for a drink and couldn't get it out."

Bridie knew her grin pleased her mother-in-law, even momentarily.

"Lucky I was in the kitchen and heard the racket outside and rescued him. You should have seen him. Thrashing about in a right panic with it stuck on his head." She paused. "I think I hear Dan."

Bridie straightened up, looking towards the door.

"Do I smell the tae?"

"You do indeed. If there's muck on them boots, don't go bringing it in here."

"Hello there, Bridie. Will you come here and give me a hand to pull them off before she goes mad."

She got up and went to him. Glad of the distraction and not to have to go straight to the point of her visit, she welcomed the pulling and tugging of the boots. Dan staggered slightly, holding onto the frame of the door, as the second boot released his foot with a sudden plop.

"Steady on there, steady on!" Dan chuckled and padded across to the table in his stockinged feet.

"You going to eat with them hands?"

"There're the only ones I've got." He winked at Bridie and, changing direction, headed towards the basin.

As they drank the tea she remained quiet while they exchanged a bit of farmyard talk, not sure how she was going to break the news. Their chat went over her head as she waited for a good time to make her announcement. With each passing topic it got harder. The longer she held back, the more she realised there wasn't going to be a suitable gap.

Stasia stood up and refilled the kettle.

"Maybe you'd clear the table, Bridie. I'll make a bit of bread. We're down to the last of it."

Dan pushed his chair back. "I might need a hand to put these boots back on first."

Bridie stayed seated and looked over at him. Nothing for it but to plunge in before the opportunity disappeared. There would be no good time. She knew she had to say it. Sooner or later. Better to get it over with.

"I will. In a minute." She paused. "Sit down, Dan. There's something I want to talk to you about. Talk to you both about."

Dan sat back down on the chair and gave her his full attention.

"I can't stay. I can't stay here."

"What do you mean, Bridie?" Dan looked puzzled.

"I need to go home to Wexford."

There was a pause as Stasia returned with the kettle.

"But you're only just back, Bridie," said Stasia. "And that can't have been easy. Leaving them all so soon after the funeral and your poor parents devastated after their little child." She paused. "Is that why?"

"I'm not sure. Maybe." Bridie paused. "I did a bit of thinking. Somehow it was easier to think over there."

"Maybe you're right, love." She settled the kettle on the

hook over the fire. "Maybe it would be a good idea to go back to your parents for a few weeks."

"No, I don't mean for a break. I mean for good." She hoped it hadn't come out like the slap it felt. They'd taken it up wrong.

Stasia raised her eyebrows and glanced across at Dan, her expression confirming an understanding of any earlier agitation that might have been evident. Why Bridie had needed them both together. It meant she wouldn't have to go through the same thing twice.

Dan's mouth opened as if to say something. Nothing came out. Stunned, he looked at her, his eyes wide as a child's. Rooted to the chair, she could see the hope that he'd misunderstood. Someone who'd loved Joseph as much as they had. She was all they had left of him. He wanted to keep her close. She knew why. This girl his son had loved. Wanted that link to continue. But here she was, about to cut them adrift.

It was Stasia who recovered first.

"Are you sure about this, Bridie? Is it too soon to be making a big decision like that? You've been through a very hard time. Your little sister now, and that happening while you're still grieving your husband. Are you giving yourself enough time? Would you be better waiting? It has to get easier."

"I've tried. I've really tried but I can't do it anymore." Bridie's voice wobbled. "Everywhere I go, everyone I meet. It's all connected to Joseph. I thought that was what I wanted, what I needed, to feel he was still here. But it's not working. I'm sorry it's not working." She paused. "Maybe if I go home to Wexford it'll be easier. It just seemed a little easier when I was there."

"Well, maybe it would be no harm to try it." Stasia came across from the fire and put her arm around Bridie. "Sure you can always come back here if it doesn't work out."

"I need to be somewhere that doesn't have any links with him, at least not every single day or every place I go to. Just so I can build some sort of a life without him." Bridie looked at Dan. "I don't want to forget him. I'll never, ever forget him."

"We know you won't, Bridie."

The guilt of his own selfishness, his wanting to hold her to this place bothered him. She could see that written all over his face. The understanding that they'd had their lives and that she was entitled to hers. She might not know what she wanted but they couldn't provide it. Of that she was certain.

"She has to do what's best for herself, Stasia." He looked up at his wife, his face stricken. "Sure there's not much left for her here now. She might be better off with her own people." His eyes filled as he saw Bridie's lip tremble. "You do what you have to do, pet. You do what you have to." He reached across and squeezed her hand, his big calloused one chafing her soft skin. "We'll miss you here but we'll manage. Somehow we'll muddle along. And you know you'll always be welcome."

Chapter 30

County Wexford

The usual letter with the American stamp arrived at Christmas from Johanna. It was enclosed with her Christmas card.

Bridie scraped the metal on the hearth as she scooped up the ashes into the bucket. She coughed as the dust caught her throat. Tilting the bucket away from her, she emptied the last shovelful more gently into it.

She was annoyed that her business was being discussed. It seemed that everyone was involved in trying to find a solution to the 'What'll we do with Bridie' question. And now it appeared that her dilemma had travelled across the Atlantic.

"I wish you hadn't said anything to her," Bridie accused her mother. "I'll sort myself out."

She caught Maude's glance that suggested she didn't think she was making much of a job of that and was relieved that her mother managed to hold back the comment. Voicing it wasn't going to help matters.

"I was only trying to help." Maude shrugged. "Maybe you should think about it?"

The question of emigration or work had never come up before but the pointed mention of there being lots of employment in America for young women had triggered the argument.

"I don't want to go." She knew she sounded sulky. "It's too far."

"Well, what do you want to do? Have you any idea?"

"I don't know. I don't know. Just leave me be, can't you?"

"Well, you need to think about it. You could always stay with Johanna for a while. You know she'd be delighted to have you."

"Are you sure? I know she's my aunt but I don't even know her." Picking up the ash bucket, she went out to the yard to empty it.

Moving back home to Wexford had seemed the sensible thing to do. She hadn't been long enough in Clare for it to become home. Not long enough to establish a life for herself, not a life without Joseph anyway. Moving home had seemed the most practical solution but now that she was back it wasn't really working. Aimless months under her parents' feet were beginning to irritate everyone. She was just drifting. Powerless to go forward. Unable to go backwards. There was nothing there for her.

The letter was read to the neighbours. Nothing unusual about this. They were always interested in news from abroad. It brightened up the evenings when they dropped in to sit around the fire talking. She suspected that her mother had primed them.

"Sounds like a great life." There was always one to drag it in by the scruff of the neck.

"Very fashionable over there, I believe, to have a housekeeper. I could do with one myself." They would always try to make light of it as if to disguise the fact that it was for her benefit. Or that Maude wasn't behind the plot to persuade her.

She suspected the exchange of these bits of information were saved up until she was within earshot. She didn't want to go. Hadn't ever thought about it as a possible option. There had never been a need. But the more it was talked about, the less alien it seemed. The conversation about her Aunt Maria who had gone over and was working for a well-heeled American family and the exotic places they took her seemed to be introduced more often than usual and between this and all others who had made good over there she could feel a softening of her resolve. The boxes of fancy clothes that arrived home to families every so often began to sound attractive. It wasn't as though she herself had come up with a better plan. Maybe she could stay with Aunt Johanna, until she got fixed up.

"I've been thinking. Maybe I'll go."

"Where?"

Maude had dropped the subject in the face of Bridie's resistance. Not easy for her to admit defeat. It had been weeks since the letter arrived, so the morning her daughter made the announcement over the breakfast table she had all but forgotten it.

"Where do you think? To America. Isn't that what you've been pushing? You should be pleased."

Her father looked over the top of the newspaper, his attention suddenly on his daughter. He glanced at Maude's slightly raised eyebrow. A delicate moment. Easy to say the wrong thing.

"Oh, I am." Maude smiled.

"That sounds like a good idea, Bridie." Her father smiled gently at her. "Broaden your horizons."

Bridie saw him shoot a warning look at his wife. No doubt he hoped she would manage not to look too pleased that her badgering had finally reaped a reward.

"I'll try it anyway." Bridie looked a bit uncertain now that she'd voiced it. "For a while."

121

"When are you planning to go?"

She could see her mother wanted the practicalities sorted before her daughter changed her mind. "I don't know. You're sounding very anxious to get rid of me? I'm still only thinking about it."

"We'll help you with the fare, Bridie."

The undue haste with which her father jumped in told her a lot. Well used to Maude's practical attitude, he could see the response forming in his wife's head even before she opened her mouth. She could hear it herself . . . "the time for thinking is over". The last thing she needed to be told.

She was pleased that he'd got involved. Happy, she knew, to give her the money, anything to help her take the next step and move on. He could probably see that any delay might halt the progress and have her changing her mind.

"I'll pay you back when I get a job. It might take a while though."

"In time, in time."

He hadn't said very much since she came home. Just let her be, with the odd pat on the shoulder and gentle comment that told her he understood what it had all cost her. She caught his stern look across the table to his wife. The one that indicated that no more needed to be said on the subject for the moment.

"Any more tea in that pot there, Maude?"

"I thought you were finished." She clicked her tongue at him before turning to get the kettle to top up the teapot.

Cornelius turned to his daughter. "It's alright, Bridie. Don't worry about the money for the moment. It will take you a while to get on your feet out there." He added a drop of milk to his mug before going back to his newspaper.

She watched her father, hoping it was relief that she was reading on his face, comforted perhaps by the new lightness in his daughter. At least someone was happy.

Chapter 31

1898

It was one of the close neighbours, Harry, who drove her to the station. There had been a lot of talk about who would deliver her to the train, whether her father could change his day off in order to do it. Her mother had suggested going with her in the horse and trap and Cornelius could meet them in Gorey. It would save him having to take the day off work.

Bridie could imagine the farewell on the station platform. Her mother, businesslike, not wanting to show emotion, now that she'd got her way, and her father, rigid in his Head Constable's uniform, unable to. Cornelius would check his watch every minute even though they would be half an hour early. He was a stickler when it came to timekeeping. She could see him already. He would walk to the edge of the platform, looking up and down the track as if the train might approach from either direction. Maude would make her check her bag a thousand times to ensure she had her tickets and money until Bridie would lose patience and snap at her. When the train pulled into the station she could imagine them not wanting her to go, but rushing her to climb aboard for fear it would pull off without her. She would have to be the one to step forward to hug them or else face the awkwardness of waiting for one of them to do so first. Or worse still, they would shake hands with her.

"I'd prefer to say my goodbyes here at home. It'll be easier. Best for everyone." Bridie had already asked Harry if he might do the journey with her. He'd often been the one to drop her to the station when she was going to Clare and she liked his quiet way. No fuss.

"No problem, child. I'll drop you in to the train. I have to go to Gorey anyway this week so it might as well be tomorrow as any other day."

They drove along. The lack of conversation was companionable with neither feeling the need to fill the silence. It was as if he read her thoughts. Never asked why she wanted him to drive her rather than her parents. Didn't seem to consider it odd. No explanation needed. He knew them well enough to picture the scene if they had taken her.

She wondered why she had always thought of him as an elderly man – he was not much older than her parents. Maybe to her childish eyes it had been the shock of white hair. She glanced across at him now, pretending she was looking at the passing scenery and realised he was probably only in his fifties. Not young, but not as old as she'd always believed.

The father of four boys, she had never given much thought to him before. He was always there. She'd just accepted him as a lovely grandfatherly addition to her life, without the parental need to correct or criticise.

It crossed her mind now for the first time if perhaps Harry had wanted a daughter. If that was why he took an interest in her, why he allowed her into his life? She expected he had no idea what a magical part of her world he was. The way he always included her when he wanted to show his boys lots of nature's little delights. Explaining things in that way of his that made everything so straightforward and simple. She was going to miss him.

The little things that had never seemed important were what she was going to miss on the other side of the ocean. The connections. The links. The distance from all that was familiar suddenly seemed frightening. She had an urge to tell him how important he was to her, but she couldn't, it would be too embarrassing. For both of them. And it might sound like a betrayal of her own father.

Cornelius and Maude had objected at first, considering it their familial duty to see her off, but Bridie was insistent and she knew they were relieved. Not about the inconvenience but about the distress of the farewell. Not just parting, but parting in public, with the inevitable delay between the goodbyes and the train pulling out of the station. The waiting on the platform, looking for their daughter through the carriage windows and she on the other side of the glass, smiling and waving to them, struggling to be brave.

She had blown hot and cold about it after she'd made the decision. But there was no going back and there was no future at home. She had thought of it simply as emigrating to a different country without the slightest understanding of what that meant in reality.

Alighting from the train and leaving the station behind caused a flutter of nerves. The last familiar part of her travels behind her.

It was as she stood at the port counter looking down at the sailing ticket and checking the date that her head went completely into a spin. What if she'd come on the wrong day? What if that date was tomorrow, or worse still yesterday?

125

The ticket clerk, a kindly man with grey hair sticking out from under his cap, smiled at her. He'd had seen many such girls stand in front of him, emotions ranging from panic to eager anticipation on their faces. Most, he knew, would not be back.

"Have a good voyage."

The momentary thrill took her by surprise. Like something new was about to happen. She raised her head and smiled back at him.

"Thank you. I will. At least I hope I will." There was no changing her mind now.

She had plenty of time to think during the journey. Not a sign of land for days. Nothing but miles and miles of ocean to contemplate. As far as the eye could see. With hours to idle away, nothing but the sound of the waves and the hum of engines to interrupt the thoughts of what she was facing. She wished she'd given it more thought. She only knew Aunt Johanna from her letters as she had gone away to America before she was born. An unnerving little niggle crept in. Not a worry that she hadn't met Johanna as much as the thought that her aunt might not like her. What if they didn't get on? An uneasiness surfaced. The possibility that this meeting might be a disappointment. For either or both of them.

Johanna's letters had always been sensible, like someone well anchored to the earth. Written in a hand that was confident in the knowledge that what news she wrote would be of interest to the folks back home. The warmth with which the stories were related always had created the effect that she was sitting at the far side of the fireplace relating the incidents.

She'd always liked the sound of her. A bit like her grandmother. She'd assumed that. Without ever hearing it, she thought she even knew Aunt Johanna's voice. But as the boat neared the docks the doubts started. And there was still a train journey to go.

Boston, Massachusetts, USA

She needn't have worried. The moment they met in Boston she knew it was going to be alright. The voice was different, a slight American twang to the odd word but hardly noticeable under the Clare accent.

She returned Bridie's hug with the affection of someone who had known her all her life, but had been waiting for this moment to envelop her in a big soft hold. Bridie felt disloyal even thinking it of her own mother but, despite the similarity, to her relief, Johanna was a warmer version of Maude.

"Let me look at you." Johanna stepped back, holding her niece at arm's length and studying her. A smile played around the corners of her mouth. "Aren't you lovely – your mother never told me you were as beautiful as you are. And so tall. Like a mannequin."

Bridie blushed, unused to such fulsome praise. Joseph had been the only one who'd ever told her she was beautiful. Certainly not her mother. She moved in to give Johanna another hug to hide her embarrassment, while the doubts on the journey momentarily diminished. It was only later that she thought about the relevance of the black coat and hat. It had only been about five or six years since her aunt too had lost her husband. So wrapped up in her own tragedy, she'd not given a thought to the person whose home she was about to live in.

It wasn't until she'd arrived in Boston that Bridie realised she had never experienced life in a city before. Short visits

127

to Dublin and once to Galway with Joseph – day trips, so rare as to be exciting new experiences. Different if you'd been going there for good.

It was something about her aunt and the way she seemed to fit into this throng that stopped Bridie turning and heading straight back to Ireland without even unpacking her trunk. The speed of things around her reminded her of the merry-go-round at the carnival in Courtown, when young hoodlums made it revolve too fast. She knew the fear of wanting to get on but not being quite ready or brave enough to step onto the fast-moving platform.

The crowds on that first day frightened her as they swept past in the street, all intent on getting their business done. The fact that she could not escape them was what alarmed her. There was no edge to the city. The peace of the countryside lay far, far away. She had no clue exactly how far but she had a fair idea it wasn't just a long walk down the road to find it.

JOHANNA

Chapter 32

Johanna had been shocked at Bridie's fragility when she met her at the train station. It was difficult to recognise the glowing girl from the wedding picture. Easy enough to see the effect the loss of her young husband had had. All but drained the life out of her. Maude's worry about her daughter was not without foundation. This was going to need some work.

She'd warned Maude not to labour the topic of her daughter getting employment.

"Just give her enough money to tide her over for a while. I'll sort out the job," Johanna had advised. "Sounds like she doesn't need an overload of information at this point. I know myself how frightening it is to leave behind everything you know and I was a lot tougher than poor Bridie."

"I know someone who can sort you out with an interview." Johanna was anxious to get her started. She'd waited until the next day, afraid any delay might give too much time for her to dwell on things and take fright.

"Oh, I don't know." Bridie faltered. She hoped Aunt Johanna wouldn't rush her. Would give her time to catch her breath.

"Well, believe me I do." Firmness was needed if she

was to help this hollow-eyed girl who clearly had no plan. "Nothing for it but to plunge in and get a start. You'll feel the better of it once you're anchored."

Remembering the knock her confidence had taken after Mattie died, she knew the struggle that lay ahead for a young widow. Too many echoes deep in her own heart. She worried that Bridie might lose whatever little confidence she might have if she didn't throw her in at the deep end.

"I met her in the shop this morning and she told me of a woman looking for someone to look after the children. Their nurse is away, gone back home for a few months to look after her mother. It would get you a start and a bit of experience. She's not looking for a trained nanny or anything. Just someone honest and reliable."

"It's a bit soon. I think I need to find my way about first."

"Alright then, maybe we'll leave it for now." Satisfied she'd planted the seed, she left her niece to acclimatise to the idea of moving forward with her life. "Maybe you're right. There'll be plenty more, so we needn't rush into anything."

BRIDIE

Chapter 33

Everything was different. The people and their accents. The clothes. The buildings. The novelty of it all gave her an energy she hadn't felt for a long time. Something new every day. Enough to keep her focussed on this fresh start.

For the first week Bridie set herself an agenda each day. Partly to familiarise herself with the layout of the city but also to keep out of Aunt Johanna's way. She didn't want to outstay her welcome too soon and she could only help with the household chores for so long without becoming a nuisance.

She decided to walk a few undiscovered streets each day and see where they led and to check out what they might have to offer. In an effort to link them all up together she walked some streets she had previously explored and hoped that in time they would become as familiar as the country roads and lanes in Wexford or Clare.

There were days she despaired she would ever become part of it. On these she ended her walk in Copley Square. Partly because she could sit on the steps of the Public Library and while away an hour or two without anyone noticing and thus avoid returning to the house too early. She would think about what news she had to bring home to Johanna, something she had learned about the city. If she could do that her day wasn't wasted.

It puzzled her that it was called a square. With so much attacking her senses, to her it looked more like a series of triangles. She looked across at the building opposite. The decorative façade of Trinity Church had an intimidating presence. It looked like the sort of place you'd have to pay into or else have a special invitation. While beautiful in its ornamentation it exuded an impression that you would have to be someone very important to enter. Not exactly what the Lord would have approved of.

A few couples wandered around the square admiring the surrounding buildings. Families strolled along the pathways. A young mother passed, walking slowly while rocking the carriage in an effort to get her fretful baby to sleep.

A man in a soft hat and dark overcoat stood reading his newspaper, leaning against a pillar of the library. He glanced up occasionally to survey the scene around him before resuming his perusal of the news. He reminded her of Uncle Hugh, the same air of owning the world about him. Probably reading the financial market reports to see how his stocks were doing.

Uncle Hugh looked a bit fearsome. Although fearsome was probably too strong a word for it. Her first impression when Aunt Johanna had taken her around to the store to meet him was that he was not someone who would be interested in her woes. She couldn't be sure if he even knew anything about them. He'd given no hint.

"So another one of the Irish relations. Maude's daughter this time?"

Despite his polite smile she knew immediately that she wasn't going to have a close relationship with her uncle.

"That's right. Bridie." Even as she told him her name she knew. To him she would be just that. Another relative.

132

She suspected that he wouldn't even remember her name.

"Well, I hope you'll like it over here with us, Bridie." He leaned across the counter and shook hands with her and smiled before turning to a boy in a brown coat who had just appeared out from an archway behind the counter. "Will you bring up another box of those cereals from the stockroom?" He turned back to the two women. "And how is your mother? Well, I hope?"

"Oh, she's fine. Says I'm to give you her best regards."

It was when he barely gave her time to reply she knew he was not one for unproductive chit-chat.

"And Cornelius? Still as straight as ever, I presume, upholding the law of the land?"

It wasn't said unkindly. Just a polite effort at conversation. He was busy, but she knew he had already moved on from her in his head and she just gave a mumbled reply, knowing he wouldn't notice.

"Well, we'll be off then. We won't keep you from your work. Hugh?" It was something in the way Johanna added his name that made him look up. Her glare, directed at him, was not missed by Bridie. "I just thought you'd like to meet Bridie now. She must have been a baby when you went back on that visit to Ireland, so you'd hardly remember her. Maybe you'd ask the twins if either of them would be free on Sunday and maybe come over for tea. They'd be nice company for her. She doesn't know anyone yet. Say about five if that suits them. You can let me know."

Pausing, before dipping the pen in the black ink again, Bridie gazed out the window, picturing the excitement at home. The postman arriving, her mother wiping her hands on her apron going out to meet him.

"The one you've been waiting for, Mrs. Redmond. Amerikay. Judging by the postage stamps."

Her mother would not have been able to wait for Cornelius to come home from work. Bridie could picture her, making the pot of tea and sitting down at the scrubbed kitchen table to read the letter. Just like she used to do with Johanna's letters. She would have her sleeves rolled up, probably caught in the middle of washing the clothes or making the cake of bread. Whatever the chore, it would have dropped to the bottom of the priority list once the foreign-stamped letter arrived. She could picture Maude tearing open the envelope with her finger, leaving the edges jagged. Her father would tut-tut when he saw it. Left to him he would have taken the time to remove a knife from the drawer and close it again before using the sharp edge to slit open the envelope neatly

Holding the letter in both hands at arm's length her mother would settle back in her chair to read the news from abroad.

It was for this reason that Bridie felt she could write only positive things. She could only say that she missed them all. Couldn't write that she was dying of loneliness, would prefer to be at home squabbling with her mother over the kitchen table. Couldn't say that she had made the biggest mistake of her life in coming to America. That she was frozen with the cold in the snowy Boston winter and that she had no friends. Uncle Hugh was too busy and Johanna was great but she couldn't impose herself there every day as her aunt had her own life to deal with. Her cousins were nice but very American. What else could be expected? They had their own lives with their college friends and she didn't fit in. Didn't feel comfortable and had nothing much to contribute to the conversation on the occasions when she had met up with them. At least nothing that they could relate to. She could hardly tell them that she was a widow or what it was like to clean out the cow shed or pick spuds when they thought that potatoes could only be bought in a shop or a 'store' as they would say. She felt so much older than any of them even though they were much the same age.

"There's a letter there from Bridie."

"Oh, is there? I'll read it when I change out of this uniform."

She could hear their voices. She knew her father's apparent lack of excitement would annoy her mother, but suspected Maude would know that he wanted to be settled just right and comfortable in order to savour it. Just as much as she herself had.

After Cornelius had read the letter he would make a few "*Hrrumphs*" before acknowledging that Bridie seemed to be making a life for herself over there. He would place the letter back in its envelope and examine the stamps before propping it against the sugar bowl on the table again. That was the way her mother liked it. Strategically placed so that the unusual stamps would initiate a question from visiting neighbours. Bridie wished she was there. At that end of the letter.

She went back to her writing and thought up things to tell them. The afternoon tea with Aunt Johanna in the newly opened tea-rooms. The wander down the fashionable streets, not buying, just looking at the window displays. Her father would worry if she said she had gone into these stores to buy anything. Wasting her money. His money. The picnic with Uncle Hugh along the lakeside at Jamaica Pond one Sunday. He had surprised her with the invitation. His house was big and beautiful, overlooking the lake, but it had a strange sadness about it, as though it was a showpiece rather than a home. She decided to leave this bit out, instead telling them that the area reminded her of Glendalough in County Wicklow, backed as it was by

135

woodland and mountains. Not that she had ever been to Glendalough but she'd seen pictures of it.

All these bits and pieces she knew would keep them going for weeks until the next letter arrived. But she was going to have to do something to make life happen if they were not to get bored by the repetition.

A young woman sat on a bench in the square, her handbag clutched on her lap. Bridie admired the pink and purple flowers decorating the hat. They matched the purple dress she wore under her stylish navy coat. She caught a glimpse of it when the coat slid open as the woman released her grip on the handbag and reached up to adjust the brim of her hat. Once satisfied with the hat's angle, she settled her coat and resumed her position, back straight, hands clasped on the bag on her lap again. Every so often she turned her head to look in the direction of the church and then back towards the library. Bridie saw a young man, coat flying open, come round the corner of the building and head towards the woman, waving. She was close enough to see the woman smile as she stood up and Bridie watched as she began to walk towards him.

Unlike the floral-hatted young woman, Bridie was waiting for no-one. Nothing to do, no-one to meet. That was going to have to change and today was the day she'd have to do that. She had already decided what that change was going to be. Although it was a small step it would be in the right direction. She was going to enter that building across the square where the late afternoon sunshine was warming the face of the church. She persuaded herself that it was doing so in an attempt to draw her over. Maybe if she did it, answered the call, it would lead her on to something else. Perhaps it would reveal to her what the next move might be. And the next. And the next.

The size of the exterior was off-putting. If she walked up the steps everyone in the square would see her. Tall as she was, her height couldn't save her. She would be dwarfed by the great big empty frontage. The very thought of it was as frightening as if she were to strip naked and expose herself to the Saturday strollers. She waited until she saw a woman and child mount the steps and without giving herself time to think she sprang from the bench and half ran towards the building. Realising her speed, she slowed down to a brisk walk and following the pair up to the entrance told herself that she had as much right as anyone else to go inside.

The dark inner womb of the church surprised her and she stopped a moment, allowing her sun-filled eyes to adjust before slipping into one of the back benches.

Her heartbeat slowed as she took a few deep breaths. She felt the hard wood of the seat under her. She smiled to herself. She'd done it and the world hadn't ended. The foolishness of her fear amused her. Would an American be afraid to enter the doors of the little church in Riverchapel? She doubted it.

Apart from a desire to conquer her fear she now wondered what it was that had drawn her in. She had no idea. It didn't matter. Now that she was here she contented herself with looking around. It might reveal itself in time.

The interior was dull. She had expected something amazing. Not nearly so impressive as the façade. A bit disappointing. And there was something different about it. Different to the churches at home. Something she couldn't quite put a finger on.

She sat and watched the woman and child wandering around the church. The woman took the little girl's hand and pointed to the stained-glass windows. She shook herself free and walked backwards down the aisle to get a better look before returning to her mother's side. She looked up into her face, whispering a question that Bridie couldn't hear.

The church returned to silence as the echo of their shoes faded as they left and Bridie was alone. With no distractions she had an opportunity to plan. She wasn't leaving until she had formulated a plan. A direction. It didn't matter what it was except that it had to be forward.

A lot had happened in the short time she'd been in Boston. It should have been easy, but now as she sat there going over it all, having released the thoughts, given them their freedom, all she had was a head swirling with a mixture of things that she couldn't get hold of. She needed to get a grip on them. To corral them and sort them out. The ones that needed sorting. If she could pick out just one thing and deal with it that might be the best way forward. The way she'd coped with things in Clare. One step at a time. That had sort of worked. That system had grounded her and resulted in her being here. Progress of a sort. As she pondered on it, the breeze from the door opening behind her brought her back into the present.

Maybe I'd better leave it for now. No point in wondering if I've done the right thing. Didn't I get myself to America? And I have achieved something today. I'm in here. Satisfied with that thought she stood up and stepping out of the pew genuflected in the direction of the altar.

As she approached the door, she directed a confident smile at the man holding it open for her, his family already starting up the side aisle.

She stopped to read the noticeboard outside. Not a Catholic Church. That was the difference. And she had genuflected! Or maybe they did that too? She laughed at the thought of the parish priest in Riverchapel. If he could see her now, having committed a mortal sin, he'd have her excommunicated.

Chapter 34

Once she'd got started, it wasn't long before things began to fall into place.

The day a woman stopped her in the street and asked directions to Boston Common was when she felt the first major shift. A simple question. Even though she wasn't sure, she'd been able to send her in the right direction. The fact that the woman had selected her to ask for help made all the difference. The first manifestation that the isolation of not belonging was no longer part of her. She must be beginning to look part of the place. To look as if she should be here. Confirmation enough that she'd done the right thing in coming. Nothing here reminded her of Joseph, no association with the place at all. A lonely feeling, but for the best.

She still thought of him, but the pain no longer gutted her. It had happened slowly. A gradual thaw until it had turned into a soft nest of memories that comforted her in bed. She took one out each night. On those nights she had difficulty sleeping. She turned it over in her head and looked at it. She talked to him, sometimes out loud, hoping that Aunt Johanna in the next room couldn't hear their conversation. She knew she was recovering when she woke in the morning and realised she had fallen asleep before ever getting to the end of her story with Joseph.

She was surprised by the job offer, coming as it did from such an unlikely source, a few weeks after her arrival. Not having expected to register on his horizon at all.

"Your Uncle Hugh wants you to go into the shop for an interview." Johanna made the announcement on her return home from work. Plonking the bag of groceries on the kitchen table she took off her hat and proceeded to remove her coat.

"What?" Bridie looked at her, arm outstretched to take Johanna's coat.

"You heard." Johanna patted her hair as she handed over the coat. "Well?"

"I didn't think I'd made any impression on him whatsoever." Bridie turned and walked out to the hallstand. Flattered that he'd noticed her, she was glad of the distraction as she took her time hanging up the coat. She went back to the kitchen. "Sure I've no experience working in a shop."

"You needn't worry – he's not expecting you to run the place." Johanna unpacked the foodstuffs and put them into the cupboard. "You can take it from me he's well capable of doing that. Single-handed."

"I suppose it's only an interview though." She paused. The doubts began to creep in. "Does he know I've never worked outside of home?"

"He does. The interview is just him checking you out to see if you've a brain in your head – can you weigh stuff, tot up a list of groceries and give the correct change."

"I'm not sure I can . . . "

"Oh, you needn't worry. You'll be trained. His way." Johanna didn't wait for her to put up any objection. "For the interview all you need to do is give him the impression that you can learn. He just needs to be reassured that you won't run his business into the ground in your first week." She looked around at Bridie and smiled. "Do you think you can manage to persuade him of that?"

"Well, when you put it like that it doesn't sound so bad. It might take me only two weeks to achieve that." Bridie laughed as she put the teapot on the table. "Look, I'll try. I'll practise my times tables. Sit down there, you must be tired. The eggs will be ready in a minute."

Johanna pulled out a chair and eased herself onto it.

"That's great, love. I'm looking forward to this. Just sitting down and having it handed to me." She glanced at Bridie. "I'll miss that when you get the job."

Johanna had been working on Saturdays since the children became old enough to be left on their own for a day. It was one of Hugh's busiest days and he needed extra staff.

Bridie had a suspicion, but wasn't going to voice it, that Johanna might have forced the issue of her interview. She was impressed with her aunt, the way she didn't seem the slightest bit intimidated by her brother.

Her black skirt and jacket were a bit loose with the weight she'd lost over the year, but they were the smartest clothes she had and Johanna assured her they would be most suitable for the interview. She'd taken special care with her hair, pinning it back in a soft chignon. But she needn't have worried. Her uncle didn't appear to notice, just asked a half a dozen questions before telling her that she had the job.

"Come in on Monday and ask for Miss Doyle. She'll sort you out with a uniform and start your training."

"Thanks, Uncle Hugh. I really appreciate the opportunity." She wondered if it was her answers that convinced him that she wasn't a complete ignoramus or if it was her demeanour. She'd taken Johanna's advice. But more probably he'd given her the job just because she was a relative.

"Don't thank me. Just work hard, be polite to the customers and don't bankrupt me. And we'll all be happy." He stood and gave her a brief smile.

"I hope so." Bridie smiled back at him and, taking her cue, stood up. The interview was clearly over.

"If you have any problems don't come to me with them. I'll expect you to sort them. Any questions refer to Miss Doyle." He walked towards the door and, holding it open, gave her a nod to go ahead. "I'll see you on Monday then."

"See you then, Uncle Hugh."

"And, Bridie – it'll be Mr. McNamara to you here at work. None of this 'Uncle Hugh'. Not in the shop."

Life changed with the job. On her feet all day, by evening she wasn't sure if her legs would get her home, but it was fun and the staff appeared to enjoy working with her. Her enthusiasm over every new thing, commonplace to them, amused them. She'd never seen such a selection.

"At home we've just one of everything in the shops. And that's if you're lucky." She laughed. "We don't have to make any decisions. Other than if you are buying jam, you might get a choice of which fruit."

Determined to speed up she made a bit of a joke about being something of a slow learner.

"Quite the contrary. You're very quick on the uptake," Miss Doyle assured her. "What you learned in a week I've often seen other juniors take a month to learn."

She was the last of the staff to go, delaying until she was sure that Hugh had his coat on and was leaving. He raised an eyebrow when he saw her waiting at the door.

"You still here, Bridie? Can't get enough of us?"

"I just wanted to have a word with you."

"Is something wrong?"

"Oh no. The opposite. I love it. I just wanted to say thanks . . . you know . . . for giving me the job."

"You did well, Bridie, for your first week."

"Did I? Oh thanks, Uncle Hugh. I think Aunt Johanna was worried I might run the business into the gutter in my first week."

"Oh, Johanna likes to have her little joke." He smiled, pulling on his gloves. "She would never have recommended you if she thought that. No, Bridie, I'm impressed. If you can keep up that level of effort you'll go places."

She stepped outside as he turned out the lights and began locking the door behind them. She felt lonely as she heard the metallic clicking as the bolts shot home, all life inside suddenly switched off and locked away until next week.

He raised his hat and headed off in the direction of home. Bridie watched as the distance increased between them. She had survived that first week despite the aching legs. As she turned into the wind, the thought of her bed and a sleep on in the morning was a welcome pleasure.

HUGH

Chapter 35

He could keep an eye on the activity on the shop floor from the window of his office located up above and with the window open he could hear some of the conversations.

"Isn't that a lovely brogue you have?"

He watched as the elderly man raised his hat and chuckled as he took his leave of Bridie.

"And with that lovely red hair no need to ask where you come from."

He hadn't been the first to comment. The American customers found her accent charming, a few of the regulars had remarked on it. He sometimes saw others delaying in chat, just wanting her to talk more, as their eyes glowed with something that suggested possible reminiscences of home.

He noticed the way she'd sometimes try to continue the conversation while serving the next customer. He wasn't sure if she sensed their longing or if it was in case she felt he might be watching and thinking she was wasting time.

"Good customer service and friendly conversation brings them back, Bridie. Never be afraid to engage with them," he'd heard Miss Doyle advising her.

He knew she was anxious, but she needn't have worried. He was impressed. A few of the customers had singled out his new shop girl and he'd been proud to tell them she was his niece. Like Bridie, a lot of the relatives he had given a start to had pleased him with their performance and some had moved on to higher things. A few had disappointed him, thinking they were in for an easy ride.

From that first introduction he liked her. Much softer than her mother. He hadn't been sure about her as a possible employee when Johanna had forced the issue.

"I don't know, Johanna. I'd be worried about her history." He shook his head slowly.

"She has to get over that, Hugh. And the only way I can see to help her, is to give work."

"I can't afford another sympathy job." He sighed. "And if it doesn't work out . . . ?"

"Look, she can't be that fragile. Didn't she travel all the way over here on her own? And carrying a broken heart. We both know how that feels." Johanna could see he was weakening. "She must have a bit of spark in her if she could do that, after all she's been through."

Hugh looked at her, aware he wasn't going to be able to resist the pressure he knew Johanna was capable of exerting.

"Just interview her," Johanna pleaded. "That's all I ask."

Even though he was looking for staff, he had a fear that her good looks might distract the young male workers. All very well to have such a pleasing appearance, but it could also prove a handicap. Watching her interaction from above he was pleased to see his fears were unfounded. She was completely oblivious as to how she appeared and had the same easy relationship with both the young men and women. If she had her problems she didn't bring them in to work. He liked her spirit. Johanna had been right. Again.

JOHANNA

Chapter 36

"Hugh's not exactly the cuddly type, Bridie, but when you get to know him he's alright. A bit of an acquired taste. Like Brussels sprouts."

They'd laughed together about that. She was delighted to see the change in her niece. Full of news when she came in from work in the evenings and a bounce in her step every Monday morning.

"*See you this evening, Aunt Jo!*" Bridie shouted her goodbye before banging the door behind her.

"*Bye, love. See you this evening!*"

Johanna watched from the upstairs window as Bridie went out through the gate and turned up the road. A very different girl from the one who arrived a month ago. She would write and tell her sister.

Despite his early reservations, Hugh had been impressed.

"You need to tell her that, Hugh." Johanna was pleased. "She needs to know."

"I've already told her, Jo. You think I don't notice such things, but I recognise when someone needs encouragement. And I've given her that." He smiled. "She's earned it."

Miss Doyle had also had a quiet word in her ear. "Your niece is a pleasure to have around."

Yes, she'd plenty to tell Maude and Cornelius.

An air of relaxed industry permeated the kitchen. Johanna sat at the fire knitting while Bridie ran the smoothing iron over her blouses, getting them ready for the next week.

"Hugh says you're working out well in the job."

"Yeah. He seems pleased with me. Although it's hard to know. He's a bit stern, isn't he?"

"Oh, his bark is worse than his bite. Take no notice. Just keep working hard and you'll get on just fine with him. Hard work. That's all he knows about." Johanna paused as she drew out a length of wool from the ball and began a new row. The periodic hiss of the hot iron on the damp material and the click of the knitting needles lent an air of cosy domesticity, the perfect setting to allow Johanna move things along. "Have you made any friends at work yet?"

It had been good to watch Bridie over the weeks gain a foothold on life again and see her progress. But what she was seeing now concerned her. Sitting in on a Saturday night with your aunt was not what she saw as fit for a young girl. It was as if her niece was satisfied with her achievements, as if she had arrived at a destination with no necessity to build on the successful start. A bit of pressure might be needed to stop complacency setting in. Now that she had settled at work it was clear that the next step wasn't going to happen without a push.

"Oh, I have. They're all very nice. Well, most of them anyway. There's an Irish girl from Clare. She works in the office. Her name is Claire too!"

"Yes, I know her. Nice girl. Very friendly. She's always there on Saturday mornings when I go in. Why don't you invite her here for tea some evening?"

"I never thought of that."

"Well, sure ask her over next Friday after work. I'll

147

make a few potato cakes for the tea. Remind her of home."

Claire was delighted with the invitation. Something Johanna had guessed would go down well. She'd told her that she reminded her of her own mother. Had the same look.

They ran home from work in the rain, arriving in like two drowned rats. Johanna handed them towels to dry their hair. She took their coats and hung them on the back of two chairs, leaving them to steam in front of the stove.

"This would remind you of home." Claire turned her head sideways to look at Johanna.

"What? The rain or the tea?" Johanna turned the potato cakes with the spatula.

"Both."

They laughed as Johanna broke the eggs onto the pan, the damp smell mingling with the aroma of the cooking.

"These will be ready in two minutes. Sit in the pair of you and pour out the tea."

The girls cleared the table and began washing the dishes.

"You can leave them to drain. We'll put them away later." Johanna passed over the last of the delph from the table. "I'll check on that fire in the parlour."

By the time the girls joined her the room had heated up. Johanna threw a log on the fire. She sat back in the armchair and watched it catch, throwing a fresh blaze up the chimney. Not a good idea to jump in with her enquiries immediately, she thought, better to listen to the girls chatting amongst themselves for a while.

"What do you usually do on Saturday nights, Claire?" She had held back as long as she could. It was getting late and she was concerned she might miss her opportunity if the girl suddenly announced she should be going home.

Bridie shot a look across at her aunt. A look that

148

suggested that the question could only be heading one direction, the way Johanna had crashed it in.

"Oh, there's a club we go to, a dancehall. They've a dance there every weekend. All the Irish go."

Johanna watched as Bridie glanced across at Claire, a check to see if the question had jarred on her friend.

"I'm always asking her to come with us. It's great."

Johanna beamed at Claire. Her niece was trapped.

"You should go with them, Bridie."

No escape as both looked at Bridie, waiting for an answer.

"I don't know . . ."

"You don't know what? There's nothing stopping you. A young one like you! You never know – you might even enjoy yourself!" Johanna pressed home, confident of Claire's backing.

"Yeah. Why don't you come with us tomorrow night? There's a group of us going. I'll call in for you. I'll be passing here anyway."

Bridie opened her mouth, but before she had a chance to utter a word, Johanna jumped in.

"Well, there you are, Bridie!" Johanna beamed. "She'll be ready for you, Claire."

"Claire?" Bridie frowned at her. "I'm beginning to think you and Aunt Jo have been plotting?"

The two heads swung in her direction.

"*Never!*" they chorused.

They had her cornered.

BRIDIE

Chapter 37

It was easy to single out the young Irishmen. The walk. It always gave them away. The awkward stooped shoulders as they loped over to ask a girl to dance, like they were apologising. It was that, and the sandy hair and freckles. But most of all it was that, the "sorry for being alive" thing that marked them out.

The first time Bridie set eyes on Seán Ryan she was bowled over. His dark hair and olive skin were not the only things that made him conspicuous amongst the dancers. His strong Galway accent, and the fact that he didn't try to hide it, displayed a confidence the others lacked. Many acquired an American twang before they were a wet week in the States in an effort to shake off what they thought sounded like their peasant brogue. They did so in the vain hope that it might bestow on them an assurance that would make them stand out in a crowd and appear more attractive to the girls, while at the same time wishing that the new accent would allow them blend in.

Bridie was good at the Irish set dances. Being a head taller than most of the girls, it was easy to spot her auburn curls dancing in the line further down the ballroom. By the time her row of dancers had advanced forward through several troops in the Siege of Ennis, Seán was well ready for her. She didn't know it but he'd had her under surveillance for the whole battle. Ducking, she passed under the arch of arms and as she arrived through and straightened up she met his eyes, almost level. And from that moment those big blue eyes hypnotised her.

As their round finished and he raised his arm to allow the advancing line to pass under his arch he winked at her before moving on to the next set of dancers.

She caught up with Claire as they returned to their seats.

"He looks interesting?" Claire grinned at her as Bridie looked back over her shoulder and saw him heading towards the bar.

"Yes, he does, doesn't he?"

"I've seen him here before. A bit of a regular. Always the first with the latest dance steps." Claire sat down and picked up her drink. "All this dancing would make you terrible thirsty."

Bridie drained her glass as the rhythm changed. She watched as Seán walked across the dancefloor. Stopping in front of their table, he put his glass down.

He extended his hand and smiled at Bridie. "May I have the next dance?"

Bridie stood up and, glancing back at Claire, hoped he didn't see the broad wink her friend gave her.

She could see what Claire meant about the latest dance steps. Hoping she didn't appear too clumsy she tried to follow him as he strutted his stuff, guiding her around the floor. For the first time in ages Bridie was having fun. She was alive again.

Chapter 38

Every single thing around Bridie seemed to have taken on a life of its own, like she was caught up in a series of whirlwinds that she was powerless to control. But it was exciting. Not something she had any desire to control. She wanted them to take her along in whichever direction they chose to blow and she was happy to go with the flow.

Working as a barman, Seán was busy most evenings so they only had a short time to meet up between both their jobs. Hardly time to eat a meal as she raced in from work each evening.

"You're in some hurry, child!" she could hear Johanna commenting as she loped up the stairs to change and beautify herself before running out the door to meet him.

"I am!"

"Would you not eat something before you go out again?"

"I'm only going out for a short while, Aunt Jo. I'll eat when I get back. Seán has to be at work at eight."

Within a few months they had planned their marriage.

There was only one thing bothering her. One thing that was taking the gloss off her new happiness. That was having to tell Joseph's parents. She had written to them a few times since coming to Boston but since meeting Seán her letters had become less frequent. Aware of it, she had pushed away the guilt. Blamed it on lack of time. Busy at work. And now with her wedding imminent it became a problem, a problem that she could ignore no longer.

Mary Ann had agreed not to say anything to Joseph's parents when her granddaughter had written to her for advice. It would be wiser to leave it to Bridie to break the news.

"Just be straight about it, Bridie. There's no easy way to tell them. They are going to be upset but they are sensible people. But what's this about feeling betrayed? They won't. What is there to feel betrayed about? They often talk about you but they've said to me that while they miss you, they hope you are getting on with your life over there in America. You're young and they know you can't stay in mourning forever.

It might be a good idea when you've written the letter to show it to Johanna before you send it. She has a sensible head on her and might have a suggestion as to how you can soften the blow. But do it soon before they hear it from another source. That would be too cruel . . ."

Johanna suggested a few changes, getting her to add a sentence or two in before she jumped into the announcement.

"You can leave it on the stand in the hall and I'll post it for you when I'm out later."

Bridie knew the offer was to ensure there was no opportunity for second thoughts at the post-box.

JOHANNA

Chapter 39

Johanna had worried at the speed things were progressing but, having encouraged her niece to move on with her life, she was reluctant to put a damper on her delight. She just had to suffer the uneasy feeling that she was watching a very out-of-control spinning-top whirling Bridie away from her sadness and into another life. She hoped it was the right one.

"Any letters for me?" It was the first thing Bridie asked each day when she returned from work.

"Don't get yourself into a knot, child. There won't be anything for a few weeks, if at all. But you can't do anything about that." Johanna could feel the tension in the question, unlike the tone of the enquiries about the usual letters from home.

A few weeks later it arrived. Stasia's black spidery writing was unmistakeable.

Johanna watched Bridie's hands shake as she looked at the envelope. She turned it over a few times as if she could change the handwriting to be that of someone else.

"Open it, Bridie. Stalling is not going to change what they have to say one way or another."

Bridie hesitated a moment. Johanna watched her take a deep breath before slitting the envelope with her finger and unfolded the thin paper within. She scanned her niece's face as she waited for an indication as to its contents but all she could see were Bridie's frantic eyes darting back and forwards along the lines.

"Oh, Aunt Jo, they don't mind at all. They are pleased for me!" Bridie put her hand over her mouth, her eyes filling with tears of relief. "Can you believe it? They are happy for me and they wish us well. Here, read it." She passed the letter across the table and, taking out her hanky, blew her nose.

Johanna could feel her eyes on her as she scanned the letter, as if watching for any indication that she might have taken the wrong meaning from it and maybe they were upset.

"I'm right, aren't I? They are happy for me?"

"They are, love. They're big-hearted people."

It was to be a small wedding on a Friday in winter. Hugh and Johanna were most unhappy with the arrangements when they heard it was not taking place in the Catholic Church. A Registry Office had already been booked by Seán.

It was only a few weeks before the wedding when Bridie admitted to Johanna that he had been married before and it had ended in divorce.

BRIDIE

Chapter 40

She'd been shocked herself when he told her. He had waited months before breaking the news, by which time it was too late. She was totally besotted.

"Why didn't you tell me this earlier? Before I got involved with you," she said, as she wept. "That would have been fairer."

"Because you wouldn't have, would you? Got involved with me. I liked you the minute we met and I wasn't prepared to risk it."

"But the choice should have been mine," she argued back. "You know what it's like at home. I'll never be able to tell them."

"I know, but I wasn't prepared to lose you at that early stage. I wanted you to get to know me before you made up your mind." He smiled at her. "I didn't want that little fact to put me out of the running. And anyway there are ways around it. It's just a bit of an inconvenience."

"It's not a *'little'* fact and well you know it."

The arguments continued for a few weeks until he won her over. It was only when she told them the full story that Hugh and Johanna understood why Seán had dug in his heels on the location.

"And what have your parents to say about this?"

She knew that Johanna already knew the answer to this. Would have been in no doubt that this arrangement could never have had their blessing.

"They don't know."

"They don't know you're getting married? Or they don't know you are getting married in a Registry Office?"

"They know we're getting married but not where and you're not to tell them, Aunt Jo. It's not like they'll be travelling over for the wedding."

"I take it they don't know you're marrying a divorced man either?"

"Well, what do you think? They don't need to know anyway."

"I'm not happy about this, Bridie. Not happy at all. You can do what you like, I'm not your mother, but I don't like keeping this from them."

"But I can't tell them. They'd go mad."

"Believe me it'll slip out some time. Sooner or later. These things have a habit of that." She paused. "I'm not telling you what to do, but I feel you need to think about this and tell them. I'll leave it up to you and your conscience. But you can't hide it forever."

Hugh and Johanna attended the wedding. Reluctantly. Claire was the bridesmaid. Seán's parents were dead so it was just his sister and brother and a friend attending. After the ceremony they went to a restaurant for a meal which Hugh paid for and it was straight back to work on Monday for both of them. With no time for a honeymoon, they spent the weekend settling into their new home, a small rented ground-floor apartment in a house about ten minutes' walk from Johanna's.

Chapter 41

1900

Mary Josephine was born shortly after Bridie's twenty-first birthday, on the eve of their first anniversary, just as the world moved into the new century.

From her hospital bed she could hear the chimes of the church bells and the ships' horns in the distance. The sound of revelry in the street below coaxed her from her bed. It was as if the celebrations were especially for her and her new baby. She leaned on the windowsill and looked down at the cheering crowd, envying the couples standing entwined in the street. Too late for Seán. He hadn't mentioned the New Year when he'd visited earlier in the evening and she was in such discomfort that she had forgotten. She wondered if he was missing her now.

Carried along on the euphoria of the birth she knew without doubt that this was the biggest, most overwhelming thing that could ever happen to her. More powerful than anything that had gone before. Had anyone told her this a year or two earlier she would never have believed them.

She found it hard to take her eyes off her daughter. Every tiny movement, every change of breath was an event of the utmost amazement. A miracle. She wondered if her own mother had felt the same with the birth of her children. Had Maude spent hours staring at her in her crib, marvelling at her every stir. Probably not, seeing that there were the three boys born before her.

Seán arrived to take herself and Mary Jo home from hospital. Walking along the corridor with his beautiful pale-faced wife carrying his child, he smiled around at everyone they met, as if he was the first father to have ever walked through the doors of the hospital. Bridie, with eyes for no-one but her baby, gazing down at the little crumpled pink face swathed in the blanket in her arms, didn't notice the proud look on her husband's face that said 'Look at me. I'm a real man now'.

It wasn't until the hall door of their apartment closed behind them that she realised there was no going back. The euphoria had been short-lived. The responsibility for this little life was now hers. She wasn't sure exactly how she'd arrived at this thought. It was not something she'd considered in the hospital with nurses and doctors around. With the world now outside the closed door, and she and Seán and the baby alone in the house to fend for themselves, all she felt was an urge to open the door again and run and run and run.

She glanced at Seán. Oblivious, he held the baby while she took off her coat and went into the bedroom to deposit her hospital bag.

"I'm dying for a cup of tea." She came back into the kitchen and went straight to the tap to fill the kettle. "It's only like water, the stuff they serve in the hospital."

A whimper came from the pink bundle.

"Here. Don't leave me standing here like this. Take her."

She looked around. Seán was holding out the bundle towards her, staring at her, his eyes tense with fright. In that instant she realised that he expected her to know what to do.

It was the next day, when he went off to work and she was left alone with the baby, that she knew everything had changed. The child too expected her to know what to do. Delicate and helpless as she appeared, Bridie knew without a doubt that the relaxed sleeping cherub in her arms held all the cards. This tiny innocent scrap had all the power and she terrified Bridie.

In the way that everything had happened so fast in the last year, the constant spinning, now as reality set in life seemed to have slowed down almost to stopping-point, even sometimes it seemed to her to go into reverse. Like when someone in the family dies and the world seems to come to a halt, all other things so important before no longer of any consequence. In some ways it was good. There was no need to rush at things now. No getting ready to go out to work. No schedule to keep. Just as well because she didn't have the energy.

It took forever to feed Mary Jo. One feeding time seemed to merge into the next. Bathe her, change her, dress her, and then it was time to start all over again. With no time to rest in between or to do anything unrelated to the baby, it took a while for her to recognise that she was lonely.

"They keep asking me about you at the store," Johanna told her. "They want to see the baby. Why don't you call in with Mary Jo?"

If she didn't count cooing at Mary Jo, it would often be days since she had spoken to anyone other than Seán and Aunt Johanna. It was true she needed more adult company but it was something she didn't have the strength to do anything about. Not for the moment anyway.

Despite the sunshine there was a nip in the morning air. It

was two weeks since Johanna had made the suggestion and today was the day she would force herself to go.

She had been up since six, exhausted but unable to get back to sleep after feeding Mary Jo. She lay in the bed, waiting until it was a reasonable hour to dress the baby and go out walking with the baby carriage.

She smiled as the women in the shop all admired the sleeping child and said how good she was while the men served the customers.

Hugh saw her from the window of his office and came down to say hello and congratulate her.

"Good to see you out and about again, Bridie. And the little one."

He gave a half-glance at Mary Jo before moving away quickly to check on stocks with staff before returning to his office.

It was only when he appeared down onto the shop floor the second time that she felt his disapproval of her disrupting the business of the store. She had overstayed her welcome. She said her goodbyes and fumbled at the door, unable to manage negotiating both it and the baby carriage. Miss Doyle saw her struggle and came across to hold the door open.

"Come in again with the baby, won't you, Bridie?"

"I will. See you soon." Even as she said it, she knew she wouldn't.

The visit to the shop made her aware that people had their own lives to get on with, more on their minds than cooing at her little bundle – but it gave her a start, something to build on.

On the days when she had the energy, she walked around to have a cup of tea with her aunt. She always felt better after she'd made the effort. Something about Johanna's practical attitude made things seem possible and

161

she always left motivated to try harder. But by the time the next morning arrived that wave of enthusiasm had drifted away, disappearing somewhere in the dark night and the effort was just too much.

JOHANNA

Chapter 42

Johanna hadn't seen Bridie for two weeks.

She had watched the lethargy descend and allowing for the natural tiredness of a new mother didn't worry too much on those first few visits. She was reluctant to go knocking on Bridie's door in case she was taking the opportunity to rest when the baby was asleep. Might be the only relaxation she was getting. But now it was worrying – her absence was going on too long. Time to call around to the house.

It took several knocks before Bridie opened the door and Johanna was shocked at the pale, almost transparent face that stood before her. She hadn't time to recover, to even think about hiding her dismay, before the white face in front of her crumpled and dissolved into tears.

"What's the matter, child? Things can't be that bad."

"No, they're not. I don't know why I'm crying." Bridie let her hands drop to her sides and stood there, planted, blocking the way into the hall.

"Well, if you'd step aside and let me in we might be able to work it out." Johanna hoped hearing the lightness in her voice might help Bridie realise that all was not lost. She smiled at the moist half smile on Bridie's face, an expression halfway between tragedy and comedy, as she stepped aside to let Johanna enter.

"That's more like it. Now let me have a look at this little one. Where is she?"

"I think she's asleep."

"Well then, you put on the kettle and we'll enjoy the bit of peace while she is."

They walked up the hallway and, with her hand on the knob of the kitchen door, Bridie stopped and turned to her aunt. "Oh, Aunt Jo, the place is in a bit of a state." She pushed the door open.

"Oh, I'm sure it can't be that bad." One glance was enough for Johanna to note the understatement. "Nothing that can't be fixed between us."

After that she called in to see Bridie twice a week and helped her get organised. She cleared surfaces, removing everything that didn't have a function. She sorted the baby clothes that needed washing and took a bundle away with her. They came back a few days later, everything washed, ironed and neatly folded.

She'd had a word with Seán, suggesting that he keep an eye on her. Didn't want to get between them but she wondered how much help he was with the baby.

"I'm worried, Johanna, but there's not a lot I can do when I'm working such long hours. I do my best when I'm there but she doesn't seem to be coping." His concern sounded genuine. "I don't know much about these things. I've tried to be patient and I've tried being tougher – I know that sounds awful, but nothing seems to be getting through."

"Just encourage her, Seán, and maybe keep an eye on the baby and send Bridie around to me occasionally for an hour – just to give her a bit of time for herself without any responsibility."

"I'll do my best."

She wondered how good his best was going to be.

164

BRIDIE

Chapter 43

It became a welcome ritual. Everything seemed easy when her aunt listed the chores and got her started, like normality had been injected into the situation, but as soon as Johanna disappeared it was as if she took all common sense and routine away with her.

The regularity of the visits provided an anchor in Bridie's life that kept her from drifting off into the unknown. It got her up in the morning, not wanting Johanna to see her at her worst. On the days in between it was evening before she washed herself and put clothes on in time for Seán's return from work, a pretence that she had been up and about and was on top of things. Some days she didn't bother to wash herself at all, just threw on the clothes minutes before he was due home.

Bridie had been the one to pick the name, well, half of it anyway. Seán had wanted to call her Mary after his mother, but he agreed to the Josephine bit which Bridie had chosen and the joining of the two.

Even though she was happy with the compromise, Bridie could still only think of her as "it" or "the baby". Never Mary Jo. Hard to believe that she was a person, this baby that she might break or drop or not be able to stop crying or starve or overfeed. Sometimes she even thought she hated her when she wouldn't stop screaming. A mother was supposed to love her baby but Bridie didn't think she did. She just wanted her life back. She wanted someone to come and take this baby away and for things to return to the way they had been. To return to life before "the baby", when Seán loved her and she loved Seán and Joseph looked down from above and smiled on her and was no more than a happy memory.

Then it happened. The day the crying of the baby woke her. She jumped from the bed and ran towards the kitchen to check the time, her bare feet hitting the cold tiles.

Seán walked in the door before she could get there.

"What are you doing still in your nightdress?"

With no idea what time of the day it was, Bridie couldn't think up a plausible lie. His very presence told her it was probably after six and he'd be looking for his dinner. But she couldn't be sure as he worked irregular hours.

"I wasn't well so I went back to bed." It sounded like a lie, even to her.

The baby's crying coming from the bedroom reached a crescendo as if to highlight the fib.

"*Huh.* You'd want to start getting out of it in the first place. Have you even bothered to feed the child today?"

"Of course I have. She's only just started to cry." To her horror she heard her voice reduced to a whimper as another possible lie escaped. She had no clue how long the baby had been crying or when she'd last fed her.

"Yeah, sounds like it. Looks to me like she's had plenty of practice. Jesus, will you just pull yourself together, Bridie? I'll go out and get us something to eat but this is the last time. I'm warning you, Bridie. You can't go on like this."

She wasn't sure if she sensed a growl in his voice. She found it hard to judge things these days. But there was something in the word *'warning'* a slight threat, real or imagined, that bothered her. It was the echo of this that had her managing to cobble together some sort of a dinner for him most days after that, although she knew it wasn't the occasional lack of a meal on the table that annoyed him.

It was the once or twice that she slipped up that she noticed a look that had started to appear in his eyes. It only happened when she failed. It wasn't something she'd noticed in the early days following Mary Jo's birth when she just couldn't get anything done. No, it wasn't there then. It was a look that had crept in gradually as the months went on. A cold stare that he held for a few seconds more than was comfortable. She wasn't sure quite what it was that made her nervous and she was too tired to work it out.

That was until the day his patience snapped and he hit her. She couldn't blame him. It was her own fault.

SEÁN

Chapter 44

The doctor diagnosed postpartum depression and put her on medication. Seán apologised and never hit her again. It didn't come easy to him but he managed to bite his tongue whenever he felt a reproach coming on. Sometimes when a sentence managed to escape he would rescue the criticism halfway and turning it on its head translated it into something more positive.

"What's that smell? Did you not . . ." He turned his attention to Mary Jo. "Have you a stinky little bottie? We'll have to tell your mammy, won't we, so she can do something about it?"

From a shaky start, with a little practice he had become good with the baby. Once she began to take notice and respond he got even better.

"She's smiling at me. Did you see that, Bridie? She gave me a smile. That's her first."

Bridie came across to take a look.

"Ah, you know your daddy, don't you now?" He beamed back at her. "Say bye-bye now, baby! Your daddy has to go off to work." He continued waving, watching her smile, as he backed out of the kitchen. "I'll be home about six, Bridie. See you all later." And with a final blown kiss to

Mary Jo he was off.

When he came in from work he was happy to play with Mary Jo and sing to her while Bridie prepared the meal. Sometimes when he was not working they would all go out for a walk together.

"Come on, Bridie. It's a lovely day. Dolly yourself up there and we'll all go to the Common and parade with the glamourous people." He hoped she'd pick up the hint.

And so for the summer months he returned to his usual charming self. When they met others, he was delighted to show off his baby and his pale, lifeless, but still beautiful wife.

To onlookers they were the perfect couple.

BRIDIE

Chapter 45

She too had mistaken Mary Jo's smile of recognition when it happened the first time, but not wanting to deny him his moment of glory she said nothing about having seen that grimace of wind many times.

In the weeks that followed, when the medication kicked in, she noticed the difference. She still didn't feel anything. Not happy, not sad, her mood was still flat, but the slight improvement made her more able to keep going through the motions. Looking after the house at a superficial level became easier as did being alert to the needs of the baby. An outward appearance of someone recovering.

The first identifiable sign she could remember was one evening when Seán arrived in from work. She heard the hall door bang.

"How's my girl?"

Bridie was mashing the potatoes as he came through into the kitchen. She looked up from the saucepan with a smile. His arms were outstretched, his eyes trained on Mary Jo sitting up in her baby carriage at the far side of the table. As the baby grinned at him and dribbled down her front Bridie knew that she herself was invisible. A stab of jealousy pierced her as annoyance and disappointment mingled. She could only blame herself. Couldn't even be annoyed at Seán. He was oblivious. What sort of a mother was she? What type of woman would be envious of her own child? Her own baby. And it wasn't the first time.

The change between them had come about gradually. So gradual she didn't know quite when it started or what had triggered it, if anything. His efforts at being nice over the past few months, holding back the criticism had not gone unnoticed. Nor had his lapses when he could no longer sustain it.

It was just little things she noticed. If she were to describe the incidents to anyone they would have thought her foolish. That she was imagining it. None of any importance, they were just petty little things, but as they mounted, she could feel them began to erode what little self-belief she'd manage to build up.

"Lavish with the money, aren't we?"

The surprise of the shop cake she'd bought to celebrate his birthday suddenly turned stale as she held the knife ready to cut a slice.

"Isn't it well for you? No financial worries, I dare say."

"I think I'd like to go back to work. Uncle Hugh says my job is there for me if I want it."

"Why? Did you go in asking him?"

"No. I went in to buy your birthday cake and he asked me. He'd like me to go back." She sank the knife into the cake, the icing cracking under it.

"And how exactly are you going to manage that? You've a child to look after."

"Well, I was thinking maybe just on a Saturday when you're free you could mind her. For starters anyway." She ignored the scowl as she passed the plate across the table.

"Aunt Jo thinks it would do me good. A bit of adult company for a few hours."

"Does she now? Maybe she should mind her own business." He ignored her outstretched hand, forcing her to lay the plate on the table in front of him. "I don't need her to organise my one free day for me, thank you very much." His face darkened in silence as he picked up the slice of cake and bit into it. "You seem to have discussed it with everyone so. Didn't consider that you might talk to me first. Ask me what I think? *Huh.*"

Bridie recognised when a subject was closed. She knew better than to try and defend herself when he was in this mood.

It wasn't all the time. Just on days when he was in a foul mood and she never knew when that might be. At first it was only when they were alone. No audience. That was until one evening when Johanna came around to visit with a young man in tow.

"Bridie. Meet Brendan. He's son of the Lacey's from the village. The shop Laceys."

"Which shop?"

"Ah, Bridie! I forget that you're a Wexford woman. But you must have gone down to it often enough from your grandmother's. She always did her shopping there."

"Oh, I know now. The little grocery shop with the pub attached."

"The very one." Johanna had her anchored. "Brendan, this is Seán, Bridie's husband. A Galway man."

The two men shook hands and Seán sat back down in the armchair beside the fire, indicating the one opposite for Brendan.

"Brendan has only recently come over from Clare so everything is new to him. You might be able to give him a few tips, Seán." Seeing the two men settled comfortably,

Johanna grinned. "I suppose Bridie and myself will look after bringing in the tea then?" She gave her niece a wink and a jerk of the head. "Come on."

Having finished the tea and scones they all moved from the table to sit around the fire. Not often having visitors, Bridie felt the lift in her spirits and she was aware of her aunt watching her come to life on hearing all the news from Clare. Maybe this was something she should try more often.

When the conversation turned to matters of the world, encouraged by her newfound confidence she ventured an opinion on a newspaper topic.

"And sure what would *you* know?"

The stress on the '*you*' hit her like a slap. The dismissive tone hit the mark as she felt herself shrinking into the armchair, wanting to burrow under its cushion and out of sight. Johanna rescued the situation with diplomacy, but her intervention only served to make Bridie feel worse. The fact that there had been witnesses.

Over recent weeks, when they were alone, Bridie had begun to note every minor incident and the increase in their regularity. Every day or so now some little jibe or other. To the point now where he no longer tried to disguise his thoughts. Never tried to twist his words, manipulate them into positives. All pretence was gone. Little left now but contempt. At least that was how it seemed to her. A single click of the tongue and a slow shake of his head from side to side was enough to indicate that he couldn't believe her stupidity. His comments, delivered in a tone he reserved only for her, were designed to sting.

Since Mary Jo's birth she'd had difficulty feeling anything. But with each incident, she felt the barb. But she was trying to override them. Her head told her she loved him. That they had just lost their way. Temporarily. That it must

173

still be in there somewhere. But her heart wasn't telling her anything. She just couldn't feel it at the moment. All she could sense was another little bit of her love for him dying. Each time. It puzzled her that she could feel the soul-destroying death of each little piece of her love but not its existence? How could she tell anyone that? They would think she was deluded.

And now this new departure. A put-down in front of guests. She never expected that to happen. That he would deliberately humiliate her in front of others. Not for her sake but for his own. She didn't think he'd drop his façade and let himself down to that extent. She was mortified but it didn't seem to embarrass him in the slightest.

Even when he wasn't cutting with his disparaging remarks Seán's unspoken criticisms were transmitted across the dinner table in his silence. The way he attacked his dinner, sighing as he made hard work of cutting the meat. Sometimes it was just a throwing of his cutlery with a clatter and pushing the almost empty plate away as if it was a dog's dinner he'd just eaten

Bridie refused to engage with him when he was like this. She hummed to herself as she cleared the table as if oblivious to his mood. At times she ignored him and took refuge in her head. It became easy to transport herself on a journey to another place and another time when she was appreciated. Even though herself and Joseph had only been married a short time, she stretched it out in a slow-motion daydream that had no ending, a daydream with the horror of its final sequence edited out.

Chapter 46

Bridie went to Boston Common regularly. It was on the doctor's recommendation that she get out of the house at least once a day. It didn't matter where she went, just out. Anywhere. Baby dressed, into the pram, coat on, don't sit down again, just one foot in front of the other and out. *Don't think about it. Just do it.*

She went through this routine every day when it wasn't raining. It seemed pointless, but because she had been told to, she did it. She herself had come up with no better solution. And also because she was too tired to think of an alternative other than to sit down and look at the four walls, it was better to do as recommended and get out into the fresh air.

Their uniforms bestowed on them an air of superiority. In fact in most cases they weren't even uniforms, just navy or black coats with a glimpse of crisp white blouse showing at the neckline. Their smart appearance and distinctive style just gave that impression. It meant that an onlooker could not mistake them for anything other than nurses or nannies with their charges in tow and pushing stylish baby carriages. Employed by people who could afford them, unlike the slightly harassed look of mothers with their children, in a hurry to get home and put on the dinner. Most walked straight-backed, heads held high on swanlike necks, slowly turning right and left as their eyes surveyed the surroundings with a leisure and a confidence as if they owned the city. They were probably nice enough, but in her frame of mind everyone she passed seemed to hold an air of authority, to be of superior standing. Unlike herself they looked like they were meant to be here, had every right to be.

She was half relieved that they ignored her. Invisible. To stay there, to not draw attention by making eye contact allowed her to wallow in her misery. There were days when she pondered her situation, wondering if anyone ever just disappeared into invisibility? She certainly wanted to. And that frightened her.

She sat on the park bench gazing into the distance. Her eyelids began to droop. Such an effort to hold them open. The gentle warmth on her face felt good, making her want to just let them close and drift asleep. Her body was thawing in the heat that had only recently come into the sun. Or so it seemed to her. If the winter had been as long as it felt was something she was unsure of. She wasn't certain of anything anymore.

She forced her eyes open and glanced into the pram. Mary Jo lay there, eyes closed, totally relaxed and in no danger of smothering under the blankets. Her eyelids flickered slightly as if her slumbers were nearing an end. It would be unwise to fall asleep. What if the baby carriage rolled away or someone took the baby? Stifling a yawn she stood up and, stretching her neck, rotated it to get rid of the stiffness that had settled.

Mary Jo stirred, chubby fists appeared above the cover to rub her eyes. As her mother's face appeared in her line of vision the pink baby lips trembled and broadened into the makings of a smile. Bridie's eyes filled, overflowing as she reached in and gently stroked the downy head. With this cherubic recognition of her she could feel her heart turn over in relief. The first penetration of the deadness inside since the birth which seemed a lifetime ago. Mary Jo blinked in surprise as the tears from above splashed onto her pearly skin.

She could explain it to no-one but it was as if the world outside her had shifted too. Had jostled her out of the clutches of whatever lethargy and dullness that had paralysed her for the last year or so. Time to build on that.

When she'd first arrived in Boston, she looked at people as they approached and smiled and wondered at the way most of them blanked her.

"That's the way in cities, Bridie. Sure you couldn't be saying hello or smiling at everyone you meet. If you keep that up you'll soon have a pain in your face," Aunt Johanna had advised her with a laugh. "That was one of the first things I had to learn when I came over."

Johanna had explained that people rarely spoke to each other in public in America unless they were acquainted or had business that gave reason for them to engage. Unlike at home where everyone in the village knew each other. Even in a town like Gorey most people would have a few words to say to each other. And even if they weren't familiar, they always had a nod to throw to the stranger as they passed.

The next day she felt it as she sat on the bench and watched the nurses and young mothers in the distance. Some of them turned off down a different path before they reached her. She watch others select a bench and sit down. Sometimes two of them together with their charges would sit and chat. She would like to be one of those. Today she wanted some of them, even just one of them to see her.

Propped up against her pillow in the baby carriage

Mary Jo gurgled as she chewed her fist. The redness had gone out of her cheek now that her third tooth had appeared.

"Well, baby, what do you want to do?" Bridie smiled across at her. "Will we play a little game?" She reached across with the facecloth and wiped the bubbles, some of which had already burst and rolled down to drip off her chin. "Now, there, isn't that better. Do you know what I think? I think we'll try and make a friend today. How about that?" She stowed the cloth at the foot of the carriage. "Time to see if we can conjure up some magic." She sat back on the bench and looked around. "We can't rush into this now. We'll have to pick the right one."

Mary Jo, happy playing with her rattle, gurgled each time Bridie made a comment.

"I think it's time to make our selection. What do you think, Mary Jo?" She had spotted the nurse, her brown hair poking out from under her neat navy hat. A sensible-looking candidate, a younger version of Aunt Johanna, but slightly older than most of the other nannies around. A likely one to try her magic on. To get some practice anyway even if it didn't work first time. A face that wavered between pretty and plain, all average and matching, with no one feature remarkable it made her less intimidating. A certain softness in the face that could be described as "kind" looking. That would suffice for today – it was just what she needed.

As the woman approached, walking along talking to her little charge, Bridie watched her push the hood of the pram back slightly. She could see a child sitting up waving its hands around in answer to the nurse's cooing. Engrossed in the little boy, the nurse leaned forward towards him, oblivious to her surroundings.

Bridie stared hard at her in an effort to cast a spell. A spell that willed herself to become visible, just to one person.

178

She would be satisfied with that. Fixing her stare on the eyes, she concentrated. She held back a smile in readiness. Didn't want to come across as a grinning idiot. The nurse almost alongside the park bench now, Bridie's hope began to recede. It looked as if the chuckling little boy had more power over his nurse. She began to feel stupid. Just about to drop her gaze, she felt her hidden smile melt back into her. At that moment the woman glanced up from the baby. It was as if she felt the light of Bridie's stare boring into her.

"Hello." Seizing her opportunity, she smiled up at the nurse.

"Hello. Lovely day, isn't it?" The nurse smiled back.

"Absolutely gorgeous, thank God," Bridie responded, amazed that it had worked.

The nurse stopped, stretching her back. She glanced at the pram parked alongside the bench.

"Is this your baby?"

"It is, yes. My first."

Bridie adjusted the blanket on the pram. She didn't know why she did it. A reflex action. To indicate which baby, but there was no other, or maybe to denote ownership? She couldn't tell. It didn't matter. She brushed the foolish debate from her head as the nurse moved over and looked in at Mary Jo.

"And what's your name?" Experience had clearly taught her never to assume the sex.

"Mary Josephine. We call her Mary Jo."

Bridie realised that apart from her time in the hospital and when other tenants who rented rooms in the house asked, she'd hardly spoken Mary Jo's name to an outsider until now.

"Aren't you beautiful, Mary Jo, and what a lovely name?" The nurse smiled down and was rewarded with a gummy beam. "And look at those lovely teeth. "How old is she?"

"She's fifteen months now."

"A turning point. They get interesting after that."

"They do. Yes, they do." Happier having made some human contact, Bridie got up to walk alongside her new friend. She was afraid that if conversation dried as she sat on the bench the nurse might walk on. Best to make the most of this opportunity. Easier now to build on the progress. Getting started was the difficult bit and she had passed that test. The magic had worked.

"If you're going this way I'll be as far as the exit with you?"

"Well, I was going to do another round of the Common. Keep him out a bit longer in the fresh air, it's such a nice day. The winter was long enough."

"Maybe I'll do another round with you. If you don't mind, that is?"

"Not at all. I'd like the company. Conversation here is a bit limited. You can't talk yet . . . sure you can't." She leaned forward to include the baby in the exchange. "And I get a bit tired talking to myself." She chuckled at him. "Isn't that right, little man?"

Walking along in the company of the nurse the chat became relaxed. In the odd lull she breathed easily, looking around the park and wondering if any of the other young mothers and nurses noticed she had a friend. She guessed some of them must have seen her alone in the park over the weeks. As she recognised most of them, they must also recognise her as vaguely familiar. Not as invisible as she'd thought then. She smiled to herself.

Get interesting, she thought. If, as the nurse had suggested, the babies can become more interesting as they get older, that's the key to it. So must I. It can't be that difficult.

Chapter 47

Bridie sang to herself as she walked along the streets leading from the Common.

"Mellow the moonlight to shine is beginning,
Close by the window young Bridie was spinning,
Bent o'er the fire her blind grandmother sitting,
Crooning and moaning and drowsily knitting."

By the time she turned into her own street, what had started out at lullaby speed had upped to a bouncing pace, a tempo most unsuited to the sound of "The Spinning Wheel". Had there been anyone listening they'd have thought she was daft.

The late-afternoon sun had come out from behind the clouds where it had started to play hide and seek. It didn't worry her that the new spring in her step threatened to waken Mary Jo in her carriage as she barrelled along. She needed someone to share her good news. She had made a new friend and was about to step out into the world once more. A fresh start. Ready to work on making Seán see her again.

"She said a new word today."

Best to begin by telling him little details of her daily life and Mary Jo's. Too sudden a change might alarm him.

"What?" Seán took off his coat, shaking the drops off it

before hanging it on the back of the door.

"She had a new word. It was 'home'."

"She's too young. You must have imagined it."

"I didn't. She said it clearly. We were coming up the road and she pointed. There was no imagining it." She looked at him, surprised at the negativity towards his daughter. Pausing a moment, she was determined to stand her ground. "I'm telling you she said it. She kept saying it and pointing to the door. And she has a new tooth."

He went over to the carriage and smiled in at Mary Jo, tweaking her pink cheek. He was rewarded with a big sloppy grin as she pushed her wet fist into her mouth.

"What are you saying at all, at all? And let Daddy have a look at that new tooth." He took her hand gently out of her mouth. "Oh, look at that tootsie-wootsie!"

Mary Jo gurgled back at him through the wet dribbles, a mumbling jumble of sound.

"She was probably just testing out her vocal cords."

Jealous that he hadn't been the one to experience the expansion of his daughter's vocabulary. For once could he not just give her the satisfaction? She left it at that and got up to wet the tea.

Over the following weeks she told him about the people she spoke to during the day. If there was nothing particularly unusual about the encounters, she searched for a detail that would make each little event sound exciting. At first, he looked up from his newspaper and listened, surprise stamped on his face at the new bright Bridie before him.

She became more alert, watching out for things that might amuse him. Things that might make her appear more interesting. She stored them up for entertainment in the long evenings after he had had his dinner, releasing them one by one as she felt necessary to keep up the momentum. Sometimes she held back one or two just in case she had no new experiences to relate the next evening.

It would take time to win back what she had lost but she was prepared to work hard at it. Happy to put the effort in, however long it would take. That was before the new signs began to appear. Subtle little indicators that all was not what it seemed. They were gradually slipped in, like her introducing topics to make herself interesting. It took time for her to notice, but the increasing regularity made her wonder if it was unconscious on his part, or if it was something he deliberately stuck into the conversation. The way he said "I see" with a slight inflection on the "I" and the drop in the end of the "see" told her he had tuned out. He didn't see, he simply wasn't with her at all. That subtle little indication and the fact that more often than not he didn't bother to look up from the newspaper or avert his gaze from the fire when she told her stories.

"You're not even listening." Not the first time she'd accused him.

"I am listening. You were talking to your Uncle Hugh in the grocery store." He remained behind his newspaper as if to prove that he could do two things at once.

His way of always being able to repeat the skeleton of the event, but missing the nuances entirely left her stewing in a mixture of hurt and irritation that she had wasted her story.

She began setting little traps when she suspected he wasn't listening. Instead of accusing him she would simply stop mid-story and wait. He never noticed. She knew she was good in her telling of amusing incidents and remembered a time when he found her recounting of them hilarious. Now they just fell flat. When she challenged him there was something in the way he would tell the joke back to her in a monotonous voice that made her feel foolish for having considered it entertaining in the first place. There was no doubting that he had no desire whatsoever to relate in any way to her experiences, no interest in her efforts to restore any real attachment between them. It had moved on from that. It was now clear that he was deliberately trying to thwart them and by persisting the only one she was tormenting was herself, but she'd started so she'd keep going. It came hard to her to give up. If she did, there'd be no going back to it.

It took a few months more of perseverance before she abandoned all attempts. She knew for certain that the fresh start was over when he gave no indication that he had even noticed that she'd stopped trying, that she had finally admitted defeat.

The only thing that got her out of the bed in the morning now was Mary Jo and her demands. She was glad that it was essential to respond. That Mary Jo didn't tolerate ignoring. But even Mary Jo wasn't enough. During the day she found herself thinking too much. All thinking and no feeling other than that of slipping backwards. It was the lack of emotion that bothered her most. She didn't want to return to that. Not happy, not sad, not suicidal – just a lack of joy or any feeling of happiness. It was all gone.

Most days she just about managed to keep the basics going. More often she was experiencing a strong desire to bow out. No energy left to claw her way back in.

She sat on the park bench, idle thoughts drifting by as she rocked the pram. The occasional meeting with her new friend on the Common, and a couple of others she'd become acquainted with there had never gone any further and those little encounters were no longer enough to sustain her. Where had it all gone? All the pleasure in life. Maybe you only get a certain ration. It frightened her to think she had used up hers already. All spent. Nothing left

184

now but this endless nothingness. Not yet twenty-three, a bride, a widow, a move to America, a bride again, a child, a husband who was tired of her. She didn't blame him. She was tired herself. Tired of herself. Wanted nothing more than to go to sleep, let this weariness wash over her and not wake up again.

Chapter 48

Bridie had never seen a black man before she went to America. There weren't any in Ireland, at least not any that she had encountered, so black men never crossed her path. They were people she had learned about at school. Pagans from darkest Africa, that Irish missionary nuns and priests went over to convert. They were more like mythical people.

When she was seven, she received a black doll from Harry and his wife. They'd been to Dublin with their boys on a rare holiday and had brought her back a present. They'd never given her a present before. Well, that wasn't quite true, but they'd never bought one for her. Harry had once given her a bird's nest that had fallen out of a tree in his garden during a storm. She'd worried that the birds would come back looking for their home but he assured her that they had abandoned it a long time ago. He'd pointed out all the intricate latticework and the way the birds had lined it with soft fluff and bits and pieces they had found.

It wasn't Christmas nor was it her birthday so she was a bit surprised.

"Thank you, thank you, Harry." She was delighted when he gave her the doll. "I love it."

186

"Well, don't thank me, Bridie. It was the wife picked it out for you. She'll be back later and you can thank her. I don't think buying cars or trains for the boys gives her much pleasure. Mollie leaves that to me. She's very fond of you and she thought you'd like this doll."

Her other dolls looked pale and uninteresting beside this beautiful chocolate-colour creature, with strands of black hair moulded into her skull. She named her Polly, not being familiar with names that babies in Africa were called. Polly had arrived one summer and slept and woke and had her clothes changed and her pretend feeds for a year before a terrible disaster befell her.

Bridie sat on the granite seat happily crooning to her baby doll. The seat felt a bit scratchy on her bare legs but the heat of the afternoon sun, having shone on it all afternoon, made up for that.

"Mammy says you're to go in and help her." Dorothy appeared out from the house.

"Why don't you help her? I'm busy, can't you see I'm feeding Polly."

"Because she says you're to do it."

"Alright." Bridie knew better than to draw her mother on her. "We'll go in, Polly, and we'll help Mammy make the tea."

"Here give her to me. I'll mind her." Dorothy reached out for the doll.

"No, she's coming with me."

Dorothy grabbed Polly's white lace dress.

Reluctant to release her precious treasure into the care of her young sister, Bridie reached out to remove the grasping hand but Dorothy had a firm grip on the dress.

"No, I want to mind her. Mammy says you're to go in." Dorothy's half whinge was accompanied by a sharp tug.

Bridie felt Polly slipping from her arms and with an

unexpected freedom the swinging doll smashed the back of her head on the corner of the granite block.

A stunned silence from a wide-eyed Dorothy, breathless with shock, was accompanied by a high-pitched wail from Bridie as she saw the perfect "V" cut out of the base of Polly's beautiful brown skull. An injury so severe it would render her neck incapable forevermore of supporting her head

Bridie's aria only lasted a few bars before Maude came to the door to investigate the commotion. Seeing her mother, Bridie came down from her high note and wept.

"*Mammy, look what Dorothy's done!*" The words jerked out between her heartbroken sobs.

Charles Black was the first black man Bridie had ever spoken to. Funny how his name was also Black. She always noticed these coincidences. These links.

She'd first seen him on Boston Common while pushing Mary Jo in her carriage. Noticed the way he carried himself. His back straight and proud as he walked. It was neither a stroll nor a brisk walk but something elegant in between. He was there on some days but not others. It was usually the days she arrived early for a morning walk that she saw him, always with a folded newspaper under his arm. When the sun shone, she noticed the way he had of holding his face up to it as he walked, sometimes pausing a moment and closing his eyes momentarily. He appeared to be taking a deep breath in through his wide nostrils, like a man reliving a memory.

Bridie rocked the baby carriage. Mary Jo hadn't settled and was grizzling. She stood up and pulling back the covers took her out of the pram and began rubbing her back. It took a few minutes but as she sang gently into her ear she could feel the tension beginning to ease from her daughter's body.

She moved to put her back in the carriage and Mary Jo's face crumpled again. Too soon to chance it she sat back down on the park bench and began to rock her.

"You're tired in that thing. You just want to look around, don't you?" She settled her more comfortably on her knee. "It's much more interesting up here, isn't it?"

The black man caught her eye as he passed and she was surprised when he smiled. She smiled back.

A few days later he smiled and said "hello" and continued walking. It wasn't until the following week that he actually paused and made a comment about the beautiful sunny morning before continuing his walk. The next day he sat down on the bench, leaving space for one and a half people in between.

"I see you here regularly with your baby. You must live locally?"

Bridie had welcomed the previous smiles and "hellos" but a slight prickling of discomfort made her unsure if she wanted any closer communication.

"Charles. Charles Black is the name."

It felt dangerous. Not Charles, he seemed a perfect gentleman. Dangerous might be too strong a word for it. Maybe unsafe for this risky shift into something unknown.

"Bridie. Bridie Ryan." She heard herself respond before she had a chance to work out what that unknown might be. Not to have done so might have seemed unfriendly, so surprised by the development that she didn't know how to deflect it without seeming rude.

"Bridie? That's an unusual name?"

"Not where I come from?" It just slipped out.

She wished he'd move on. She jiggled Mary Jo on her knee, half wishing she would begin grizzling again to give her an excuse to go. As her child gurgled contentedly she was torn between being rude by cutting the conversation

189

short and standing up or continuing in a situation where she resented having been pressured to introduce herself.

"It's short for Bridget." Conflicted, she was trapped into politeness. Caught into allowing further intrusion into her life.

"Well, Bridget . . . or Bridie, with an accent like that I guessed you didn't come from these parts."

"I'm from Ireland."

"Very pleased to meet you, Bridie Ryan from Ireland."

And that was how the affair began.

Chapter 49

She stood at the sink, washing the breakfast dishes. She propped the last plate against the cup on the draining board and ran her finger over the suds, directing them down the back of the plate. There were days when all motivation seemed to drain out of her and today was one of those.

She had been the one to establish a routine but it was Mary Jo who kept it going. She didn't worry about initiating things anymore because she knew that the routine would fall into place when Mary Jo decided.

Looking up, she gazed at the raindrops running down the windowpane. Life suddenly seemed very long stretching out before her. Dull days like this were the worst. Not being able to go outdoors, not even for a short walk. It left her with no encounters or happenings to differentiate one day from another. There wasn't a break in the sky, just one flat blanket of grey, not even a passing cloud to disrupt its evenness.

She dried her hands on the damp tea towel and walked over to the sofa. She could feel the familiar lumpiness in the seat as she sat back into its soft cushions. Mary Jo was back in her crib having a nap before her next feed. Just as well. It was difficult to keep the goo-gooing going. Seán was good with the baby. She had to acknowledge that. She stared into space, pondering whether it was his fondness for his daughter that had her tolerate her lot or simply that she couldn't think of an alternative. Just a pity that things couldn't be fixed between themselves.

It was easy to pretend she didn't notice that Seán often came home from work late. He never gave a reason. She never asked for one. Not anymore. The arguing was long over. The red lipstick on his shirt one evening told her what she needed to know. She still said nothing. It meant that he left her alone.

She thought back to last night. A rare occasion when he expected his rights. A rare occasion when her body screamed for release from her loneliness. It suited them both but as her physical relief melted away she was left with an even emptier void in her heart.

A faint whimper came from the bedroom. She sat quietly, waiting a moment, hoping it was only a cry in her sleep and her daughter might not waken yet. There was silence from the room. She guessed that Mary Jo was also listening on the far side for a movement to tell her that her mother was coming to attend to her. Another minute passed before the whimpering began. The slightly more urgent ones that followed told her it was time to move before it reached a pitch that was more difficult to come back from.

"*I'm coming. I'm coming, love!*" She used her sing-song tone that always worked. "*Mammy is coming!*"

She went to the sink and took the baby bottle from the drainer. It was still miserable outside. She traced a fat teardrop of rain as it travelled slowly down the windowpane towards the wooden frame. Just like herself. Going nowhere.

She was in this lonely state of ripeness when Charles Black entered her life. Handsome, charming, warm and exotic.

When he was with her she had his full attention. His brown velvet eyes drank in her very soul and gave balm to her heart. Such a long time since she had been confident in her power to fill up someone's senses just as he did hers.

Charles was a gentleman's valet, or at least that's what he told her. She met him mostly for walks in the park and on his day off he took her to a tea-room. He didn't mind that she had to bring Mary Jo along.

"What you think of this big black head looking at you?" he was happy to coo at her. "What you thinking, little girl? You haven't seen too many of these."

On days when she grizzled, all he had to do was open his eyes wide and roll them around and tickle her under her chin to have her face turn into a dribbly smile.

"Would you like to come in for coffee before you go back to work?" As soon as the words were out she regretted them.

"You sure?" His eyes opened wide.

She wasn't sure. Her brave moment hadn't lasted.

He noticed the hesitation before she answered.

"Let me walk ahead and let myself in. Then give me a minute or two before you knock on the door."

"Afraid of the neighbours?"

"Absolutely. Look, you just hang on here and give me time to go around the corner and walk to the house."

Seán walked into the kitchen. He put his arm into his coat sleeve and began buttoning his coat.

"You going somewhere?"

"What?" The question took her by surprise. "Out for a walk with Mary Jo." She looked around at him, puzzled. "Where else would I be going? Why do you ask?"

"The hair. Looks like you've dolled it up?"

Big mistake. She hadn't considered that Seán might notice the renewed interest she was taking in her appearance. He never seemed to notice when she did it for him. She touched the chignon resting at the back of her neck. She shouldn't have changed her hairstyle. Too early in the morning. He couldn't possibly guess, surely?

"No. Just experimenting."

"Suits you."

"Thanks. Aunt Jo thinks so too." She glanced in the mirror, relieved to have been able to bat that one off.

"Well, I'm off now."

"Right. Bye then. See you later."

She stayed preening in front of the mirror as the door closed behind him. Since Mary Jo's birth her hair had grown long by default. She had thought about having it cut but Charles's fascination with the colour and his comments about what he called "her mane" made her hesitant to change it. She had decided leave it long and try out some of the hairstyles of the stylish women she observed around the city.

"And who is this elegant lady at my door?" Her aunt was pleased to see her. "Have you just stepped out of a magazine?"

"Oh, a bit of effort goes a long way, Auntie Jo. You should try it." She gave her aunt a playful puck.

"You cheeky thing! Come in here 'til I give you a slap."

Johanna's smile told her the contents of the next letter she'd be sending to Maude. She could feel the same glow radiating from within her that she knew her aunt was witnessing. She only hoped Johanna wouldn't be questioning from whence it came.

It was the first time she managed to meet Charles without the baby. She had arranged to join him at the Tremont

Street junction of the Common. She arrived early and was surprised to see that he had arrived before her. As she came through the gate she saw him seated on a bench under a tree. His skin like polished mahogany drinking in the heat of the afternoon sun, head tilted upwards in a position she'd come to associate with him.

Walking slowly to the bench she felt shy. It would have been easier had he been watching for her. She hoped he would open his eyes before she got to him. She stopped as a bird flew down to retrieve a grain on the ground in front of her and watched it peck some invisible treats. When she looked up she saw Charles's head turn. The corners of his eyes crinkled and his mouth widened into a brilliant white smile as he stood up to greet her.

"No Mary Jo today?"

"She's with Aunt Johanna. I told her I was meeting a friend and she said she would mind her for a couple of hours to give me a break."

"Did you tell her which friend?"

"No, indeed I did not. I just said it was someone I met on my morning walks with the baby. She probably assumed it was another mother or a nurse because she said it was nice that I had made a friend, so I didn't enlighten her."

"And nice that I have made a friend too." He smiled down at her and slipped her arm under his.

"What are you doing, Charles? Someone might see us." Bridie pulled her arm away. "Let's just walk side by side."

"You told me you didn't know many in Boston."

"Well, you just don't know – it's unlikely we'll meet anyone but you never know."

Charles walked along beside her in a silence Bridie knew to be a sulk. She was disappointed but there was nothing she could do about it. Well, there was but she wasn't going to. She wasn't going to fall into the trap of humouring him. That was one lesson she had learned from Seán. It didn't work in the long term. But she hoped he wasn't going to spoil their short time together.

Ignoring it, she concentrated on the ground. The leaves of the trees that formed an archway along the mall threw a dappled dancing pattern on the pathway as they blew about in the light breeze. She had walked this way before on dull days and found it tunnel-like, dark and depressing. But today with the start of the autumn fall, the sun penetrated the canopy, casting a golden glow.

"Let's cross over to the Public Garden and see the boats," She glanced at him.

"Perhaps madam would like to go on a voyage?" His mood had lifted.

"That would be lovely. Do you know I haven't had a ride in a swan boat since Seán took . . . well, since I first came over here?" She didn't know why she'd corrected herself, why she'd hid it. Charles was aware of her situation and it didn't seem to bother him, although for her there was an undercurrent, a low-level guilt, not enough to spoil her pleasure, but there all the same.

Crossing the road that divided the Common from the Garden she felt his protective hand touch her back as they weaved their way between the carriages. It wasn't necessary as there were few vehicles on the road but she liked the way the caring gesture made her feel precious and valued.

The queue was short and they had a boat to themselves. She'd have preferred if a third person had joined them, just in case they were seen. As it drifted along the smooth surface the diamond sparkle on the water thrilled her. The sounds of people retreated as they moved to the middle of the lake and the soft reflections of the old weeping willows soothed her soul. The tight knot inside her slowly unravelled and for the first time in weeks she was free to be happy. At peace with the world and glad Charles didn't feel the need to talk, she just wanted to relax and listen to the lapping of the water. She would have liked to trail her hand in it but it was too far below her reach. As she gazed at the reflections of the clouds on its surface, she thought how nice it was to have someone to drift along with her, someone who wanted to be in her company. When he reached over to take her hand, this time she didn't object.

"I take it madam is happy?"

"Oh, I am." Bridie smiled up at him. "Very."

The only words spoken in the boat and this time the silence felt right.

Chapter 50

"Baby, you can't be. I was very careful." He paused a moment. "You sure this baby ain't your husband's?"

Bridie looked at him, disappointment emanating from her eyes.

"I couldn't be surer." She was absolutely certain. Seán hadn't touched her in over two months.

"No, no, *nooo*, don't look at me like that, Bridie." Charles held her at arm's length and shook his head slowly from side to side, never taking his eyes off her.

She watched them widen until she could see the whites completely surround the dark velvet irises. Not sure what she'd expected him to say, she could feel her own eyes redden.

"Bridie, Bridie, this was never the plan."

"I wasn't aware there was a plan?" She certainly didn't have one. The tears began to spill. She knew that whatever plan he had it didn't include her.

"Ah, don't cry, baby." He put his arm around her in a hug. "We'll work something out."

Her nose began to run as the tears cascaded. He released his hold on her, fishing out a crisp cotton handkerchief from his pocket.

"Here, don't cry, Bridie. We'll think of something." He handed her the white square but as she wiped her wet face and blew her nose, she noticed he didn't replace his arm around her shoulders. "Let's talk about this tomorrow. I have to get to work now. We'll work it out. Don't you worry."

She was relieved when Seán went out again after his tea. It was his evening off and she had hoped he'd have a plan to go out.

"Don't wait up for me. I may be late."

She didn't query where he was going. The pretence that he was working late suited them both. She was further relieved that he didn't come home again until long after midnight.

She lay pretending to be asleep. She listened as he crept about in the dark, taking off his clothes. Keeping her eyes closed, she pictured him folding his trousers over the back of the chair and hanging his jacket carefully over them. He climbed into the bed beside her, lifting the covers gently in order not to disturb her. She knew by the way he went through the motions so quietly that he expected the arrangement to be acceptable to her. No questions asked. No answers required.

It was difficult to keep up the pretence of sleep but she tried to remain still and not toss and turn as her mind and body wished her to do. It was only a few minutes before she heard his regular snoring, allowing her to move about and try and find some physical comfort in their shared bed. Her body settled but she could do nothing about her whirling mind.

Getting up to check on Mary Jo gave her an excuse to move about if he should wonder. The baby was happily sleeping, so she stood at the window for a few minutes, holding back the edge of the curtain and gazing out at the grey smoky dawn beginning to break outside. She wanted it to be time to rise but it was still too early to get up without arousing suspicion. Before getting back into bed she went to the mirror to check that the dark circles under her eyes weren't too obvious.

She wished Seán would hurry with his breakfast. She stood at the table, fiddling about, removing things she thought he was finished with.

"Would you sit down and have your breakfast and let me have mine in peace?"

As he picked up the last piece of toast she took the plate away and put it in the sink. "I'm not hungry."

"Well, sit down or go and see to the child. You're hovering." He looked around at her. "What's wrong with you? Am I in your way or something?"

"There's nothing wrong with me. I'm not hovering."

"Well, it feels like it."

Afraid he would suspect something, she poured herself a cup of tea and joined him at the table. Mary Jo was already fed and changed and playing with her toys on the floor. It was too early to go to the park. If she did she would have to sit in the cold waiting for him.

As soon as Seán left for work she put the baby into her carriage and headed for the Common. She sat on the bench and waited. When his usual time came and went she wondered if something had happened him, if he'd had an accident or had been delayed by his employer.

She stood up and pushed the carriage a few yards up the pathway in front of the bench, stamping her feet to heat them up. She turned and walked back to the bench again. She considered doing a lap of the Common but not wanting to move too far in case he came and thought he'd missed her, she just moved up and down a bit further each time from the seat before sitting down again.

The minutes drifted into an hour. It was too cold to sit. She must have done a million laps of the same green area but she had kept the bench in her sights from each pathway. With each turn she felt her anxiety slowly dissolve into disappointment. It was only when she was almost frozen to the bone that she resigned herself to the truth. The 'valet' had disappeared and she wondered if his 'gentleman' had ever existed.

A grey cloud that had been looming overhead drifted in her direction. It began to drizzle. Had it not been for that she might have stayed there until lunchtime in the vain hope that he would eventually come. She watched the hood of the baby carriage darken as it absorbed the light mist. People walked along the pathways through the Common, intent on getting to their destinations on the far side as fast as possible. She was the only person left sitting on a park bench. No longer caring what anyone thought. She gave up looking for him, her head tilting down as her face melted to misery. Seeing nothing in particular except the gravel she asked herself how much she actually knew about him. His grandparents had lived somewhere in Africa. All dead now. What she hadn't realised 'til now, had never questioned, was that he hadn't told her where he himself lived.

Chapter 51

1902

Her journey downwards accelerated. It was a familiar one. A route she had been on before and a destination that terrified her.

It wasn't the fact that the child was born dead that hastened the fall into the abyss. At least she didn't think so. In a way, the baby being born dead made things simpler. Not that she was glad. She wanted the child but was afraid. It was all too complicated, too much of a mess.

Seán never saw the dead baby. She made sure of that. It wouldn't have taken him long to realise it wasn't his. And things were bad enough as it was. Had he discovered he might have killed her. Well, maybe not kill her, but he'd definitely dump her. Where that would lead was anyone's guess.

Unlike the excitement of her first pregnancy, this baby was carried in turmoil. She prayed for a miscarriage but her prayers went unanswered. She endured the full nine months, hopping from one plan to another, knowing there was no plausible explanation. And by the time the pains started one morning before Seán left for work she still hadn't come up with a believable one.

"It's too early, Seán. It can't be happening yet." She

cringed as another pain gripped her. "It's not due for another couple of months."

The first seed was planted. Hopefully he hadn't been keeping an accurate tally.

Despite her protests that they needed the money, Seán was insistent on taking time off from his job for the birth.

"There's no need, Seán, it's probably just a false alarm. They'll most likely send me home. Just leave Mary Jo over with Aunt Johanna." She saw his hesitation. "You can drop me off at the hospital and go to work after that. Aunt Jo will mind her until you pick her up later."

"And what if it's not a false alarm? If they keep you in?"

"It will be a false alarm, Seán, but there's no problem anyway. She's already offered – we've already talked about it. She's happy to keep her for the few days if I am kept in."

"I suppose."

She couldn't risk his hanging around the hospital. Too many opportunities for questions. Her brain had seized in terror as to what she was going to say but as another pain gripped her she couldn't worry about that for the moment.

The pains were real. It was no false alarm but the baby was in no hurry. She wondered if her anxiety had anything to do with the baby taking almost two days' labour to make its appearance into the world. Between waves of agony, she was thankful for the delay and grateful also for the fact that Seán had just gone on duty in the bar when her baby boy was born. Born dead. Seán wouldn't be back to the hospital for hours.

Following Mary Jo's birth, after the initial elation, Bridie felt nothing but exhaustion. This time her insides exploded in relief and she prayed to God in thanksgiving. She made the nurse promise not to let Seán see the body of the baby when he returned to the hospital. Said it would just upset him too much. The curly black hair might have been a giveaway and while she had curls and Seán had black hair it was safer that he never saw the child.

No one mentioned the blue-black tinge of the baby's skin. It could have been mistaken for the fact that his heart was defective. A blue baby. But she knew it was the talk of the nurses' station. They and she knew otherwise. She just hoped none of them would take it upon themselves to say anything to Seán when he arrived.

"You did tell the other nurses that Seán isn't to see the baby? And they are not to say anything about him." She couldn't take the chance. She had to be sure the nurse had left no room for a blunder. She didn't care what they thought. She was never going to see any of them again. "I'll tell him the bad news myself. They are to leave it to me."

She lay back on the pillows. There was nothing she could do now but work out a way to tell him. The worst was over. She couldn't allow herself to feel anything about the loss of the baby. There wasn't time and it would serve no purpose.

She rehearsed the lines a few times and had perfected them by the time she saw him appear in the doorway and walk towards her, ignoring the other women as he passed along the row of beds. His face was anxious but it held the expression of a man questioning rather than one who'd been met with any sort of news.

"Look, nobody could have done anything. It's probably because he wasn't full term." She smothered the nagging guilt of the lie as she made an effort to comfort Seán in his grief. "It's hard but maybe it's for the best." The tremble in her voice was genuine, a quiver of relief that her panic was over. "He might have had a lot of problems if he'd survived."

He believed her. His face told her that. She would have to live with the shame of her wrongdoing. It was a small price to pay.

* * *

She channelled her energies into cooking his favourite meals and making home a place of comfort to which he could return after work.

For the first few weeks after she returned, he sank into a disappointment which rendered him unable to return to the tension of his previous undermining campaign. He'd dropped it during her unexpected pregnancy, as if the anticipation had him forgetting all about that.

His newspaper laid down beside him, seeing his faraway gaze into the fire, she knew this time it was not designed to exclude her and her heart softened. Maybe they had a chance.

"Can you do nothing right?" The cessation of hostilities hadn't lasted.

A burnt dinner. She had forgotten the meat in the oven. He'd walked in on her as she tried to remove the burnt crackling and rescue some of the remains.

Things returned to normal with something different to criticise each day. Her hopes of a turning point were finally doused when Seán returned to belittle her mothering skills with Mary Jo, and the anger that seemed to have set in over her birthing skills in relation to his dead son John Thomas Ryan frightened her.

"I've lost a child too, you know." He wasn't to know she didn't share the same grief. "Where's your consideration of that. It's not just you who has?"

Her loss was a lot more complex. Not to be shared with anyone. She sometimes wondered if he might suspect something but nothing in his behaviour suggested he did. It was just business as usual for him where she was concerned.

205

While Seán grieved for his son that never was, he didn't seem to notice that each criticism was shaving away at her being, like a wood plane shearing another little sliver off a plank, eroding whatever little bit of herself she had left. Or maybe he just didn't care. She had no idea how or what he thought. It didn't happen overnight. Just a slow drip, drip, dripping over the months.

There were days when she felt like an empty shell. A white translucent shell with its insides sucked out. The fact that no-one seemed to notice, that Seán didn't see how she was disappearing convinced her that they'd all be better off without her. She managed to fight against it sometimes knowing that at least Mary Jo needed her. Her daughter, the only thing that kept her motivated, especially when occasionally a thought crept in that maybe she deserved his criticism. She'd been here before and survived. The difference this time was that she had very little left to fight with.

Like a drowning woman, every so often she came up for air but could feel her strength gradually diminish as she went under, deeper and deeper each time. The day came when she didn't argue back, didn't try to speak. She just lay back there in the armchair as her body went limp and she allowed his words to wash over her, no longer touching her. She no longer cared that his undermining had finally defeated her and maybe she deserved it.

Chapter 52

It tormented her the way it kept coming back into her head. This dream that took her so far into that special place but no further, always stopping short of its destination.

Bridie had always been a dreamer. It never bothered her that her dreams were only half remembered on awakening. She sometimes tried to retrieve them before she rose in the morning but it was never possible and she just left them to drift into the air.

But this one was important. It had become a tease. She couldn't leave it. Had to start the story from the beginning night after night in the hope that it might lead somewhere. Forcing it harder and harder she tried to ease off as she came close to the point where it always disappeared. Tried to relax into it in the hope that a lighter drift might allow her get a few inches further along and to a point that might identify something. This urge to go there now came between her and her sleep. This need to find the place.

The end of the dream remained missing. Like her last dollar note blowing from her hand and the wind whipping it from her reach as she chased after it. And each time she'd just caught up a fresh gust would blow it another few yards ahead. Almost, almost . . . but not quite there.

That's what her dream felt like. Always left her chasing it.

The problem was that Harry was dead. The one person who would have remembered, her old neighbour in Wexford, the only person who could have put an end to her search. The last time she saw him he had driven her to the train station on her journey to Boston. Even if she could have gone back to Ireland there was nobody there to talk to now who would know what she was talking about. None of the old neighbours left who could tell her where it was located or even if the place ever existed.

The news of his death came as a shock. Her mother had written of it. His son found him collapsed on the woodpile, the saw still in his hand. It happened outside the old shed at the end of his garden. They didn't know if the saw had slipped and caused the collapse, but they did know that he had bled to death. Her mother had written that there was a possibility that he might have had a stroke or a heart attack and had cut his artery in the fall.

"I hope that was the case, that it was quick. You remember, Bridie, when I used to advise him not to be killing himself with physical work with his heart problem and he would always say 'Sure if that happened, Maude, wouldn't I die a happy man?'"

Bridie had wept so much that the ink had run. Her whole body sagged, bereft, not quite understanding why the loss felt like it was stripping her to her core. He was only a neighbour, albeit one that she was very fond of. It was like she might need him in the future but for what she did not know.

It was after receiving the news that it became more urgent. She started to think about it in the daytime in the hope that talking herself through it might somehow throw a light on it. The more she persisted the more agitated she became and none of it helped. It made no difference. The location still eluded her. She knew if she could find it in her head, capture it, she would be able to get out of this place and start a new life there. But now Harry was gone there was no-one left to show her the way.

"I nearly had it last night. I nearly found it."

The man in the white coat seated opposite her nodded. He had heard it all before.

"I know it can't have been a dream. It was too real. I know this place exists."

"Close your eyes and go back there. Let's start at the beginning again."

At each session since she had started talking it was the same story. It had been hard to draw her out in the first couple of weeks after her admission. It was often that way with new patients but once they could see there was no benefit in silence they'd begin to talk. Only a matter of time before she would acclimatise and now that she'd started it was like a floodgate opening. Sometimes she added a little to the story. Just a detail, seemingly insignificant, but someday maybe one of these little clues would puncture the fog and she'd find the place she was looking for. A pointer to unstick her so they could move on to the next stage of her treatment. That was his hope for her. Something to help her get over her obsession so that she might perhaps be able to return to her life.

"Start at the beginning." As soon as the words were out he realised his mistake but she was off. He was reluctant to interrupt to indicate it was 'the dream' he meant. But she was off and he didn't want to interrupt her just in case an interjection might disturb her train of thought . . . and maybe this time it might all lead somewhere.

"Remember Harry? I told you about him. An old neighbour at home."

"I do. Sounds like he was a like a father figure to you, would that be right?"

"Well, no. I had one of those. My father's grand but he's very regimental. Policeman. He was great at teaching us our lessons but he was always very busy. No, Harry was different. Older, more like a grandfather – yeah, I suppose that was it, more the grandfather I never had. He used to take me places as a child and show me things. Ordinary stuff like a snail or the horseshoe marks on the bark of a horse chestnut tree but he'd make them interesting and I'd see them in a different way. I used to love being with him." She paused, her eyes soft, looking into the distance. "He loved nature. Noticed everything and I suppose because I was interested he liked showing me. I suppose he had the time and interest to do the things my father didn't have time for. Just one of those rare people, special people, that I was lucky to have in my life."

He watched her and waited.

"I remember one day in particular. I was walking along the lane. It was just as the sun was setting. I remember the sky had all these pink streaks and Harry was standing by the railings enjoying the last rays of the evening."

The psychiatrist listened. A born storyteller. He could almost paint the picture as Bridie described the scene. A shame about her fragility. He enjoyed the sessions with her. Reminded him of the way his own father reminisced about the homeland. Each meeting a different story, a vignette from her past that made him wish he'd been there himself in the idyllic world of her childhood. He must visit someday. Sad that her life had gone off the rails since.

"He was a man who had a great air of contentment about him. Harry never seemed to want much, never hankered after a life he couldn't have." Her contented expression told him she could see her friend. "I sensed that evening he was a man satisfied with his day's work. That he had earned his relaxation and knew how to enjoy such a simple thing as leaning on his gate smoking his pipe." She paused. "Funny how I picked that up." She sat back, a slight frown on her forehead. "How could I have known that – because I was only a child?" She looked puzzled. "But I did."

She looked across at the doctor as if remembering he was there for a purpose. She was wandering. But the engagement in his eyes gave her the encouragement she needed to continue.

"I suppose at the time I must have had this impression that life for adults was something that you arrive at eventually. That it just happened. Like a place that's set out for you for when you grow up and once you get there everything works out right. Does that sound stupid to you?"

"Not at all, Bridie. Not at all. But then we grow up. But wouldn't it be lovely if that were really the case?" He smiled at her. "No, I'm afraid we all set out in life, but in reality none of us quite knows where we're going."

211

Chapter 53

With so many stories the psychiatrist felt he'd met this Harry person. He liked him. A man so connected to nature. He envied Harry his life of simplicity which no doubt was not without its hardships. But a great anchor. His ability to enjoy the wonders of the world and share them with others. Something as simple as a shell on the beach was enough to fire his curiosity and pass on his knowledge of their former residents to her. Identifying the leaves he helped her collect in the autumn before sending her home to press them in a book. Just thinking about him relieved the stress of dealing with the sadness of the lives he was trying to untangle. A lot of his patients would have benefitted greatly had they had such a mentor throughout their childhood. She did seem to realise how lucky she'd been.

"Come on, Bridie, I've something to show you."

Harry took her in through the hallway. Black scuffmarks scored the wallpaper. So familiar were they that she hardly noticed as they passed along the narrow corridor. She must have been about eight.

The quiet of the house was broken by the sound of someone whirling into the hall behind them. As he hit the wall they heard the knock of a solid object.

"Hello, Victor." She didn't need to turn. It could only be Victor. His curiosity aroused by the voices.

"Where are you going? Can I come too?"

Harry looked around. The giveaway sound of the wooden handle sticking out of the pocket of his son's short trousers did not escape him.

"Of course you can, son, but leave that catapult here. You'll not be needing it where we're going."

"But I want to bring it."

"Well, then you mightn't want to come with us. Make up your mind." Harry continued walking ahead during the exchange.

Bridie looked over her shoulder and raised an eyebrow at Victor who'd hesitated. She beckoned him as she descended the two steps into the scullery.

Opening the door latch Harry stood back to let Bridie pass. Unsure if Victor intended to brazen it out with his catapult, she stood waiting in the yard. She watched as he reached the door and went to follow her out.

"Well, what's it to be then, son?" Without raising his voice or issuing any further order Harry glanced down at the weapon. "Are you coming or not?"

Bull-faced, staring down at the granite step, Victor refused to meet his father's eyes, his hand still clasping the handle of the catapult. She hoped he wasn't going to spoil the surprise. She saw him hesitate a moment and then without a word pull it from his pocket. He stepped back into the scullery and threw it on the draining board beside the basin. Then without looking at his father he passed out through the door into the soft evening light.

"Well, where is it, Harry?" She waited as he closed the door behind him. "The surprise?"

He pointed down the garden.

213

"*C'mon, race you!*" Victor said.

She glanced at him and detected a look of relief that the unpleasant moment had been averted.

"*Quiet! Quiet, children!*" Harry called after them as they ran ahead, the incident already forgotten.

Halfway down the garden Bridie stopped. Realising she didn't know where they were aiming for she turned and waited for Harry. Impatient she watched as he ambled towards them, glancing from side to side at the garden, taking in his surroundings as he walked and smiling to himself.

Victor had already reached the end of the garden. He turned and started back.

"*Whoo, whoo, chugga, chugga, whoo, whoo!*" Heading towards them with his train imitations he turned halfway, twirled in a circle and headed down the pathway to the end of the garden again.

"Victor, less of the noise. You'll have to be quiet or I can't show you."

With a last '*whoo, whoo*' of his steam train Victor came back to join them.

"Where to? What are you going to show us?"

"I told you it's a surprise," Harry whispered as he beckoned them to follow.

The old wooden shed in the corner of the garden was nearing the end of its useful life. Despite the slats that Harry had replaced, the base of each post had softened and it was beginning to sink into the mud. He led them towards it.

The door stood open a crack.

Bridie jigged about with excitement. Harry turned, putting his finger to his lips.

"Come on, you two." He opened the door slowly and gently, just enough to allow him to enter. "You'll love this."

They only barely heard the whisper through the dark.

She took Victor's hand and led him into the gloom. They could just about see Harry's bulk in the dimness and stopped just inside the door, afraid to go any further.

"Where?" Bridie whispered. "It's dark. We can't see anything."

Just as she felt Victor's hand pull away from her she felt the rough skin of Harry's catching hers.

"Where are you, Victor?" Harry whispered. "Here, catch my hand and don't fall over the garden tools."

By the slight tug on her arm Bridie could sense him reaching out in the dark to find his son's hand. As her eyes adjusted, she could see Harry looking up into the corner where the roof tiles met the stone wall at the back of the shed and followed his gaze. At first it just looked like a lump of mud stuck to the wall with bits of straw sticking out.

"Look, see the little beaks." Harry had a big beam on his face when he turned to look down at the children. "Can you see them now?"

"I can, I can!" She could just about see the beaks sticking out the top of the nest as they opened and closed in a chorus of twittering. "They're very high up, but I can see them."

"Here, I'll lift you up onto that old drum there and you'll see them better."

"Oh yeah, I can see them better now," she whispered.

"Move over a bit there, Bridie." He lifted Victor up beside her. "Now you've both got a good view. Can you see them, Victor?"

"Yeah, I can see them." He paused. "But they haven't learned to sing yet. They're only squeaking." He sounded disappointed.

"No, not yet, they're a bit young. They're only babies calling for their mother."

"Where's she gone? Has she left them?" Bridie worried.

215

"Not at all. She's just gone out for food for them."

"Can we stay and watch her feeding them?"

"Well, I think we should go out into the garden and watch from there. Maybe we'll see her coming back in to them."

"I want to stay here and watch," Victor insisted.

"But she won't come back into the shed while we're here, son. She might be outside waiting for us to be gone before she'll fly back in." He lifted them down. "Come on now."

Bridie followed Harry and Victor and turned to close the shed door behind her.

"No, Bridie, leave it open. She needs to be able to get back in to feed her babies. Leave it wide open and we'll be able to see her feeding them." Harry led them away. "Here, we'll sit here under the apple tree. We're far enough away now so she won't mind us. And we'll still be able to see."

The plank of the rough seat, bleached by the sun felt rough under her bare thighs. She sat still, worrying that a splinter might pierce her skin if she moved.

"I think that's her. Look there, on that branch," Harry whispered, pointing at the old oak tree beyond the shed. "Looks like she's got something in her beak."

"Oh yeah." Bridie watched enthralled as the mother fluttered into the shed.

"Listen now. What can you hear?" Harry looked from one to the other.

"Oh, the babies are squawking really loud now." Victor had his head cocked to one side.

"And why do you think that is?"

"They see their Ma with the food and they all want it." Victor grinned. "Like us."

They sat and watched in silence as the mother flew in and out, each time with a new tasty morsel.

"I think it's getting a bit cold, children. We'll go in home now. And your mother will be wondering where you are, Bridie." Harry went over to the shed and closed over the door until only a gap the width of his shoe remained.

Chapter 54

"It was a muddy sort of pond – we used to call it 'the marl-hole'. It's where the cattle would drink. Even when everywhere else had dried up, the marly soil would hold the water and there were always trees around it. I loved to sit beside it and watch the reflections." She paused. "There was a chestnut tree." She sat upright in the chair and stretched her arms out wide, looking into the distance. "It was huge and the big branches spread out overhead."

He watched her from where he sat behind his desk where he'd been making a few notes. Her arms slowly beginning to droop. She was somewhere else, no longer in the room. She had described it so well in previous sessions, he knew exactly where. Across the laneway at the end of Harry's garden and through a small woodland glade. In wet weather the hole filled with water transforming it into a pond. A perfect oasis.

He left her there and waited. He watched her lean back in the chair and gaze out the window, like a person reluctant to leave the place they were in. She would come back when she was ready. They usually did.

She turned her head from the window and looked him in the eye. He knew what she wanted. Checking to see if he seemed willing to come on this journey with her. He nodded, his chin resting on his interlocked hands.

"I loved watching the way the leaves blew in the breeze, the way they were reflected in the pond. And at the start of the summer the candle flowers, they were gorgeous the way they stood upright. They came out at the start of the summer. They were pink. That was a bit unusual because most of the other chestnut trees around had creamy white flowers."

She told him how Harry had shown her the moorhens when they came there to nest and made her promise not to disturb them and not to tell any of her friends about them. At least not until the baby birds were older.

She glanced for any sign of his attention wavering. It was important for him to see she was happy once. To see she was capable of it and that she wanted it again. She just needed help to find it. He was listening, nodding every now and then, his index fingers steepled, touching his lips.

She loved the dusty old armchair. She had been there the day his wife Mollie had complained that the springs were coming through the upholstery and she wanted it removed out of her kitchen, out of the house entirely.

Harry had taken it to his shed and put a pile of old cushions on the seat to prevent the springs from piercing through. He had salvaged them from the house, the cobweb thin squares of the cushions were worn to a thread from people sitting on them. Some already with a hole worn through revealing the lining beneath.

Bridie loved them, imagining each patch holding a story. The floral material might have been someone's summer dress, the checked squares perhaps a shirt. The armchair became her favourite place to sit watching him do his woodwork, making garden seats from fencing poles or driftwood he found on the beach.

To increase the light Harry had removed part of the shed's wooden door and replaced the laths with glass panels. She knew he sometimes couldn't sleep because he often told her stories about those nights when he would go down to his shed and sit in the armchair. He could see the marl-hole from his throne and in the still of the dark he'd watch the badgers slide into the pond.

Bridie never went to the shed in the night. He wouldn't allow her. But he often showed her the badger excavations and their slide runs on what he called "their nature walks" and would let her collect the lovely soft clay they'd unearthed.

"What do I need it for?"

"I'll show you. We can work together. Bring me over those old clay pots. We'll need about three of them." He stood aside. "Now stand in at the table and fill them with the badgers' soil."

He reached up and, brushing aside a cobweb, took a box down from the shelf.

"Now, remember the day on The Burrow when we collected the wildflowers seeds?" He looked down at her. "Well, now is the time to sow them."

She could almost hear Harry's voice: "Look, children, see the rabbits." She supposed that's how the name stuck, but it was the sea of wild bluebells that she loved best. A magic carpet that turned The Burrow blue around May each year.

"Let's move on to the dream. Or the dream that you say isn't a dream."

Bridie, reluctant to exit her memories, gave herself a little shake.

"Right." She exhaled heavily and forced herself to refocus. "One day Harry said he wanted to show me a lovely place. I was older then. Must have been about sixteen. We were walking along a sort of rocky plinth, with the sea on our left and I remember a stone wall on the right about the height of my shoulder." She reached out her hand and raised it to demonstrate. "The rocks were a protection to keep the tide back from the wall. But they came to an end and I wondered was that it? I couldn't see what it was he'd taken me there for until he pointed to a little stile built into the wall and told me to climb over it."

He watched as she used her hands to draw the picture in the air.

"On the other side of the wall there was a grassy pathway that ran alongside the railway track. It was only grassy because there were centuries of weeds growing between the stones."

The doctor leaned his head against the leather back of his chair and closed his eyes.

"The old red-brick station building was across the track but there was no-one on the platform. It was like a ghost place. I don't know if there was even a stationmaster on duty but then there weren't many trains so I suppose that would have been normal."

The doctor was tired coming towards the end of the day and although he'd heard all this before it was in some way like a meditation. He allowed her to go back over it again without interruption and lead him along step by step. Could have recited it himself but she was his last patient of the afternoon and as he had no plans for the evening it didn't matter if the session over-ran a little.

What he'd noticed and particularly liked about her, once she'd begun to open up, was that she never blamed anyone for her misfortunes. She took full responsibility for her own bad decisions. All she wanted was help to find her way out of the mess and to be given hope that she wouldn't be punished forever for her mistakes. He hoped he'd helped her find that even if he never managed to locate the elusive end to her dream.

"We had walked along for a few hundred yards when the railway track divided in two, like this – in a V."

Her gesture reminded him of a priest on an altar turning to the congregation – hands apart *'et cum spiritu tuo'*. He didn't even know if his recollection of the gesture and the words matched, so far back as it was, buried in his own past.

He knew this track, the one they followed. He knew it so intimately at this stage that he believed it must exist. Could almost believe he'd been there himself, so vivid was its siding that swerved off up to the right behind a high wall and out of sight. He tried to listen with a fresh ear in case an extra piece of the puzzle emerged.

"I was a bit nervous because we had to jump down onto the track." She laughed. "I don't know why I was nervous because everywhere was so quiet you'd have heard if a train was coming even if it was miles away. We crossed over to the siding but I couldn't get up again onto the plinth so Harry cupped his hands like a stirrup and I put my foot in and he raised me up 'til I had a good grip and was able to scramble onto the walkway again. He was very tall so he was able to get up no problem."

The psychiatrist scratched an itchy spot behind his ear and waited for her to move on.

"There was this house further along across the track. It had a creamy wall which seemed really bright and warm with the sun shining on it. I tried to work out how the sun was lighting up the house like this because I'd have expected the high wall on our side to have cast a shadow on it. Then I remember Harry had been very specific that we go in the morning at a certain time. I knew then it was because the sun only had a short time when it threw light on both the wall behind us and the wall of the house opposite at the same time. I knew then that's what he wanted me to see." She looked over at the psychiatrist. He was still with her. That was good. She sometimes worried that he might lose interest with her repetition.

"He knew a lot about science and things although I don't think he had much schooling."

"What happened then?"

"We sat down on the edge of the plinth looking over at the house. I thought at first it might be the stationmaster's house, but it didn't look lived in. The inside shutters were closed and while it didn't look unkempt or anything, the outside paintwork was fresh enough, I could see a few cobwebs on the windows." She stopped, her brow furrowing slightly as she tried to remember other details about the house. Maybe just one detail might come this time that would unblock her.

He said nothing, just sat there silently waiting for her. She rubbed her temples in a slow circular movement. A long sigh emerged before she continued in a hushed voice like she was listening for something.

"The place was really quiet, like life outside of us had stopped. And although the sea was only a few steps away the waves were silent and there wasn't a bird to be heard although I knew there were gulls about. I know it sounds like it might have been eerie, but it wasn't, it was beautiful. We sat with our legs hanging over the edge onto the track. All I can remember is the sun heating us, like it was beating off the wall behind us and bouncing its warmth onto our backs. I don't know how long we sat but it seemed like forever. And I knew I didn't want to move from there."

The doctor allowed the silence to continue for a minute. He watched her as she gazed out the window, until he was sure she had nothing more to add for today.

223

"Well, we'll leave it there for the moment, Bridie, and I'll see you again in a few days." He stood up quietly and walked towards the door.

"Oh." She looked at him, her mind returning to the room. "Oh sorry, I'm delaying you."

"No, no, it's fine but I think we've done enough for today." He smiled at her. "You're making good progress. It won't be long now and you'll be out of here. Just a few more sessions."

"Do you really think so?" She stopped in the doorway and gave him an uncertain look. "Well, thanks. I'll see you soon."

"Don't look so worried, Bridie." He smiled again. "It'll all be fine. Believe me."

Chapter 55

He allowed the silence fall as he watched the girl in front of him, reluctant to disturb her. It was going to be one of their last sessions anyway as she was almost ready to be discharged from the hospital. He'd miss her when that happened although he was pleased for her.

Looking at her now, from the pale shadow that had arrived into his room, the transformation into the auburn beauty before him amazed him. The blankness that she'd arrived with replaced by this glow he'd seen slowly warming her over the weeks pleased him. One of his successes.

She appeared totally relaxed. He wondered what she was contemplating. If it might be enough to realise that in her memories the sun always seemed to be shining. She could go to that place, to those places of comfort whenever she needed to. It really didn't matter where they were. What they were was priceless. It didn't matter if one of them was only in her head.

She became aware of the quiet of the room, like they had both drifted asleep in the warmth. Keeping her head still she opened her eyes to check. Moving only her eyes she observed her surroundings. To see the doctor opposite her, head back against the headrest of his chair with his eyes closed, embarrassed her. She felt foolish that the drone of her ramblings might have put him to sleep. She wondered if she should give a little cough, but before she had a chance to decide he opened his eyes and looked at her, a query on his face.

"Did something happen when you were there?"

"No, nothing happened. That's the thing." Relieved that she hadn't bored him rigid, that he thought she had just come to a standstill, she relaxed. "Neither of us spoke but I knew why he'd brought me there. It was heaven."

The serenity returned to her face and he left her to think about it for a few moments before continuing, not wanting to snatch it away from her.

"Can you remember revisiting it?" He hoped this time something might trigger a memory that would move her on.

"I tried to. With my mother. I remember wanting to share it with her and we walked there one day but she couldn't get over the stile and then it started to rain so we didn't go any further. So no, I never actually went back. I sort of forgot about it because I came to America and had a different life."

"What made you remember it?"

"When things started going wrong for me I began to dream about it, but I could never find where it was. It was gone. It had disappeared from my head. Not the actual place, but the location of it. I think about it a lot but I can never quite catch it. My mother, well, she didn't even remember going there with me. Maybe I imagined that too. I meant to get her back on that again to jog her memory but I forgot. I didn't really need to ask anyone 'til now. And anyway, she doesn't know I've a problem. She might think I'm mad."

"Where do you think it is?"

"I tried to work it out logically, to narrow it down. I'd

never been out of County Wexford with Harry so it had to be there. For some reason I thought it was near where we lived and I seem to keep homing in on that and feeling I'm getting closer."

"Well, maybe it is?"

"But it can't be. We lived beside the coast alright but there is no railway running along there. At least not that close, the tracks are more inland, going through the towns. No, there have never been tracks where we live."

"Have you considered the possibility that you dreamed it and that it never existed? Maybe you never actually visited it with Harry?"

"I think that all the time. Maybe I was never there. But then I think about the time I tried to take my mother there. Could I possibly have had two dreams about the same place that never existed?"

"Maybe."

"It's like two chapters of a book. Maybe I'm just crazy. Have you ever come across anyone else who dreamed in episodes?" She smiled at him.

"Well, no, but that doesn't mean it isn't possible." He grinned back at her. Her sense of humour pleased him. He'd noticed it was becoming a more frequent feature of their recent sessions.

He paused a moment. It was time for her to take the leap and move on. He hoped his judgement would prove correct.

"How would you feel if it were just a dream?"

"I suppose I'd be disappointed. Yes, I suppose I would. I don't think I'd want that confirmed."

He waited and watched as she gazed at the far wall. He hoped it was the look of someone for whom the wall was no barrier, someone who could perhaps see something beyond.

227

"Yes, I would feel it's a pity, because it was nice there. But do you think I'll have to make a decision about it if I'm ever to get out of here and move on?"

"Do you think you're ready to make that decision?"

"I'll never be ready. That I know. And there is another thing I'm certain of." Bridie stood up and looked him straight in the eye. "It's in Ireland. If it exists at all it's definitely there. I know for certain now that I'll never find it here."

Chapter 56

By the time Bridie came out of the hospital Seán had started divorce proceedings.

She wasn't entirely surprised. He'd dropped enough hints for her to be aware that he'd investigated the process before she ever said anything about leaving America and she didn't fool herself that there was a chance he would come back to Ireland with her. She knew what his choice would be. The next decision was hers and hers alone and it tore her apart.

Mary Jo.

Seán applied for custody of their child and got it, using Bridie's delicate mental state as leverage.

"Look, you know I love her," she said.

"That's not the problem, Bridie. That's not in dispute." His voice was quiet. She detected a compassion in the way he shook his head slowly as he looked at her. "So do I. Equally."

"But you can't do this to me, Seán." Her pleading sounded weak, even to herself as she tried to drown the niggling doubt at the back of her mind.

"I can, Bridie, and I will. I have to, for her sake. She's going on three. Here is all she's ever known. You're in no position to fight me on this and you know it." His voice was firm. "You're not taking her to Ireland and that's that."

Despite the harsh words she recognised the flash of sympathy that crossed his face as he held her shoulders. They'd had this out so many times, but this time she knew she'd nothing left to fight with, knew that she was beaten.

"I have to go. I can't stay here."

"And what about me? I'm her father. I can't just up and off like that."

"Would you not just think about it, coming home and starting a new life in Ireland?"

"No. Absolutely not. I've already told you that. I've a life here. A good job. There is no chance whatsoever I'm going back and there won't ever be, so get that out of your head. There's nothing there for me."

She turned her face away and tried to push him off, but he held her firm. Lowering his voice, he continued.

"Look at me, Bridie. Look at me. I'm not trying to be cruel and I don't want to fight with you."

She knew he meant it. The fight was gone out of him too. That was clear. But he was capable of standing firm on this. She was in no doubt about that.

"No, I know that and neither do I want to fight, but you can't look after her. You have to work." She threw the words at him, realising as she did that she sounded like a petulant child. She yanked herself from his grasp.

"Look at me, Bridie. We can't go on like this, we have to sort this out." He caught her by the arm and forced her to face him. "I'll make arrangements. If you're worried she'll be neglected you needn't, she'll be well looked after." Determined to get her to focus and accept the inevitable he continued. "I managed to see to that. She was well cared for all the while you were in hospital and you can see for yourself that she's happy."

"Well, I'm back now and she was always happy with me too."

"Look, I'm not questioning that but you haven't thought this through. You're her mother. If you want to see her, you'll have to stay here. I'm not trying to take her from her mother. Stay here. That would be the best thing for her. Best for everyone. Both of us nearby."

"And if I do stay, she lives with me?"

"But are you fit to look after her on your own? You can't look after yourself." He paused. "We can discuss that when you decide to stay. What's best for her will be the deciding factor."

The misery etched on Bridie's pale face caused him a moment's uncertainty. She spotted the slight softening of his eyes. Only a momentary thing but seeing her opportunity she pressed home for one last try.

"Please don't do this to me, Seán. Please. Don't."

"I don't want to, Bridie. I can assure you it gives me no pleasure, but if you stay, nothing is going to happen overnight. Whatever is decided you'll be able to see her and mind her whenever you want." He paused. "I can't say fairer than that. The decision is yours."

She knew he wasn't doing this with the purpose of hurting her. That was all in the past. But one thing hadn't changed. His opinion was the only one that counted. Not what she thought was best for their daughter, it was what he thought. With all that had happened some things still hadn't changed. While Mary Jo was his priority there was still the doubt in her mind that most of all he was doing what was best for himself and that he had already decided and there would be no changing his mind.

It wasn't difficult to get the former routine going again. She returned to her usual activities with Mary Jo and Seán took to minding the child on his days off.

"It'll give you a break." He helped Mary Jo put her arm into her coat. "We'll go out and feed the ducks and give your mammy a rest, won't we? And maybe we'll go 'visiting'."

She suspected it was to the owner of the lipstick but it didn't much matter.

"Where did the pair of you go today?"

"Just out and about and we called in on a friend."

Best to slip it in gradually, get in before Mary Jo said anything. He always mentioned the activity first. What they'd done. Like going for a ride on the trolley or playing ball in the park. But he never named the friend. And Bridie didn't ask. It was pointless. It might only raise a row. What mattered was that she had effectively lost Mary Jo and she recognised that the matter was out of her hands and there was very little she could do about it. She had lost too much ground. Was gone too long out of the picture.

The dilemma hopped around her head for weeks. Backwards and forwards, forwards and back. Having pondered over it for a day, she'd go to bed having reached one decision only to wake up to a completely different conclusion by the next morning. She wavered between a resentment at the unfairness that made her want to go to war on the matter to the logic that told her that her child was young enough to establish a new life without her. The idea of a new mother in her daughter's life was the thing she couldn't come to terms with.

Her head told her that to stay in America would mean another round of mental problems and no chance of getting permanent custody of her child when the time came. Going home was the only possible saviour of her sanity but her heart told her it wouldn't take very long for Mary Jo to have forgotten that she had ever been her mother. She would grow up never knowing how loved she had been by her for the first three years of her young life.

She hadn't the strength to enter a battle where the weight of evidence against her was indisputable. And so she surrendered. And that acceptance of her redundancy instigated another spell in hospital and effectively sealed her fate.

Her stay in treatment was short this time. Just a couple of weeks. And by the time she was ready for discharge she knew things were different. Something within herself had changed. It came to her with startling clarity. For the first time in her life she knew she was ready to take control of her future.

"What do you want? Do you even know what it is you want?"

It was as simple as that. The nurse stood there looking at her.

"I never thought about it like that. Everything has just been going round and round in my head."

"Well, think about it now. Make up your mind what exactly it is you want to happen, what you want to do, where you want your life to go."

She paused in her packing. Realising she had never asked herself that question, just plunging along from one crisis to another. Drifting, aimlessly in between.

"I want to start again but that's not possible. Too much has happened."

"Well, you're only young. You could do that. Start again. There's plenty of time. What's stopping you?" The nurse leaned on the metal rail at the end of the bed, her arms rigid. "You can't change the past but you sure as hell can shape the future."

She had seen Bridie in and out of the hospital. The

challenge on her face was clear to Bridie. There was no escape this time. Not without a plan.

"Do you want to spend the rest of your life in and out of this place?" She eyeballed Bridie. "No, I thought not. So, what's stopping you starting again?"

"I'm afraid my secret will come out. My secrets." She glanced away, her face miserable as she counted them stacking up. She hadn't told them at home about this latest readmission. She wouldn't have told them about the first one but Aunt Johanna had kept them posted. But that was the least of her problems.

"You could tell them. Get rid of them. You'll feel lighter. Believe me you will."

"*No.*" She realised she'd almost shouted it out. "No." Calmer this time. "I couldn't do that. It's Ireland we're talking about."

The nurse nodded. "Do you think I don't know what it's like? With an accent like this." She teased a smile out of Bridie, forcing her to look up at her.

"Well, then, you'll know that if I told them I could never go back."

"Yeah, you're probably right there." The nurse thought for a moment, rubbing her chin before resuming her stance at the end of the bed. "So?" She looked straight at Bridie.

"So what?"

"So, what are you going to do to stop your secrets coming out then?"

"I'll have to think about that one. But I'll come up with something."

"Good girl. That's what I like to hear."

By the time she was released from the hospital she was ready to move on. But first she would discuss the details of the 'arrangements' again with Seán.

* * *

"What?" Johanna looked at her in amazement.

"I know it doesn't make sense, Aunt Jo, but just don't mention me in letters home."

"Why ever not, Bridie?"

"It's the only way I can make a fresh start. I don't want any of them dragging stuff up. I need to leave it all behind me. Here."

"Well, what am I allowed to say then?"

"You can ask how I'm getting on at home but don't say anything about my life here in America when you write to mother or Granny and don't mention Seán or Mary Jo. I'll work out what to tell them myself about that. Promise me."

"And what if someone else does?"

"You're the only one who writes home. Uncle Hugh only sends a Christmas card and an occasional photograph. He never gives any news. Even about his own family."

"You're right, Bridie, it doesn't make any sense. What if I already have?"

"Already have what?"

"Mentioned your . . . escapades."

Her scalp prickled at the use of the word.

"I'm hoping you haven't." She glanced at Johanna, unsure now how much her aunt was aware of.

"No. You're lucky. I left that to you."

"Look, I know, I can't explain it but please don't. Mention anything. I'll write to you separately myself. Promise me, Aunt Jo."

They stood there side by side looking at the liner, misery etched on their slack faces.

"I can't stay here, Seán. I wish I could, but I'd go mad." Her voice was flat. Nothing more to be said. They had had it out over and over again. All anger, all resentment used up.

The wave of sadness that washed over him surprised even Seán himself as he handed over her diminished trunk on the dock. She stood there, unsure of what to do next.

"Just join the queue. I'll go. We'll say our goodbyes and I'll be off. It'll be less difficult. For both of us. It wasn't all bad, sure it wasn't." He reached over and gave her a hug. "Go on now, Bridie. I'll write and let you know all about Mary Jo, how she's getting on." He gave her arm a squeeze. "And sure you never know in the future . . ."

As he walked away in the direction of the exit he glanced back. Something in the way she just stood there, dwarfed by the ship caused him to hesitate and go back. He dipped into his breast pocket and produced a bundle of notes.

"You might just need this to help you get settled when you get home." It was the best he could do to assuage the trickle of guilt that had been bothering him since they arrived on the dock.

"I have money. You've already given me some."

"Yes, but you mightn't have enough. Here take it."

As she took the money, it felt dirty. Like she had just sold her child.

She hadn't wanted to take anything from the house, just photographs and a few clothes of Mary Jo's. On the boat journey home, she took out the christening gown each night before she climbed onto her bunk. She probably should have given it back to Johanna before she left.

"Take it, child. Sure I'll have no more use for it." Johanna had stood before her in her black widow's dress, holding out the gown. Said with an absolute certainty, Bridie didn't argue. The crisp tissue paper had crinkled in the silence as she passed it over. Handmade by Johanna for her own children, Bridie had been reluctant to accept it. Such a precious garment but Johanna was insistent that Mary Jo should have it.

The cotton was soft against her face as she smelled it. Maybe she should have returned it to Johanna for her future grandchildren. It hadn't needed to be washed after the christening. Mary Jo had only worn it in the church, but she had given it a wash before putting it back in storage. She regretted that now as she buried her face in it, hoping there might still be a trace of her baby somewhere within its folds.

Bridie fingered the lace knots around the edging for a long time. It reminded her of counting the beads of a Rosary and this nightly ritual gave her comfort. She rolled to the edge of the bunk and got out. Giving the gown one last smell she replaced it carefully at the top of her luggage for easy access.

Like a shadow wandering around the ship, she offered a faint smile as she passed other passengers whose faces had become familiar. She didn't encourage conversation and no-one intruded other than to exchange daily pleasantries about the weather. A few young men made overtures, attracted by the mystery of this tall beauty travelling alone. Attempting to engage her in chat on her strolls around the deck, her pale face and monosyllabic answers discouraged them from persisting further. In most cases they could read the signs. They would make an excuse that they were going to meet someone before politely bidding her farewell.

She worried over her story. Divorce was unheard of in Ireland. She wondered if they were even familiar with the word. A big mortal sin. If she told her parents that her husband had made her a divorcee, that she had allowed him to take her child and give her to another woman to mother, they would probably show her the door. That she had slept with another man and had his child would have her in Hell. There was only one thing for it. She would now have to concentrate on rewriting her history. She had plenty of time on the journey home to do it.

By evening she leaned on the ship's rail, looking down into the dark water, allowing her heartbreak fall into the sea below. By day, as she gazed down with the light breaking through the clouds and sparkling on the sea's surface, she imagined the same waves swallowing it all up, absorbing every drop of that pain and despair. She watched them below, washing the surface beneath her in a cleansing rhythm. She had made her decision and there was no going back.

What surprised her most was that once that decision had been made it became easier to go ahead. No longer moving one step forward then two steps backwards, swaying betwixt and between and going nowhere as she had been, her feet weighed down, as if stuck in a bog.

And so, alone, she returned to Ireland determined not to look back.

Chapter 57

County Wexford

She wondered just how many times one could start a new life. One so utterly different to that which went before. How many times were you expected to do it in the course of your lifetime?

She was weary. Not sure if it was just the travelling that had exhausted her, or if it was the thought of how much energy would be needed to yet again lay the foundations for a fresh start. But it had to be done.

Only now could she see that the effort she had to put in to create a new life in America had maybe been easier than what faced her now. There had been the excitement of the unknown as well as a certain freedom in starting again where few had been aware of her history. Her life ahead then had been a blank canvas. This time it was different. Her returning home was quite the opposite. She was coming back to a place where everyone knew her seed, breed and generation. They knew her and along with that they would think they knew her story. The few years' gap would suffice to leave them with that assumption. They were only going to be told what she wanted them to know. She would hold back something of herself, a lot of herself. It didn't come naturally but she'd had experience in being secretive in the interval. Now was the time to perfect that skill. She had no choice now but to start a new life, well, almost a new life, despite her loss. Departing her home place had had its benefits and now perhaps returning would help her to move on.

It was a long journey each day but it was good to be able to cycle. She held up her face to the drizzle that had started to fall. The misty damp on her face was cleansing. A washing away of her sins. The light breeze played with her hair. She peddled faster. The damp would have her head springing with curls if it got any wetter. She was almost there anyway so it wouldn't do too much damage.

It was only now she was home that she saw how her travels had widened her experience. Just as her father had said. Working for Uncle Hugh had given her a career and the skills she had learned were useful. She had hardly time to draw a breath before she had landed a job as cashier in the Farmer's Mart. Something to give her a reason to get out of bed each morning. The regular routine was a help. The staff expected her to have so much confidence in the Mart as a result of her experience in America that it worried her that they had an inflated sense of her abilities. Fear of making expensive mistakes kept her focused on the mechanics of the job for the first week. The money was different. More complicated than the dollar, the pounds shillings and pence that had seemed so simple before. Funny how fast you forget. It should come back to her easily enough but she needed to concentrate for the moment.

Joan, the retiring cashier, had great patience going over the bookkeeping system and allowing her to make all the entries as they arose.

"Don't worry. You won't make any mistakes while I'm watching you and you'll soon get the hang of it."

Joan introduced her to all the customers as 'the new girl' and once they realised she had been in America she could see an added interest brighten their faces.

"Oh, I've a niece over there. In New York. Don't suppose you'd have come across her?"

"Ah, no, sure I was in Boston. And I didn't even know too many there."

By the second week, Joan would go off for ten or twenty minutes and leave Bridie alone to deal with the farmers and their purchases. The first few slow transactions had her nerves on edge. She double-checked everything and kept apologising for the delays.

"Stop worrying about delaying them, Bridie. Just talk to them. Sure they love the bit of chat."

"Oh, I don't know, Joan. I'm very slow."

"You'd frighten them if you were doing it fast like in America. Look, you're new here, they're delighted. They see you as exotic." She laughed. "They've been looking at my ugly mug for a lifetime. You've given them a great lift. Believe me you've perked up their lives no end. So don't be rushing them."

"Maybe you're right. But 'exotic' I'm not." She laughed. "But yes, maybe you're right."

"I know I am. And anyway, the half of them wish they'd had the courage to do what you did and see the world. It's too late for a lot of them so they're thrilled to be hearing about it now, even second hand. Do you really think they're coming in here every day or so just to get a handful of nails or screws?"

This new insight changed everything. With a fresh confidence she tried out Joan's theory and it worked. Once she had completed a transaction, if there wasn't a queue she would fold her arms on the counter in front of her as if ready for a chat and as the banter began to develop she relaxed into the slower pace. It worried her slightly that the management might see her as wasting time.

It was coming up to closing. The last customer had left with his new spade. She had spent the last five minutes chatting to him about the plans for his vegetable garden. She saw the shop manager walking towards the cash desk. He had waited until the door had closed behind the man.

"Well, Bridie, you've certainly brought new life to the shop." He began emptying the cash. "We'd only see some of those old farmers coming in once every six months before, now they're coming in once a week." He winked at her. "I wonder why that is now?"

"I've no idea, Mr. Doyle." She laughed. A relief to know that she had got something right. She was going to enjoy this.

The family didn't question her much in the first few days following her arrival from America. They gave her time to lay her head under her parents' roof and rest after her journey, quietly sympathetic that her child had died. She had little choice but to push aside the guilt, knowing that they believed Mary Jo was dead. She had never actually said it, never mentioned the name. They had just assumed it when she told them the baby had died, so it was only half a lie. She would never enlighten them. Didn't need to as she'd never told them about her second pregnancy.

"I can't talk about it." The technique for ending the conversation worked well. Stopped any further probing. As soon as they asked an awkward question, she used the same response. It was easier than expected. They never pushed further. The tears were real. As soon as they saw the threat of them spilling, they pulled back.

She told them about her spells in the mental hospital. In

a strange way it helped hide the other big secrets. Not sure where the limit was, they didn't ask too much, not wanting to tip her too close to the edge again. They allowed her, in her own time, to show them the photographs and the baby clothes.

She didn't care that they believed Seán Ryan was also dead. She just told a straight lie about that. As far as she was concerned, he was dead. Aunt Johanna had promised never to mention him and she had to trust her. It was easy to explain away the occasional letters from America – just a few friends keeping in contact. The only ones from which she read extracts to them were from Johanna and occasionally she would drop them a little titbit from one of her friends in the grocery store to knock them off the scent.

"Are you coming down to Confession?" Maude had her coat on and was sitting on the chair, tying her shoelace.

"Ah no, I've a few things to do."

"Come on, the walk will do you good now that the rain has stopped. And sure, you haven't been since you came home. I hope you haven't lost your religion over there in America?"

This was something she was going to have to face at some stage. She knew her parents were already wondering why she hadn't gone up to the altar to receive Holy Communion at the Mass on Sunday. Better get it over with before her mother started asking too many questions.

"Right, just give me a minute and I'll be with you." Not having been to Confession was the excuse but it wasn't going to suffice forever.

As they walked along the damp road, avoiding the puddles, Bridie was glad her mother wasn't in a talkative mood. Considering what she might say to the priest was causing her a major dilemma, enough to fill her head. Registry Office marriage, infidelity, a baby out of wedlock, a divorce and abandoning her child. She was going to have to lie to cover up the tower of deception she had already built. She ran it through her head as she walked along.

"*Bless me, Father, for I have sinned. I lied to my parents.*"

"*How many times?*"

One big lie or lots of little ones under the same umbrella? How are they counted?

"*Just once.*"

"*Are you sorry and do you intend to refrain from doing it again?*"

I won't need to. The subject is closed. Am I sorry? Can't answer that. I'll have to lie. She tossed it around, silently rehearsing it until it came as near the truth as she could manage.

The greyness of the church added to the damp feel as they entered. She shivered slightly. The pew creaked as the two women walked along the kneeling board to join those already waiting outside the double-sided Confessional. Doors opened and closed on sinners whispering their transgressions in the dark. Sibilant sounds emanated through the metal grill on the doors, followed by the quiet drone of the priest as he murmured absolution to the penitents.

The door opened and an elderly woman in a felt hat emerged, leaning on her walking stick, eyes downcast watching her step. The young woman next in the queue stood up, waiting for her to pass before entering the Confession Box. The tapping of the old woman's walking stick on the tiles as she made her way slowly to the altar to pray out her penance was interrupted by a raised voice coming from the Confessional.

"*How long?*" The priest's angry voice echoed through the church. "*That's a disgrace. You need to be going more often than that.*" His voice lowered as one or two people waiting affected a cough in order to cover the young woman's shame.

Bridie wondered how long the unfortunate had told him it was since her last confession to exact such a reprimand. Had he intended those seated outside to hear? Could he read her mind? Another lie began to form in her head as the woman opened the door, a hot flush on her cheeks as she made her way to the back of the church. Bridie cringed for her. Only for her mother being in the pew beside her blocking her way, she would have melted out of the church and joined the girl.

MARY ANN

Chapter 58

1912

Maria's drowning was the thing she found hardest to accept. And all the boasting that had preceded it. *"God himself couldn't sink this ship."* That's what they said. But God had had his revenge. The unfairness of it. She really didn't deserve this.

She took to her bed and allowed the weeks to drift past. She'd often heard her parents talking about people who'd taken to their beds and never got up. She'd never comprehended it, had wondered at their strangeness. Now she understood, understood them completely.

No-one would wonder about her. At ninety her body was worn out. Reason enough to take to her bed without further explanation.

She lay on her side in the bed, the crisp clean sheets smelling of the outdoors. They had changed the bed linen that morning and she could now feel the starched lace of the pillowcase against her cheek. She moved her head slowly, rubbing it against the coarse texture of the lace in the hope that the abrasiveness would distract her from the pain and ease her agitation. She sighed as she realised that the mere consciousness of the action ensured its failure.

Her muscles ached. Her bones creaked as she rolled

onto her back and she could feel some of them scraping against each other. She rotated her shoulders, something she did regularly to keep them from seizing up completely. Not sure if she was doing more harm than good. Recently the grinding felt like it was turning them to chalk.

She inhaled deeply, pausing a moment before stretching her muscles gently. She bent her knees to ease the stiffness in her back and manoeuvred a spare pillow under them to keep them propped up. Yes, that was better. More comfortable.

Concentrating on her breathing, settled now, she allowed her mind to wander back through her life. She didn't mind the fact that it drifted from one thought to the other without seeing any one sequence through. She glided in and out of a doze, picking up where she left off. Sometimes in the middle, sometimes beginning a new story. A lot of stories. A lot of dramas. Of no consequence to others but it was her life.

The loneliness at the loss of Patrick. Those awful empty days, eased only slightly by the blessing of their children. She had been so despairing. Never thought she would get over it. It had been hard to manage alone. No choice, if she were truthful. She had to cope if they were all to survive. Looking back there must have been a certain comfort in the necessity. No, comfort was not the word. The fact that they needed her was the only thing that had kept her going. That sense of dependence, a spur that drove her on.

Emigration had swallowed several of the children. Tough each time. Didn't become easier with repetition either. Every farewell had torn the heart out of her, something she'd kept hidden from them as much as she could. Now that she thought about it, maybe it had been the wrong thing to do. Might they have thought that she didn't care, wouldn't miss them? She'd have to rectify that.

She studied the ceiling as she pondered. Maybe she would get Maude to write a letter to them all. No, not Maude. Her daughter was always so matter-of-fact about everything. She would think it too sentimental. No, the granddaughter would be better at that sort of thing. Yes, Bridie was the one. She would dictate the letters to Bridie and say what she should have said to them all those years ago. It was too late now for some of them but not for all. Yes, letters would fix that as best it could be fixed at this stage. Even if they didn't arrive until after she was gone. At least they would know that it hadn't been easy to see them off, not when she loved them so much. And as much as she missed them she accepted it was what they had to do with their lives. What they were entitled to do if it made them happy. That eventually she'd got used to the separation of the Atlantic Ocean between them and looked forward to receiving the letters. She'd tell them how much pleasure she got to see the postman coming up the driveway. Wouldn't mention the grief of one year of letters running into another with promises to visit home that were not possible to keep. The loneliness of knowing that she would never see some of them in the flesh ever again. Hugh wasn't one for letters but the cards and the photographs he sent were just as welcome and there was that one visit.

Yes, she would do that when Bridie arrived.

So many had been lost in the tragedy. Selfish perhaps to feel she was the only soul on earth to have lost a loved one. Knowing she was part of a larger community on whom the world's interest focussed and sympathised was no comfort to her in the loss of her youngest child.

A bittersweet thought. That Maria had returned home for a visit after so many years when Mary Ann had despaired of ever seeing her again. Had she not returned to Ireland she would still be alive.

Maria's life so full of incidents and experiences. Exotic compared to her own. The letters closed the chasm, bursting with detail as they were, down to descriptions of their glamorous clothes and what they had eaten at banquets. So vivid were they that Mary Ann might have been looking in a window watching her daughter in the centre of the activity. A life so remote from her own.

The joy of seeing her so recently snuffed out in one almighty icy collision as she returned to America. No more the hope that she would make a return visit home at any time in the future. No more letters.

They kept the newspapers from her. She never asked to see them. Never wanted to read the detail of the sinking of the *Titanic*. The unsinkable.

When the reporter from the newspaper called, they didn't tell her. Just gave him as much information as they felt sufficient for him to do his newsman's job and for Maria not to be forgotten. He wanted access to their mother but they refused. Just said she wasn't well. The same was told to the well-meaning neighbours, knowing she didn't want to talk to anyone, didn't want to see anyone other than the immediate family. And even that was questionable.

Her lungs full of the spores of damp hay harvests, her fight for breath became a feature of her last days. Some days easier than others with only a few breathless spasms. She was content in bed with nothing expected of her but to while away her hours, alone with her thoughts. No questions asked. No prospect of her suddenly rising up and becoming active again.

Lying there saving her energy she could examine each life slowly and in fine detail. Plenty of time to allow each of her children their season of glory.

She wanted to think about Maria but tried not to. Too recent. Too raw. The images of her final moments too vivid. She pushed the thoughts away with a force that belied her weakened state, a strength that came from a need to survive through memories of all her children, eldest to youngest. A small mercy that Maria was the youngest. Usually too tired before she arrived there to get farther than the memories of Maria's endless childhood questions. She could still hear the little voice, tinkling up at her. The endless '*why*' from a child filled with curiosity about the world.

The infants who'd only had a few moments of life were given their time. More time than they'd ever had on earth. They'd made their mark. Thinking about them was easier. All so long ago. Had they lived, what might have been? Little Daniel, John and Mary. And baby Flora. No more than a puff of breath in this world. One of them might have been a famous singer or inventor. No matter if not. They'd all have left a footprint on the earth however small. Maybe no more than gentle or kind. But she had no doubt it would have been a good one.

Sometimes she thought about these first and left those living to take their places at the end of the queue. They would be easy and there was a lot to think about. Whichever order they fell into she forced herself always to leave Maria until last.

With each child the thoughts floated past. She made no effort to capture any in particular. She just went with it and whichever one landed she allowed it to settle on her mind like a feather. Meandering in and out and through she let the children lead her wherever they wished, visiting laneways and fields. Exploring forests and seashores. She could see the face of each child shining up at her. Art,

Maude and Catherine still in Ireland. Only Hugh and Johanna left now in America.

Poor James had died over there, never the chance to come back home for a visit. Found dead in his sleep. Heart attack like his father. Never married, no children. His journey ended all too soon.

Her thoughts brought her back to the day of a visit to Ennis with a few of the children. Little James had stood beside her as she chatted in the street to an old friend. She could still feel the warmth of his tiny hand in hers as she said goodbye and made to walk away. Could still hear the little voice ringing out.

"Mama, why did you say to that lady . . . this is my eldest son Art and this is my daughter Catherine and this is James?"

"But you are James, aren't you?"

"But why am I just James and nothing else. You always say it like that. Am I no-one?"

The sight of the little freckled face and the innocent blue eyes looking up at her broke her heart. She glanced around, checking on the others. Art was still looking in a shop window holding Catherine by the hand, pointing out an item to her.

"Of course you are, James. Of course you are someone. Someone very important." Mary Ann bent down and holding him by the shoulders, leaned in and whispered into his ear. "You're my special boy, but I can't say that or the others might be upset. You're my one and only James, my very special James."

She thought now of the way his face lit up as he scrunched his shoulders up until they almost touched his ears.

"Am I really, Mama?" His eyes widened.

"You are, but let's just keep it our little secret."

251

She hoped he'd forgiven and forgotten the thoughtless neglect. That it was not something that had followed him to adulthood.

A snack arrived up on a tray, rousing her from her doze. A bowl of potato soup and some soda bread. They varied the meals in the hope of tempting her waning appetite. Sometimes it was scrambled eggs or tea and toast or stewed apples and custard.

The grandchildren took turns in dropping by regularly. They sat on the edge of the bed, telling her their bits and pieces of news. She knew they thought they were helping so she let them prattle on, giving only half an ear to them. She no longer had much interest in hearing about things she wasn't going to be around to see. But it made them happy to share it with her so she indulged them.

"That's nice, love. You enjoy that. D'yeh know, I think I'll have a little nap now."

"I'll come and see you again tomorrow, Granny, then."

"That'd be lovely, child." Sometimes she had difficult remembering their names. "You're very good. I'll see you soon then."

Chapter 59

Bridie took a few days off work and travelled over to Clare to see if she could help breathe some life back into her grandmother.

"Your grandmother wants to see you. She says she has some job for you to do for her. I can't understand why she wants you to come across the country when one of us could just as easily do it for her. But they are her wishes so we have to respect them. You were always her favourite grandchild so come as soon as you can because she is failing more each day.

Your loving mother

Maude"

She was pleased that Mary Ann had a job for her to do. She followed her instructions and found some notepaper and envelopes in the drawer of the big mahogany sideboard. The smell of old wood as she pulled out the drawer reminded her of the fascination of looking through it as a child, examining its contents. The photographs and letters and postcards and the old sampler that had been stitched by someone she had never met.

"Read it back to me, child." Mary Ann lay back on the pillow as Bridie read the letter for Johanna.

"Yes. That'll do." She gave a short cough. "You can do

the same for Hugh but add in how proud I am of his achievements with the shops and my appreciation for his helping the relatives out with jobs."

"I'll do that, Gran." Bridie could see she was tiring. "Is there anything else you want?"

"I do, but we'll wait until tomorrow. I want to write letters to Art, Maude and Catherine." Mary Ann sighed. "But we won't be posting those. I'll want you to hold them until I'm gone." Mary Ann looked at her granddaughter and smiled. "Can you just hear your mother if she got it before then? Yes, they can be delivered after I'm gone."

Once the letters for America were posted Mary Ann appeared to give up. Bridie sat with her for hours, looking up from her book every now and then to check she was comfortable. It was difficult to watch her tire after a short conversation, all enthusiasm gone from her face. Not the grandmother of old. Not the Mary Ann she remembered, always wise with her advice. The curious and questioning woman she loved. It was like she didn't care anymore what anyone was doing, often responding where she thought she ought, but asking none of the questions she would normally have asked. Sometimes she rallied and Bridie talked about her job, told her stories about the farmers coming in and the ones who asked her to go on an outing with them. To amuse her she told of the one without a tooth in his head asking her to marry him. No preamble, no invitation to go for a mineral with him, just straight into marriage.

"Oh, I met those in my time too. After your grandfather died. Probably wanting to get their hands on a good farm." Mary Ann smiled. "But don't let life pass you by, child. Don't do that. It'll be a long and lonely one if you do."

The only sign of any real engagement. The first since

she'd written the letters for her. Bridie went downstairs not sure if she should raise their hopes, that maybe this one bit of advice was a sign that Mary Ann was coming back to herself.

Her struggle for breath, when it happened, was frightening. Her face turned black at times with the effort. The doctor had been a few times but said nothing much could be done other than to make her comfortable. His visit this morning told them that the end was near.

"Try and calm down, Mama. Just try and take slow breaths." Maude spoke in a firm tone, trying to keep her voice even, despite the panic she felt.

Mary Ann was beyond hearing or following her advice. The strength with which she flailed around and tore at her daughter, pushing her away, amazed them.

"Hold her hands there, Bridie, before she knocks the water jug off the locker!"

When the gasping fit passed, she looked around at the room, wondering for a few moments where she was. She smiled at them all, no recollection of the struggle she had just endured.

"Do you know what just happened, Mama?"

"What do you mean, Maude?"

"Do you remember you couldn't catch your breath?"

"What are you talking about, child? Sure I'm breathing fine, well, no worse than it was yesterday."

Relieved that she wasn't conscious of what had happened, no-one enlightened her further. Best not frighten her.

Maude, Bridie and Catherine took turns to stay with her at night. They dozed by her bedside, an ear alert to any sound of discomfort. Art had moved the settle bed upstairs to his mother's room so that on the nights she was comfortable they could get a few hours' sleep. Her energy ebbed and flowed, diminishing a little more each day.

"I never told you about my little Flora." Mary Ann lay in the bed, eyes closed, the way she conducted most of her conversations of late. The strength to keep her eyes focused for any length of time eluded her now.

"Who's Flora?" Maude raised her head from her crochet.

Catherine, pottering about the room, dusting the furniture and settling things, stopped and looked across at her mother in the bed.

They waited for an answer. None came.

Maude halted her lacemaking, all concentration on the intricate pattern now gone.

"Flora? Do you know who that is?" She mouthed across at her sister.

Catherine who shook her head.

"Are the primroses still there?"

They looked at each other.

"What primroses, Mama?" Catherine asked gently, unwilling to jolt her mother back to the mystery of Flora.

She didn't expand, just lay there, a faint smile moving lightly across her face. It no longer mattered to her that she had introduced a topic of such immensity.

"Ask Maggie."

"Your sister Maggie? But Aunt Maggie's gone. She's dead long ago, Mama. Don't you remember?"

Maude put aside her crochet and looked at Catherine who had come over to the bed and was now seated on the edge.

"Do you think she's beginning to imagine things?" The worried look on Catherine's face suggested that she wasn't ready for this change in events. "She's rambling, Maude. She must be rambling."

Maude stood up and leaned over her mother.

"Tell us about Flora, Mama."

"My little Flora."

"Do we know her, Mama?" She wasn't about to let this go.

Mary Ann lay there, her face serene, travelling through a different world, to a different place. Her daughters waited. It was only a few seconds before she answered, but to them it might as well have been a week.

"Ah no, child, she was born before any of you. Born before Patrick."

"You mean Art. Our brother Art? Wasn't he Patrick Art?"

"Not Art. No, not Art. Before your father Patrick. Before I met him."

"What?"

The two sisters looked at each other, mouths open, unsure if they were understanding correctly.

"And where is she now?" It was Maude who recovered first. Enough to try and focus her mother's mind.

"Near the Long Acre with the primroses."

Catherine shook her head at her sister, a frown forming on her forehead, warning her not to pursue the subject. They both knew the significance of the plot beside the Long Acre.

"And Aunt Maggie knew?" Maude was not to be stopped.

"She helped me. I moved some of the primroses to the grave when we were burying Daniel." Mary Ann spoke slowly, pausing for breath between the sentences. "Will you look after little Flora's primroses for me?"

"We will, Mama, we will."

Mary Ann sighed and rolled her head to one side.

"Have a little sleep now. You must be tired. We'll go

257

downstairs and bring you a cup of tea in a little while."
Catherine settled the covers around Mary Ann and tucked
her hands under them so she wouldn't get cold. She stood
looking down at her mother for a few moments. She
thought she could see the lines on Mary Ann's face
smoothing. "We'll be back in a little while, Mama."

She looked over at Maude and caught the look of
impatience on her sister's face as she nodded towards the
door. She followed, closing the door gently behind her.

"She looks very peaceful. Did you notice?" She was a
bit annoyed at Maude's rush to get out of the room.

They stood on the landing, looking at each other.

"Do you think she's doting?" Maude had her eyebrows
raised.

"I don't think so." Catherine shook her head. "The
primroses are on the grave alright. They're still seeding
themselves. Even after all these years."

"You're right. They are. And, d'yeh know, I often
wondered why she was so particular about watering them.
They got more attention than the other flowers."

Catherine gazed across at the landing window and
across the fields. She could see the Long Acre in the
distance. She must go down there later.

"It's all making sense now. Do you remember as
children when we went to the cemetery, if we were down
to our last drop of water in the bottle she'd make us save
it, it was the primroses that always got it. She always made
us do that. Don't you remember, Maude?"

"Yeah, I do." She paused. "But it's a pity Maggie is dead."

The sisters locked hips at the top of the stairs as they
both moved forward together. Maude stepped back to let
Catherine go down first, each too shocked to say anything
more.

BRIDIE

Chapter 60

County Wexford
1915

Just when she thought she had had her life, not that it was over or anything like that, more that she saw the future as straightforward, uneventful, no more big changes to cope with, enter Mickie Joe.

Strange how it was always a Jo that brought joy to her. Joy, that very feeling, just when she thought she might have used up her lifetime allowance. In fact, she felt she didn't deserve any more. Not with her history. Joy – the first two letters.

It was quiet in the shop. She sat at the cash desk toying with the idea that there might be a message in that? Joseph, Mary Josephine and now Mickie Joe. Otherwise known as MJ.

With his big ham-hands and shock of greying hair he was a most unlikely bearer of such a treasure. No butterflies, no bells ringing, no heart leaping. It was more a glow with Mickie Joe, whenever he appeared. Totally at ease in his company.

She tried to analyse what exactly it was about him. The only thing she could come up with was that it seemed it was he himself who exuded contentment. Not in any smug way, he didn't seem to be aware of it, but an earthy straightforwardness appeared to emanate from him. It was familiar to her, something she recognised but couldn't quite place. Had she thought more about it she might have recognised the similarity to the qualities that Harry had. A different generation but someone who knew his place in the world and was confident in that knowledge.

Almost twenty years older than Bridie, he had bought a neighbouring farm during the time she'd been in America, a farm where the original family had all died out. She only remembered it derelict. Had no recollection of who had ever lived there. Was only aware of half-remembered stories about them. Throughout her childhood the windows had always been boarded up and the barn roof was open to the elements. What remained of the mud walls of the other outhouses, half melted back into the earth, was covered with ivy. She was surprised at how he had managed to build up the farm single-handed over the few short years she was away. He had even restored the old dwelling-house to a state that it was possible to live in it.

He spent what spare time he had between his farming chores to continue working on the finishing touches.

She had seen him at Mass on Sundays but it was quite some time before she actually met him. He passed on the road a few times when she was out gardening but they simply exchanged pleasantries.

"You haven't seen my dog, have you? A black-and-white collie?" He stopped at the gate, glancing up and down the road, a bit distracted.

"I haven't. But I'm sure he'll appear back when he gets hungry," Bridie reassured him. "They usually do."

"I'm a bit worried with all the new lambs about. I wouldn't trust him. He slipped out on me the other day and Ned the Farmer brought him back. He was worried too about his sheep."

"Do you think he might be gone back in that direction again? If you like I'll put on my boots and go down there and see if I can find him and you can check a few other places."

"That'd be great. Before he does any damage."

"In case I find him, does he know his name?"

"He does. It's Collie."

"Very original." She laughed before turning and going into the house.

It was after that she noticed he had started to come in to the Farmer's Mart to do business and thus Mickie Joe had begun the process of 'wooing' her. She joked it was finding the dog for him that did it.

Bridie's healing had been slow and one of the lessons she'd learned was to take things gradually. Her past life had barrelled along at much too fast a speed, so this romance was destined to be a slow-burner. She suspected that Mickie Joe Doyle had heard rumours. He didn't have time on his side but, cautious man that he was, he seemed content to wait.

Having only ever seen him in his work clothes she was surprised he'd scrubbed up so well when she bumped into him at the Harvest Thanksgiving dance.

"May I?" He held out his hand while giving a mock bow.

"You certainly may, sir." She laughed as she stood up, her height matching his.

Her heart thumped in time to the music and left her breathless. She wasn't sure if it was just because she was out of practice or if it was for another reason. MJ didn't seem to have any problem, not a bead of sweat showed on his face. She was conscious of the little rivers of perspiration trickling down towards the hollow of her back. He just beamed at her each time they twirled around.

She smiled back, hoping that her hot face wasn't as red as it felt.

When she worked it out there really weren't any complications.

In the eyes of the Catholic Church she had only been married once before. To Joseph. Her precious Joseph. Forever young and perfect. And according to the rules and the records she was now widowed. No need to mention the bit in between.

When she thought about it, her marriage to Seán in America didn't count. That's if she had it right. The Catholic Church didn't come into it at all. They didn't recognise a Registry Office marriage. They made the rules. So as far as they were concerned her marriage to Seán never existed. Now that they were legally divorced, those events cancelled each other out. Well, they made the rules so she didn't need to draw attention to this chapter of her life. She didn't need to discuss it with anyone. To her amazement she realised that things for once were going her way. It all fitted very neatly. She may have gone off the rails, but now she was back on them. She was free.

Chapter 61

The rays of the Indian summer were balmy on her back as she walked up the pathway towards the church and entered the dim chapel porch.

In the body of the church the slanting sun filtered through the stained glass creating a jewel pattern on the plain terracotta tiles leading to the altar. She stood for a moment with her father in the cool, waiting for the priest to signal the organist to strike the opening chords of the wedding music. A veil of sadness at the memory of the white froth of her wedding to Joseph passed across her vision like a dream of long ago. That first wedding with the delicate gauzy veil, when a big wide future so full of excitement had stretched out ahead of them on a sea of innocence. Today she settled for a half-dozen creamy rosebuds studded in her hair.

The bubbles of youth had burst but there was something more solid in what lay before her now as Bridie began the walk up the aisle on Cornelius's arm for the second time. She could see it when MJ's grey head turned and his dependable face beamed light on her as she slowed her pace in time to the music.

The smiling faces of the guests became a blur as they

turned in her direction. Something that Mary Ann had said before she died came into her head.

"You always reminded me of myself, Bridie. The hair. We both started out with the same curls."

"But yours is brown, Granny?"

"That's true, but it used to be a chestnutty colour. It had a few strands of auburn, not like yours, but the few glints all the same. It turned a duller shade with each child until it was just a plain brown."

"D'you think that'll happen to mine?"

"Ah no. Sure yours is still like burnished copper and you're well over thirty now. It would have started to fade long before this if it was ever going to."

The memory just popped in from nowhere. It made her wonder what image the guests had of her. She wished Mary Ann was there to see the joke of herself and MJ. The copper head that would soon lie beside the silver one on the pillow. But what matter. This time it was different. No fluttering in her stomach. No heady fizz. Just a slow walk into a warm cocoon. A place she knew was right.

Discarded years ago, the sofa sat against the back wall inside the barn. Her father had finally agreed to Maude getting a new one despite the fact that he couldn't see the sense in it.

"We don't have to throw it out, Cornelius. Ask MJ or Bridie if they want it. I'm sure they'll have a use for it." Maude had worn him down. "It won't go to waste."

And so it sat in the barn, its arms open awaiting the time when it would come into its own. And it did. During the lambing MJ dozed at night on its dusty tattered cushions. When a birth was imminent he went back to the house and shook Bridie awake.

"C'mon, love, we're about to become parents. You can't

264

miss this." He handed her the woollen dressing gown he'd given her on their first anniversary before heading back to the barn, leaving her to follow.

She looked at it, smiling at the memory of the satisfaction on his face as he watched her opening the wrapping paper. The lack of romance in his choice of present having completely eluded him.

She loved the lambing season. The new-borns breathing their first warm misty breaths into the frost of a February morning brought tears to her eyes. The wonder and innocence of it all. The tenderness with which MJ wiped their snotty faces with his big ruddy hand as the lamb slipped from its mother's womb was like he had reached deep into her chest and massaged her very heart.

She loved the predictability of her life.

"Come on, let's join the bathers!" MJ would bound into the kitchen.

"Ah, I'm just about to bake a loaf!"

"Leave that until tomorrow can't you or 'til we get home. Sure the summer's short enough and we don't want to miss it." MJ picked up his swimming togs from the rail where the clothes were drying. "Plenty of time for baking all winter."

"I suppose you're right." She untied the belt and removed her apron. "But I'm not getting in for a swim, mind you."

MJ wrapped a towel around his waist and struggled into his bathing trunks, oblivious to the sand he scattered onto the woollen rug where she sat. She watched him jog across the beach with the dog following. She knew what was coming next and waited for it.

"*Aaghhhhhh!*" His tortured shout as he hurtled headlong straight onto the cold waves for his evening swim.

As he recovered from the shock she watched him flounder about and waited for him to wave to her. She waved back at the beaming face and watched as he splashed the water up on himself. He did it every evening during the harvest season. Loved to wash the dust off after a sweaty day working at the corn.

Collie had stopped short at the water's edge and was still sniffing the creamy foam left by an ebbing wave. He nosed about showing no enthusiasm to enter the cold water. It was only with MJ's encouragement the dog was induced into the sea.

She watched her husband swim about ten strokes out towards Wales. It no longer worried her, knowing that that was his limit, all he would swim before turning back towards the shore.

The first time she'd seen him do it she panicked. A mother's warning from her childhood. Always swim parallel to the shore. Never head out to sea. The advice rang her head as she'd watched him. But it was another thought from the past that had her worried that day. The possibility that if he swam out of his depth that he mightn't return. It had happened before. Her experience of the power of the sea so strong in her memory that on the first occasion they had joined 'the bathers' it had caused her to jump up and run towards the water. Just as she reached the edge, the water lapping at her bare toes, like he had read her fears he stopped and turned to wave back at her. The big foolish grin on his face, oblivious to her panic. She couldn't say anything to him. As he stood up, the water reached just above his thighs. The sight of it and her terror passed and she laughed. He turned and struck out again, this time swimming alongside the shore.

Bridie rubbed the goosepimples on her arms. She slipped her cardigan over her shoulders. A slight chill had crept into the evening breeze as she sat on the rug content to wait while MJ played about in the water, messing with the dog.

They worked well together. But even when working alone she was content. There was no missing him when he went off to the cattle market and she was left to her own devices at home. She knew he would be back.

In the beginning she was concerned that the peace of mind she now had might all of a sudden disappear. The way things had changed in the past. But as the months and years passed, with no evidence to support that worry, she pushed it to the back of her mind. That was then. This is now. And she was no longer annoyed by such insecurities that had been there in the background. It had taken time but she was relaxed now in the knowledge that she could be happy whether he was there or not, knowing that he was in her life.

The golden warmth of the autumn afternoon warmed her back as she clambered onto the ditch to reach up for the blackberries. Happy with her harvest, these last few luscious ones seemed to be calling 'pick me' to her. She stretched towards the juicy bunch an inch out of her reach, giving a little hop up to reach. Her foot slipped on the muddy ditch just as she grabbed them. She felt the berries burst with the reflex and squeeze through her fingers, the purple juice trickling downwards along her upstretched arm as she tried to gain a foothold. Thorns snagged the thin skin on the back of her hand as she flailed about. A row of thorns on an old briar hooked her cardigan firmly in its grip as if saving her. Once her footing was secure she tried removing the briar but the hard brown spikes were reluctant to release their captive. Bridie put down the can of fruit on the top of the ditch and used her free hand to unlock herself from the barbs. She sucked on her pierced skin to stem the bleeding. The taste of juice mingled with the blood, a pleasant warming sensation in her mouth. Looking into the can there was enough to make a few pounds of jam when mixed with the apples MJ had already collected. Plenty to keep her busy for the evening.

She applied pressure to the back of her hand where the thorns had punctured a vein, hoping that the dirt on her hands wouldn't introduce infection. Leaning back against the ditch she waited for the trickle to stop, drinking in the last of the evening's rays as she did so. The damsons could wait until next week.

The turf mountain by the side of the house was completed. As the top layer dried Mickie Joe had started transferring a barrowload at a time inside the barn, exposing the next layer to the wind and sun. He liked doing it by degrees. Sometimes it rained on the stack and he was back to square one but most times he could anticipate the showers and managed to get a load in before it got wet again. It was much more pleasant dealing with the sods when they had been dried outside. They burned more efficiently than when he had to shift them indoors while still damp.

He had started work on the woodpile in readiness for the winter. Each day when the farm work was done he went around the land and collected fallen trees. Taking them home in the cart he stacked them in a heap in the yard in readiness for cutting. By the time she got home with the blackberries he was pottering around the yard.

"Have I time to do a bit more at this wood before the tae? I want to get a few more sticks done before it gets too dark."

"You have. I'll call you when it's ready."

He loved nothing more than to work away at his

sawhorse, cutting a quantity of logs each evening, all exactly the same length. These he stacked methodically against the wall under the overhang of the barn roof, the cut ends of the logs facing out in a honeycomb pattern. When the first row had grown to about a foot high, he placed a lath of wood on top to create a shelf to support the next row of logs. He liked to get at least one row done and a basket of firing filled for the evening before he went inside.

He loved when Bridie came out to call him for his tea, the way she stood and admired his neat workmanship. They'd return to the house together and she'd pour out the tea while he washed his hands at the sink and each day he would savour the jam on the homemade bread and tell her "You wouldn't get the likes of that in the Taravie Hotel".

The predictability of his comment always made her laugh.

CORNELIUS

Chapter 62

1921

The tightness in his chest bothered him. He had been feeling it more regularly recently. It happened again today as he walked over the road to see his daughter although the farm was no distance away, just a short stroll down the road. He breathed deeply as he sauntered along, newspaper under his arm, enjoying the smell of newly mown hay in the fields around. It gave him a purpose to his walk, delivering the weekly newspaper after he'd finished reading it. No point in both houses buying it. There was a time when he would have marched briskly. A hangover from the job. Something that had taken years for him to shake off, but not anymore.

He was in no hurry so the dart of pain, so unexpected, startled him as he wandered along. So sharp this time that it almost pinned him to the road. He stepped onto the verge, wobbling slightly as his foot landed on a grassy hump. He leaned back against the ditch and waited for the pain to subside. It had frightened him this time as he'd never felt it so severe and it took several minutes for a feeling of normality to return. When it did, he decided to stay where he was for another few minutes. Just to be sure.

He settled himself into a more comfortable position

against the ditch and glanced at his newspaper. Mickie Joe would be interested in the paragraph about the local skirmish. Nothing much. Scuffles between hotheads in the town after a night's drinking, no doubt looking to play their part in the war. Just a few shots fired with minor injuries but he might possibly know those involved.

The biggest happening had been the killing of an RIC District Inspector last year, gunned down mercilessly on the roadway just outside Gorey. The brutality of it had stuck in his head. He hadn't come across him in his time in the Barracks but whatever his reputation no man deserved that. It had been different in his day. Yes, he was glad his career was long behind him. Didn't have to deal with the unrest of the last few years with revolutions and wars and the local lads who all wanted to be heroes. And the RIC men sitting targets as were the few Irish lads who went off to join the British Army and returned home to something less than a heroes' welcome.

The national newspapers were full of the fighting in other areas of the country, but the reportage of the involvement in the local neighbourhood rarely got more than a few inches except in the local paper. Hardly warranting a mention in the nationals unless there were killings. Buried amongst other events of little consequence. Nothing more than a few arms being discovered or a farmer taking a pitchfork to someone who disagreed with his politics. All minor happenings in the light of the major conflict raging in the country, the events of the war barely touching them here, but you couldn't rely on it staying so quiet.

He said nothing to Bridie about the twinge when he arrived but it didn't escape her.

"Are you okay, Papa? You look a bit pale?"

"I'm grand, child, I'm fine. Just a bit tired. Here, I've brought you the newspaper." He pulled out the chair and sat down. "Don't suppose there's a chance of a cup of tea?"

It was happening now at least twice a week. Something was squeezing his heart in a way that caused him concern and after today's incident he could ignore it no longer. He needed to have it checked out.

As he walked through the town it happened again. He'd exchanged his books in the library in Gorey, collected a prescription in the pharmacy and was walking uphill to where he had parked his bicycle when he felt the pain grip him. Not severe but it worried him enough to sit down on the seat at the junction of the Main Street and John Street and wait for the tightness to pass. Normally he would not consider sitting on any of these wooden seats which were placed at all the crossroads along Main Street. They were deemed suitable only for idlers. At least in his head. He'd been the one to start the tradition of referring to them as 'the corner boys' when he was in the barracks. He smiled at the thought that he was now joining their ranks.

He said nothing to his wife when he arrived home. Maude would only nag him to see the doctor and he didn't want to admit that he had already called to the surgery before he left town. The news was worrying. He had to have more tests. He would tell her when the time came. No point in her annoying herself for days.

Seated in the winged armchair he looked at the covers of his two library books and pondered which he was in the mood for. Selecting the historical tome, he placed the other on the side table for another time and, settling back on the cushions, he began reading. He loved this step in the process with a new book. The anticipation of being captivated by the opening lines. When that happened, he enjoyed the incongruity of being held prisoner until he reached the final page.

Concentration was difficult. The dull ache in his upper

arm persisted and the remaining hint of discomfort in his chest undermined his enthusiasm. Rubbing his sleeve, the friction of the tweed heated his palm. It would work better if he took off the jacket and massaged the arm directly but he was too tired to rouse himself.

He tried to suppress the niggling thought that this might be a problem not easily solved. The more he attempted to douse it, the more it hung on in there, pushing its way in through the periphery of his mind as if trying to gain a foothold. Like a fly that refuses to stay out after you've swatted it through the open window, it returned with each new paragraph. A pest that persisted in its attempts to get back in, batting its head each time on the window pane.

What if something happened to him? Imagine if Maude came in and found him dead in the chair, with the book having slid to the floor. He was happier now that he'd been to the doctor and had set the procedure in motion. There wasn't a lot more he could do but he was going to have to tell her. Sooner or later. He returned to his book but now that thought of Maude finding him dead had entered his head he couldn't let it go. It seemed to take on a life of its own.

What could she say about him other than the fact that he was her husband and a good provider? An upright citizen. A pillar of the community. Never put a foot wrong. Yes, these were things she might say. The very qualities that irritated the hell out of her, knowing how he took them to extremes. But what did she really know about him – she might even wonder who was this man?

There it was. He was even beginning to think of himself in the past tense.

It wasn't her fault that she hadn't managed to penetrate his shell. What had he ever revealed to her about himself

273

other than the facts – the basic particulars, the details, with all emotion and passion obliterated? And his children, what would they remember of him? Would he just exit this life without leaving a mark or a memory?

He'd overseen the children's schoolwork each evening. He might have made a good teacher, even if he thought so himself. He hadn't discovered this talent until his children came of school-going age, but you have to make choices in life and stick to them. Maybe a bit rigid, but fair. With an insistence on neatness and accuracy he was careful never to comment on their lack of achievements, just an occasional "Good" or "You're coming on well with that" when he saw effort. Lectures on the importance of education were a regular feature and after allowing a first week of freedom during their summer holidays from school he insisted that they study an hour each weekday throughout the holidays. A little less for the younger ones. Talent, education and status were important elements in life – talent being the only one that could possibly stand on its own. The talentless needed education if they were to get anywhere in life. Cornelius didn't tell the children this but he knew it to be one of the harsh facts of life.

There was a strange loneliness in the thought that no-one really knew him. No one at all. He stared out the window, eyes fixed open seeing nothing. The book lay forgotten on his lap and the prickle of the dry tears of a lifetime remained trapped at the back of his eyeballs.

Chapter 63

Being considered dull was one of Cornelius's greatest fears. Something Maude had never been aware of. The fear that was. How could she have been? He'd kept it well hidden. It wasn't something you'd boast about, not a thing you'd want anyone to know. They'd laugh at you or worse still agree.

By the age of sixteen he had learned an important lesson in life. The role of observer was much safer than being an active participant. Much less exposed. Life was simple if you just followed the rules.

When it came to choosing a career this viewpoint, as an unquestioning upholder of the law, made Cornelius the perfect candidate. His decision to train as a member of the Constabulary an easy one. Everyone said he was just the man for the job.

His serious approach to life, his honesty and reliability saw him moving up the ranks from an early age. With each step up he had moments of self-doubt which had him wondering if he would be found out. If he had reached the level of his own incompetence. But the failure never happened. His superiors had occasionally commended him on his performance.

With each promotion, once he'd settled into his new, more responsible role, he seemed to grow an inch in stature. His handlebar moustache and sculpted face gave him an aristocratic appearance of which he was totally unaware, while his height bestowed on him an aura of authority.

It was this Cornelius that Maude had met and fell in love with – this tall, enigmatic man of few words.

It was like it happened yesterday. Sixty years ago and he could still hear the harshness of the tone.

"*You* can't sing."

It was the stress on the '*you*' that was possibly the turning point in young Cornelius's life. Or at least the first of the turning points. Up until then he had always jumped head-first into any new idea that came into his mind. Fearless. Not looking forward. Not looking back. He just went for it with the enthusiasm of a ten-year-old.

Like the concerts he put on in the barn every year, gathering his young friends into lines and conducting them in a choir. When the performance was lacking or was in danger of falling apart he recognised the need for something to hold it together. He would then give up the conducting and appoint himself soloist. He would stand to the front of the choir and sing out in his boy soprano voice for all he was worth.

He scheduled the concerts for the first week after they got their summer holidays from school. It gave enough time to get the performers rehearsed and not too much time for his scattered schoolmates to lose interest. There was always the danger that if he delayed too long those who were not natural performers would forget to come. Forget that they had their role to play as 'the audience'. Just because they weren't on the stage they still had a purpose in his 'event'. Nobody was ever left out and with little else happening in the countryside they seldom forgot.

While these concerts were one of the highlights of young Cornelius's summer they were the only highlight for some of the other children. The admission price was always the same. A stone from their garden or farm. Not just any stone. It had to be an unusual one. It didn't matter how small, even if it was only a tiny pebble or shell. The rule was strictly adhered to. Anyone who forgot had to go back down the lane until they found a suitable one. No admission without the pebble.

Pressing the last stone into the mortar he completed the nought. 1860 – C.R age 10.

He stood back to admire his handiwork. The stick figure of the stone boy above the inscription was perfect. His fourth picture completed in his secret place on the ground behind the barn where no-one went. Satisfied, he went in for his tea.

He concentrated on taking the top off his boiled egg with the edge of his spoon. He liked to do it without breaking the yolk. As he lifted the lid he saw that he'd ruptured it and as a large teardrop of thick yellow dribbled over the jagged edge he caught it with his spoon. It was while licking that first delicious droplet of yolk that his mother took him by surprise.

"What were you doing putting yourself forward like that? Sure you know *you* can't sing."

His mother's sharp voice cut across the table as the egg congealed on his tongue. Its rich flavour vanished instantly.

She had been pinning clothes on the line in the yard when she'd heard the raggle-taggle choir sounds coming from the barn. At the time he could see her through the open doors and was pleased when she turned her head and spotted him holding it all together as soloist at the front.

He stabbed the spoon into the egg, pushing it right down until it came through the bottom of the shell, spattering the contents all over his plate.

"Will you watch what you're doing! Look at your shirt!"

He blinked hard to block the hot tears he felt forming behind his eyelids.

"Wipe it off. You'll be wearing that again tomorrow, egg or no egg."

He didn't know if his parents even liked him, but he supposed they probably did, at least some of the time. They fed him, clothed him, sent him to school, made sure he was washed and well dressed for Mass on Sundays. He sometimes wondered if they were ever proud of him, even just a little bit. Maybe it was just that they didn't believe in showing it in case he got above himself. He'd often heard them saying that about neighbours, but he wouldn't have. He knew that. He just needed to be told he was good at something.

They were probably not even aware what they were doing, particularly his mother. In fairness his father never said much. But he could have stood up for him when his mother had a go at him. She had a particular knack of killing any delight with her little barbs puncturing the bubbles of excitement anytime they appeared. No adults were allowed attend the concerts and that was why. He knew she'd take the fun out of it. Criticism from the other children was allowed even if it ended in a retaliatory lash of the tongue or a box on the head from the intended target. That was forgotten almost as quickly as it was the uttered. It was only when it came from his own mother that it was like the sting of a wasp.

* * *

He arrived home with his end of year report from school. Second place. Divided only by two points from the class genius's top ranking.

"Why didn't you get first?"

The sting – a little bit of which remained buried in his skin.

The next year he came first. He ran all the way home waving his report. She'd be pleased.

"Why didn't you get full marks?"

"No one ever does. That's the way the teacher works. In case we think we know it all!" he shouted. *"Even the teacher said I was excellent."*

"Don't you shout at me, you little pup!"

"Nothing I do is ever good enough for you. Maybe I won't bother next time. Maybe I'll try and come last and then you'll be happy, won't you?"

Was it just his mother or did everyone else think him foolish to believe he was any good? It was much safer to be in the middle like his brothers and sisters. Nothing was ever said when they came home with their reports. They escaped unnoticed. On one particular occasion the unfairness of the criticism stabbed him in the heart. It came from his grandmother – his mother's mother who lived with them. It had happened when he was showing her the penny whistle he had won in a raffle. His friend had taught him how to play his first Irish air.

"You won't manage that. You never stick at anything."

So it wasn't just his mother. Her mother thought the same. Something in her tone and the way she had turned away from him as he raised the whistle to his lips told him he was not his grandmother's favourite.

After that there were no more concerts. Cornelius never showed any of the adults his stone pictures and he never made any more.

MAUDE

Chapter 64

Maude loved house parties. From the time the children were old enough to behave, she organised one each winter.

She hated the long dark evenings. The short days when dusk fell early and left too few daylight hours to get much outdoor work done. She saved up any entertaining she felt she owed and spread it out to brighten the winter. The highlight of these was the annual musical evening. The neighbours enjoyed it and had come to expect it. She normally left it until the end of January when people had recovered from Christmas and were facing into a dull and dreary future.

She sent the children around the houses with the invitations. For two days each child had a job. Polishing the furniture and washing the good crockery and cutlery while Maude took charge of the crystal glasses. Bridie could never understand why she had to wash the parlour windows before these events because the curtains would be drawn and no-one would see whether the windows were clean or dirty.

"It's not a topic for debate. Not if you want to come to the party?"

Bridie knew when her mother meant business. No point in arguing.

"Call it an early spring cleaning."

She had no idea if her husband enjoyed these evenings or merely tolerated them. He never ever suggested having one. Sometimes she was unsure if he even approved, but she didn't care. Cornelius just left all the decisions and organising to her and when she presented him with the bill from the local shop for the food and drinks, he would put on his reading glasses and spend time studying it before issuing a quiet "*Hrmph.*" Later the invoice would appear on the kitchen sideboard with the required money weighting it down.

CORNELIUS

Chapter 65

Cornelius lit the turf fire early on these evenings to ensure the room was well warmed up before the arrival of the guests. He laid out the glasses on the sideboard and set up the port and sherry bottles. Standing back, he admired the reflection of the fire in their rich colours. He loved the flickering warmth it brought to the room. Bottles of stout and whiskey were set out for the men and lemonade for the non-drinkers, and the search for the bottle opener commenced.

"But you had it at Christmas. Where did you put it then?"

"I didn't do anything with it. You put it away."

It went missing each year and the same argument went back and forth until it was found.

All the children learned a musical instrument and were encouraged to play at the musical evenings. Maude ensured that each performance was mercifully short and met with a polite round of applause. She would then take them up to bed before the adult entertainment began while Cornelius poured the drinks for the guests.

The children were reluctant to leave but their treat was that their mother would give them a plate of cake to share and allow them to sit on the top step of the stairs listening for a while. Cornelius would pretend he didn't know they crept out onto the landing as they sat listening to the muffled sounds of adults performing behind the closed parlour door below.

Apart from pouring the drinks and keeping the fire fed, Cornelius wasn't an active participant in the entertainment. Maude played the piano accompanying those who wished to sing. Occasionally she herself would sing while Cornelius sat in the winged armchair beside the fire and listened, a quiet smile on his face. He loved the Thomas Moore melodies. On occasions he hummed along quietly with her when she sang "The Last Rose of Summer". He knew it amused her that he thought no-one could hear him. In the early days she tried to get him to sing, aware of his pleasant tenor voice, but he only ever released it while he shaved and generally when only she was in the house. He was glad she'd long ago given up coaxing him to perform in public.

He for his part envied her confidence. Bound as he was by rules, he marvelled at her ability to break them at will. The way she would drop down an octave when a top note was beyond her reach, giving the song her own unique arrangement, her lovely voice making the song all the sweeter to his ears.

BRIDIE

Chapter 66

1922

What happened that day changed everything for Bridie. Nothing appeared different on the outside to anyone else but it changed everything on the inside for her.

The light rain of the morning had dried up and the afternoon turned out to be a scorcher. MJ had made a wooden sun-lounger and placed it for her in the shelter of the crescent of fuchsia bushes across the yard. A little oasis that separated the kitchen garden from the fields beyond.

After the lunch she took the tartan rug from the sofa and headed out with her book and sun hat to take a break. The lounger was comfortable enough but she hadn't had the heart to tell him about the rough edges on the wood. She lay the rug on the wooden frame and settled herself, lying back to take a few rays of sun.

After ten minutes she could feel her skin reddening. Not a good look with her auburn hair. She put on the straw sun hat and picked up her book. She had only a couple of chapters to finish. As she reached the last one, she could feel her shins begin to burn. She stood up and moved the lounger around so that she was not taking the full force of the sun on her front. It didn't take long before the searing heat began to scorch the thin skin of her shoulders. Defeated she closed her book, forced to abandon her little sanctuary. The thought amused her. Waiting all year for a bit of sun and then when it comes, she can't cope with it. She checked the page number before closing the book. She'd go for a stroll and finish it out of the sun.

She crossed the road and entered the laneway opposite. It ran through the woodland that led to a clearing behind Harry's old garden. She wandered along under the trees, admiring the soft dappling on the sandy floor. There was just enough sun penetrating the leafy canopy to keep it cool but not cold.

In the middle of the clearing, two children lay on the grass beside the marl-hole. Their faces serious as they chatted, as if they were sorting the world's problems. She smiled at them as she approached, recognising them from the village. Knew the house they lived in and their parents, but their names eluded her. Just two of a large family.

"Hello, children."

The boy, his too-long blond hair flopping over his right eye sat up and rewarded her with a big beam. He followed it with the curious 'hello' of a five-year-old reluctant to let a possible interesting opportunity pass. His older sister remained lying on her back but turned her head towards Bridie.

"Hello, missus," she mumbled in the disinterested way of a fourteen-year-old, before turning away to look up at the sky through the trees.

It struck her that the girl might not have appreciated being called a child.

Walking around to the far side of the marl-hole, she sat down on a fallen tree trunk that someone had placed there as a seat. Well placed in front of a large oak which served as a backrest. She watched the sun sparkling on the surface of the water. She was surprised that the water wasn't low following the dry spell, but then there had been a lot of rain before that. She'd hoped to have the glade to herself, not wanting to share her special place with anyone. But sure it was a free country. She smiled at the thought. At least now it was and the Civil War seemed to be over, at least for the moment.

The old shed still stood at the end of what had been Harry's garden, the place he'd watched the badgers from. It was well battered now. The glass was broken in the door as if someone had thrown a stone through it and a few of the wooden laths were missing from the side wall. She caught a glimpse of the old armchair, its stuffing bursting through the upholstery, rotted and torn now with age. A couple of roof slates had slipped sideways and a few were missing, leaving jagged gaps that looked as if someone had stood on them and broken through with their weight. The shed looked cold and dank in the shade under a tangle of briars, no longer loved. If he were still around he'd never have let it have fallen into such disrepair.

She could see the boy on the far side of the marl-hole picking what she imagined were bits of leaves and bugs from the earth. She would have liked to tell them about her childhood adventures with old Harry but they wouldn't be interested. The girl anyway.

The boy had taken off his top, his white body and shoulders in stark contrast to his tanned neck and the brown of his arms below where his short sleeves had ended.

Bridie opened her book and began to read, conscious that he was wandering around exploring the woodland. He disappeared behind the trees, popping his head out every so often with a soft '*Pow*' of his imaginary gun, aimed at his sister and sometimes at Bridie. He smiled back at her when their eyes met but didn't encroach on her peace. She thought about 'powing' back at him in fun, but a niggle at the back of her mind saddened her that he had learned about guns at such a young age. Probably from overheard conversations around the fire at night when the men in his family exchanged stories of the recent wars. Nothing much had happened close to home for a child to fear. To the boy it was probably nothing more than make-believe, but near enough for the adults to be caught up in the drama of it all.

His sister lay back on the grass, not interested in his game, which soon lost its novelty without active combatants. He began exploring the woodland floor again, picking up treasures, examining them before discarding those that were of little use. A child old enough to entertain himself and young enough to be curious. To find everything of interest.

She felt her eyes heavy. Allowing them to close she rested her back against the tree. Aware of the contrast between her drowsiness and the bright twittering of the birds hidden amongst the treetops it wasn't until she heard the splashing that Bridie realised she had forgotten the presence of the children.

Looking up she saw the child's head bobbing in the middle of the marl-hole. His sister jumped up at the same time and ran towards the water shouting.

"Robbie, Robbie, what are you doing in there!"

Two brown arms were thrashing around breaking the surface of the water, his head coming up for air. His mouth opening in a gasp that only had time to catch a breath before submerging again. No time to shout. His blond hair turned dark in the muddy pond, fanned out and floating on the surface of the water.

The girl waded in as far as her waist.

287

"*He can't swim! Save him! Please save him!*" She looked
back at Bridie, her face pale with pleading. Too petrified to
take a step further into deeper water, not knowing how
bottomless the hole might be. "*I can't go any further and he
can't swim either. Please do something . . . please!*"

Bridie kicked off her sandals, slid down the bank and
waded out towards the boy, his head, thankfully, still
bobbing up and down in the middle of the pond. A poor
swimmer, but she had no fear as she knew the depth. She
had seen the cracked bottom in the summers on the rare
occasions when all the marl-holes in the district dried up
during long spells with no rainfall. As she reached the
child, she grabbed him by the legs, and, with an arm
supporting his back, raised his head above the water.

"You're alright now, I have you. You're alright, you're
going to be alright."

The child grabbed her hair, spluttering and coughing. It
felt like he would pull it out in tufts between his fingers.
He wrapped both his arms tightly around her head. She
could scarcely breathe but knew she had to get him out
before he unbalanced them both in his panic.

Tall as she was, the water was almost to her chest so she
could understand the child's terror. It would have been
unlikely that he could have touched the bottom. She felt
the heavy clay oozing through her toes and hoped their
combined weight wouldn't cause the base of the marl-hole
to suck them both under.

His sister stood rigid in the water, sobbing, her hands to
her face, rooted to the spot.

"It's alright, he's safe, don't worry, he's safe," Bridie
reassured her. "Come on now, follow me. Head for the
edge."

Turning her attention back to the boy she tried to
soothe the sobbing child as she attempted to release one

foot from the suctioning clay below.

"You're alright, luvvie, you'll be fine now. You're safe." She hoped her wobbling wouldn't set him off again in a panic. She thought about swimming to the side but as she attempted it he became frantic. The screams came in juddering gasps, the water still dripping from his nose and mouth. Not wanting to frighten him further she decided to walk with him in her arms.

Once she had one foot freed it became a little easier. She moved forward too quickly and began to topple forward causing the child to bawl. Take it slow.

"Slowly, slowly, don't worry, we'll get there." She crooned to the boy with each careful step. "We're nearly there now."

As she approached the shallower water around the perimeter, she began to lower the child, intending to hold his hand as they both walked to the bank but his terrified screams and grasping at her body forced her to scoop him up again into her arms and hold him tight as he buried his head in her shoulder.

"My parents will kill me," the girl sobbed.

"Oh, I doubt it. They'll just be glad you are both alive." Bridie smiled at her.

It was the talk of the village for weeks. Bridie hadn't said much, but by all accounts the girl had related it in full colour, no doubt enjoying the drama of the ordeal, now that they'd both survived and her parents hadn't killed her.

The headline '**Heroine Saves Drowning Child**' appeared in the local newspaper and was picked up by the national dailies. She had no idea who had given the story to the press. It embarrassed her when locals approached after Sunday Mass and congratulated her on her bravery. What would they have expected her to do? Leave the child there to drown? She didn't feel like a heroine. Any one of them would have done the same.

MJ pushed her outside to pose for her photograph with the boy when the photographer called to the house. As they stood there, she could feel Robbie's little hand warm in hers as he looked up at her in adoration. His saviour. Smiling down at the blond head it was only then she knew why she had been put here on this earth. That one act would forever more sustain her, absolve her of all her sins.

Life made sense now.

CORNELIUS & MAUDE

Chapter 67

1923

For their 50th wedding anniversary Cornelius surprised everyone. Not just his wife. It wasn't something spontaneous. That wasn't his way. But he did something unexpected, something that he'd spent months thinking about. He hired a charabanc to take himself, Maude, their children and grandchildren to Hunter's Hotel in County Wicklow for dinner. Just like she didn't discuss the details of the house parties with him, he didn't discuss this event with Maude but not for the same reasons. He didn't discuss it with anyone. Just went ahead and booked it. He then worried about it, fretting over how he was going to ensure they would all be available on the day without having to tell them too much. He hoped they wouldn't ask too many questions. That would spoil the surprise.

He checked that his adult children were available on the date and instructed them to keep it free. After he had managed to bat away any queries as to why.

"Wait and see, but you'll like it."

Any further pressing was met with "What's the meaning of surprise? You wouldn't want to spoil that now, would you?" All down to logistics then, and he was good at that.

They were given instructions to assemble at the crossroads a few hundred yards from the house on a Sunday in May 1923. They were not to come to the house. He gave them instructions to bring the grandchildren in their Sunday best and to say nothing to their mother. He refused to say anything more to them about it.

It was Saturday morning before he mentioned anything to Maude.

She had been curdling her bile for a week. He hadn't passed a remark to indicate that he was aware the occasion was imminent and she had no intention of prompting him. She wavered between hurt and fury, her rage increasing over the days that such an important landmark could be forgotten or that it should mean so little to him. She wondered how he could remain oblivious to such anger when it was almost flaming out her ears as she sat opposite him each day waiting for him to say something. Surely he could see the smoke?

She tossed around the argument as to whether it would be best to allow the volcano to erupt now, something she felt most inclined to do, or to stay silent until after the event. If nothing happened she would then be justified in giving full vent to that fury. She even found herself rehearsing the row in her head as she went about the daily chores.

He'd come in from the vegetable garden and washed the clay from his hands at the sink. They were now sitting at the kitchen table just finishing the cup of tea.

"We'll go out for dinner tomorrow, Maude. Save you cooking." He didn't mention the occasion.

"Where are you taking me?" There was an edge to her voice. She wasn't going to refer to it either but it had better be somewhere extraordinary.

292

"A surprise. Somewhere you've never been before."

"Well, I certainly hope it'll be somewhere nice." She tried to hide her irritation at his refusal to say where. She didn't want to criticise. It was unusual that he'd done things this way. His usual approach was upfront and straightforward. Rarely anything unexpected with him. She was glad she'd held her fire but it had better be good.

She stood up from the table and gathered the plates and cups. Disappointed at the low-key nature of the celebration the embers were still smouldering, only half doused. But then he didn't seem to remember it was to be a celebration. To him it might just be a dinner out. Nonetheless she would have liked a say in the choice of venue. She'd say nothing for the moment in case he thought she was ungrateful.

After his announcement she had gone to the wardrobe and debated whether to wear the navy or the maroon outfit. Selecting the navy one she took it outside, and giving it a good shake she hung it on the line in the hope that the breeze would get rid of the smell of mothballs. She possessed few clothes for social occasions as she had little need of them but the two good outfits she had, despite their age, were of a quality that rendered them timeless.

She couldn't remember when they'd last gone out for Sunday dinner. She'd worn the ensemble to a couple of weddings but it looked like there might be no more so this would be a good opportunity to give it another airing. Having waited weeks for him to bring up the subject of their anniversary and as he hadn't, and she wouldn't, there was no question of buying a new outfit even if there had been time.

It still fitted. It wasn't obvious if the soft cream inset in the V-shaped opening at the neckline formed part of the frock or if it was a separate blouse underneath. A

293

diamante-studded clasp cinched the fabric in to the low-slung waist. So long since she had worn it she had almost forgotten the feel of the soft fabric as it fell in folds caressing her legs

She laid the navy cloak on the bed and picked off the few spots of white lint from its fine wool surface. Pulling over the chair she climbed up to reach on top of the wardrobe and, easing the hatbox towards her, she stepped down. She removed the lid and took it over to the open window. Holding it at an angle she blew the dust from it and watched as most of it sailed through the opening. She ran her finger over the lid and checked. Still remnants of grey. She would need to wipe it with a damp cloth. Too long lying up there on top of the wardrobe. She needed to get out more often.

She went back to the box and took out the navy hat. She straightened the ends of the pale-blue ribbon that was tied around its crown. As good as new. Placing it on her head she cocked it slightly to the side and grinned at her reflection.

"Not bad, Cornelius, not so bad at all." He checked himself in the mirror. With one final tweak of his moustache he went down the stairs to the hall.

He handed the clothes brush to Maude to brush the collar of his jacket. She had to admit he looked impressive in his dark suit.

At the bottom of the stairs she turned to head through the kitchen and out the back door.

"Wait, Maude. We'll go out the hall door."

"Why? We never go out that way." She looked at him in surprise.

"For a change." He smiled and gave a slow nod of his head that was almost a bow. "Now that we're all dressed up."

He held the door and stepped aside to allow her pass into the front garden. Following her, he turned to check the door was firmly closed behind them. He walked down the paved pathway to where she waited at the gateway and took her hand. Threading it through his arm he placed it firmly in the crook of his elbow, giving it a pat.

"Are you ready, Mrs. Redmond?" Looking down and smiling at her, he linked her down the road. Unaccustomed to such a display of affection she never noticed the charabanc parked at the crossroads.

The rain started just as they arrived at the hotel. Inside, a fire flickered in the grate where they'd gathered, waiting to be seated.

The waitress addressed Cornelius. "If you'd come with me, please, sir. We're ready for you now."

He turned back and nodded for the family to follow down the corridor and into the dining room.

Maude knew this was special. All her previous annoyances had evaporated. She felt bad when she thought about the one-sided rehearsals of the row. She should have given him the benefit of the doubt. She'd guessed when he refused to tell her where they were going that he had something special planned.

The plates had been collected and they were waiting for the next course. He still hadn't mentioned the anniversary and she wasn't going to. She was happy now to wait for him to say something. He'd get around to it in his own time and in his own way.

They all thought there was something wrong when, after the roast beef dinner, Cornelius stood up from his place beside Maude. As he pushed back the chair it wobbled and he stumbled slightly. She reached out to steady him in a way that would have been ineffectual had there been a serious need. The clink of the cutlery ceased. His face was a bit flushed, reddened in the way it used to get whenever he was annoyed by one of the children. He rustled in his pocket and took out a piece of paper. Silence fell. There was no tapping of a glass to make an announcement. Silence just fell as all faces turned to look in his direction, unsure of what was happening.

"I'd like to say a few words." His voice came out in a hoarse murmur. He cleared his throat. "It's unusual to have you all together so I'd just like to say a few words while I have this opportunity. As you all should know, your mother and I have been married fifty years. But what you might not know is that they have been the happiest fifty years of my life." His voice wobbled.

Maude looked up at him, her mouth agape.

"I've never said this before . . . I've probably never told her, but your mother has made me a very happy man. And I just want her . . . I just want you all to know that."

The twitch at the corner of his lips was not visible under his moustache but as he glanced down Maude saw the smile in his eyes. A momentary thing but it was there. She was glad she'd held her fire.

Bridie had seen it too. How her father had looked at her mother. She hoped MJ would still be looking at her the same way in fifty years' time.

Cornelius lifted his head. He looked around him at the upturned faces, silent for a few moments as if wondering how he came to be standing up. He cleared his throat again and glanced down at the piece of paper in his hand.

"And I'm very proud of you all. Very proud indeed of each and every one of you. You may not be aware of it, but I am."

No eye contact was made with any one of his children,

just a general sweep of the room where they all swam in a mist before him. With a quick glance over his shoulder, he pulled the chair back in to him and sat down. He was aware of his wife's face turned in his direction, speechless, staring at him. At that moment he couldn't meet her eyes but he felt a tight knot dissolve inside him. He looked around for the waiter before throwing out the question to no-one in particular.

"Are they coming with the dessert or what?" He took a brief glance at her and smiled before shaking out his serviette, ready for the next course.

BRIDIE

Chapter 68

1923

The weak sunlight hit the bottom of the grave, throwing up a dazzle from the muddy brown puddle. The gravediggers had dug the hole the previous evening and overnight showers had caused the water to pool.

Bridie looked down at the yellow-streaked marly soil which had not allowed it to drain away. She wished they had bailed it out but if the rays were taking the chill out of the water that might be something. Even still, she didn't like to think of her father being delivered down there and having to lie in the cold and wet.

The occasional whisper broke the silence around her as they waited for the coffin bearers to take position. Men huddled on the periphery rubbing their hands as if to appear occupied while they stood there waiting. She heard the sudden rustle of clothing as people moved back to make a clear passage to the side of the grave for the priest. Arms shot out to catch a woman who, in her haste to make way hadn't seen the obstacle behind her and stumbled on the edge of a neighbouring plot.

A few gruff commands from self-appointed ushers were all that breached the hush of the gathered crowd as they waited by the graveside for the coffin bearers to take position. The priest stood silent, his hands crossed over the prayer book he held close to his chest.

She glanced over to where her mother stood and saw the tears running into the crevices of her weathered face. She murmured to MJ and began to move away. Two distant relatives stood between mother and daughter. Indicating that she wanted to move over to Maude, they stepped aside to allow her pass. Standing by her side, she felt her mother's arm slipping through the crook of hers as if for support. She looked down and saw the red eyes and crumpled grey handkerchief which Maude held just below her nose as if to catch the drips. Tightening the muscles of her upper arm she gave her mother a squeeze, not trusting herself to speak in case it released something long buried. The unfamiliar physical gesture seemed awkward, but she hoped that the bond of one widow to another was understood. That's if her mother even remembered. It could never have been said between them. United in grief, but each alone with their own thoughts, unique and precious to only them.

Although she stood beside her, with the hypnotic murmur of the chant Bridie's mind drifted from her mother. It wandered back to a time she was so overwhelmed with grief she could remember little of the wake and burial of Joseph, her husband of such a short time. Unable to recall who had carried the coffin or who had been there. The details of the whole event lost in her impenetrable grief. Her only memory was being held back by the two mothers, Maude and Stasia, as she screamed and struggled to go forward and into the grave with him.

She couldn't remember where her father had stood in that cemetery in County Clare. Was he beside her holding her or had he stood stiff and detached at the far side of the grave unable to show his grief? And now he himself was

299

being lowered down into the hole before her. Two graves, on opposite sides of the country.

Her alertness now to every movement gave Bridie comfort. She was confident that she would remember every detail of these last moments shared with her father. Here at his graveside she knew she would remember things with a clarity that was forever lost at Joseph's.

She had dreams afterwards of worms down in the hole, crawling on her husband's coffin, nightmares that the wood was rotting and the maggots were beginning to penetrate the softened timber. She always woke up before they managed to make their way through.

Pushing away the memory she allowed the tears to fall. Soft blobs of water quivered on her lashes for a few seconds before rolling down her cheeks. She could taste the salt as one entered her mouth, not sure for whom she was weeping. Slowly and silently they continued to roll as the men lowered the coffin to its final resting place, cleansing her inside and outside of all the sad things that had happened

"I'll take them with me and look after them for you. Enjoy your new life now. They'll be safe with me." It was as if her father had taken the weight of all the breakings of her heart into the grave with him.

As she looked down into Cornelius's grave, a spider crawled on the coffin lid. The sight of its spindly legs as it made its way towards the brass nameplate made her smile through the tears. Her father would like the company.

"There's no need to step on him. Sure isn't there room in the world for us all?"

She could hear his words when she went to crush a daddy-long-legs spider she'd found on the doorstep. She'd always have thought of the tall stately father of her childhood as her 'Daddy-Long-Legs' since that day. She would never have dreamt of telling him that in case he wouldn't have approved. She was sorry now. He might have appreciated the joke.

The movement, as a few people stepped forward, interrupted her reverie. The dull thuds sounded as each neighbour dropped a handful of earth down into the grave where they landed with a light thud on top of the coffin. MJ, having picked up a shovelful of clay, threw it into the grave to begin the backfilling. He passed the shovel on to a neighbouring man who did the same. Others edged closer in the hope of being passed the shovel and included in the ceremony, an honour equal to those who had been asked to dig the grave.

Bridie listened from her position beside her mother. How true the statements were and how comforting. She would never know what they had said about Joseph. Too late now to ask anyone. Nobody would remember. It was all too long ago.

She thought about her father's last words to her. He hadn't spoken all morning and she hadn't put any chat on him after she'd fed him a little watery porridge at breakfast time.

The doctor had been surprised that he'd survived the heart attack but had warned them to expect the end. Sitting quietly beside his bed reading her book she wasn't anticipating any conversation. It was the flutter of his hand, like a moth, the navy veins showing through the creamy parchment of his dry skin that caught her attention.

"Do you want something, Papa? What can I get you?" She put down her book on the edge of the bed, careful not to allow the weight of it near his body.

His eyes were open, looking at the ceiling. He shook his

head slowly and looked at her, his lips pushing forward in a silent "No," before whispering his last sentence. "You did a brave thing, Bridie, a very brave thing. That little child. Pulling him out of the water like that. I'm very, very proud of you."

Her eyes filled again now at the memory, a rare moment between them. She felt a hand on her shoulder. MJ looked into her face, eyebrows raised, questioning if she was ready to move. Giving him a nod, she glanced at Maude.

"Come on, Mother, I think we should move away now and leave the men to finish here."

The gravediggers had been waiting until they were sure the crowd had moved away a sufficient distance before the finishing off of the grave. Bridie could see they were getting fidgety. She hadn't wanted to see people shovelling the soil nor did she want to hear the heavy clods of earth landing on the coffin below or watch the spider crushed by the weight, but Maude had stood her ground. Now as she inched away she saw her mother bend down. She watched her take a handful of earth. Saw her pause before throwing it into the grave. Only then did she turn and nod to Bridie. She was ready now to allow her daughter to lead her away towards the pathway.

MAUDE

Chapter 69

It had been as the priest intoned the prayers at the graveside that it struck her. Probably for the first time she realised the true worth of Cornelius. With all the talk over the few days, the way the neighbours and friends had spoken of him had set her thinking. His rigid ways which had seemed boring, now transformed into endearing qualities, no longer annoying. His straightness in all his dealings. No hidden agendas. She had dismissed his twinges until the night he told her he thought he was having a heart attack. Too late now the guilt of knowing that he might not have been aware that she loved him. How could he when she didn't realise herself until this moment just how much. A good reliable man. A pity she hadn't recognised that earlier. Well, she did really, but she should have appreciated him more. Let him know he was valued.

No point in regrets now. Far too late for that. Plenty of time ahead of her now to look back and thank God for what she had had. She'd looked around at the gathering as they droned the decade of the Rosary. She'd hoped no-one could read her thoughts, as taking a deep breath she joined in.

A line formed to offer their condolences to the family.

Nobody seemed in a hurry as each approached to shake hands and murmur their sympathy.

"Sorry for your trouble, missus. A good man."

Most brief and to the point. Others chatted on, oblivious to those in the waiting queue who shuffled about a bit but seemed content enough to wait their turn.

As the villagers moved away, holding his soft hat against his chest, a tall, silver-haired man approached. He wiped his hands together and checked them before extending a hand to Maude.

"He'll be missed. You couldn't wish to meet a straighter man. Was very good to me when I worked with him in the barracks." The man gave a slow smile. "And I can tell you he'd a lot to put up with there. A lovely quiet man. Didn't say much, but when he did it made great sense."

People waved to each other across the cemetery, their expressions lighting up when they recognised a familiar face from long ago. Some skirted around graves to join up with friends and relatives they hadn't seen since previous funerals. Individuals gradually broke off from the groups and bade their farewells. The crowd gradually dwindled, people sloping off to resume their own lives, their duty done.

BRIDIE

Chapter 70

It surprised her that the weeks after the funeral hadn't been as painful as she had expected. Maybe because he was old, it was easier to accept his time was up. There was no unfairness about it. Maybe that's why when the incident happened it took her so much by surprise.

It had been busy all afternoon at the Farmer's Mart. People getting their bits and pieces before the store closed for the Bank Holiday weekend. From her position at the cash desk she'd watched him make his purchase at the counter where the screws and nails were sold, glancing over at him as she took the money from each of the customers queueing. Unusual for her not to make eye contact with them. Some of the regulars were surprised by her reluctance to chat. Not herself today. A bit distracted.

She wished she could leave her post, just for a minute, but there was no-one to relieve her. She could see only the back of his head now. Earlier she'd caught a glimpse of the turned-up end of his whiskers as he'd moved down the counter to where the garden tools were stored. She was certain it was him. But there was no rational explanation for it. Her mind flitted back and forth, trying to make sense of the impossible.

"Thank you, Murt. Here's your change. I think that's right now." She'd had to count the money twice after he'd said he thought she was giving him too much back. With a quick look over again at the back of the head in the distance she handed the change to the farmer in front of her, hoping he would just take it and leave. He had been there trying to engage her in chat for the past five minutes, allowing other customers go before him.

"Ah, go ahead, sure I'm in no hurry."

No customers behind him now, but he seemed disinclined to move.

"I think you've everything there now, Murt. Goodbye now and thank you very much. See you next week, no doubt?" She said it firmly and turned away, in an effort to get him to shift his elbow off the countertop and end his conversation.

"I suppose I'd better be off then." With an effort he heaved himself upright. "Enjoy your weekend then, Bridie."

"What? Oh yeah. You too, Murt." She came halfway out from behind the desk and, as he stepped aside to allow her pass, she was aware that he looked at her strangely. Disappointed no doubt that she wasn't in her usual chatting mood. She couldn't worry about that now.

It wasn't approved of to leave the desk unattended, but she had to. Just for a moment. Anyway, Murt was hardly likely to rob the till. She needed to get a closer look. Had to confirm it for certain, but she knew it couldn't be him. Her father was dead.

It was still bothering her when she arrived home. MJ laid down his paper and listened to her story.

"Am I going mad or what? I chased after him in the shop like a lunatic."

"Did he see you? Chasing after him?"

"Well, no, not exactly."

"Well, then, no need to worry and no, you're not going mad. I've often heard tell of that before. Sometimes you think you see them everywhere and it's not them at all."

"But I was so sure even though I knew it couldn't be. I went right up beside him and kept willing him to look around at me so I could see him full face. And when he did he was the image of my father. What must he have thought to see this one staring into his face with God knows what sort expression on hers?"

"But are you happy now it wasn't him?"

"Yes, of course I am. But the fellow behind the counter, the shop assistant, the way he was looking at me he definitely thought I was a madwoman. And we both know I've been there before." She raised her eyebrows and fixed him with a grin. "When the man left I had to tell him why I'd been following the customer around the shop and staring at him. What's worse is I have to go back in to work tomorrow – I only hope he hasn't told the others."

"Ah, no doubt he has."

"Apart from the lunacy of the idea, d'yeh know what convinced me he wasn't my father?"

"What?"

"Well, he had the *Echo* newspaper under his arm and Papa always bought the *Wexford People*. That was the only thing that convinced me it wasn't him."

"Wouldn't have been seen dead with it, I suppose?" Mickie Joe grinned over at her.

"Now you're laughing at me. Will you go away!" She nudged him with her elbow, happy that normality was restored.

Chapter 71

She'd had enough excitement in her life. More than her fill.

Mickie Joe was good for her in his easy-going way. Never looking too far backwards nor too far forward, he just went along with the comings and goings of the changing seasons. He reminded her of waves on a shore, the way the quiet lapping, regular and soothing, lulled her into her own natural rhythm. That was the steady disposition of him. It suited her. His solid companionship that provided the calm she needed to see her through the rest of her life.

He'd travelled a bit in his young days. Spent time in England as a labourer before deciding it wasn't for him. Not what he wanted to spend his life doing, nor where he wanted to spend his life living. He'd set himself a goal. Kept apart from those who worked hard over there and then in the evenings squandered their money in the inns. No, he was focused on making it count towards the life he wanted and so it was the money he made there that enabled him to buy the farm.

He never spoke much about it. There wasn't a lot to say other than he'd told her how he'd worried a bit about buying the farm. Not being from the area.

"What were you worried about? Sure wasn't your money as good as anyone else's?" she'd asked.

"Ah, well, you know yourself, the sensitivities about buying a farm."

"I do, but the family had all died out. What were you waiting for? For someone to come out of the woodwork and stake a claim on it?"

"Not just that. Some of the locals might have had their eye on it and wouldn't like a 'blow-in' outbidding them."

"Well, it lay there long enough for them to declare an interest if they were thinking of buying it."

"I know, that was the reason I went for it. But I had to wait a couple of years before I made my move. Just to be sure."

"Bet you're glad you did now." She laughed over at him.

He never asked Bridie much about America, apart from whether she ever missed her life in the States. She told him truthfully that she didn't. She told him about Mary Jo but not that she'd left her behind. Had left him believing the same as the rest of the family. Apart from that big omission, the only interruptions to her peace were the twinges of guilt that occasionally troubled her conscience. The fine detail of her history, the bits she had managed to omit, to push out and over the side, but they were small compared to the Mary Jo bit.

She told him about Joseph. The short time they'd had together in Clare. She had no problem talking about that period now. And she showed him the letters she still received from Stasia. The writing wobbly and the contents shorter now. Time had indeed healed that part of her life but she still liked to get the letters. Joseph's father was gone now. She'd been fond of Dan, a gentle man who seemed to understand her. So Stasia was now the last link to a life she could never say goodbye to.

She had given him the general outline of her life in America but was never quite sure why he didn't ask her for more detail. She suspected it could be because he thought it might be too painful.

She told him bits and pieces about things she did with Aunt Johanna and the places she saw and the people she met. Sometimes she felt the urge to tell him the full truth, but one thing that life had taught her was not to act on impulse. In the past it was rushing into things that had caused most of her problems. And she'd had quite enough of them. No point in ratchetting up more. Always best to sleep on things and review the situation in the morning and waking up to embark on a new day with MJ, it never felt right to tell him. In the cold light of morning she was glad she hadn't. Nothing to be gained. For either of them. Maybe it would only serve to invite a dark cloud into their life. That would be foolish. If he didn't take it well it would be a dark cloud that could never be blown away. Too much to risk.

Life had taught her a lot of lessons. Hard lessons for the most part. But there was something that life hadn't taught her or maybe it was just that she hadn't been paying enough attention. Something that she later realised. Nothing lasts forever. The bad spells – while they were miserable, they would eventually pass if you had the patience to wait and sit it out and keep yourself otherwise occupied. That was the best part if you just had the courage to hang in there. The worst part was that the same went for the good spells. They wouldn't last either.

Sunday was the day of rest. The day for catching up on the newspapers after Mass. Only the essential yard work was done, everything else could wait for the new week.

There was no football match being played this particular

week in the nearby field. The local team were playing 'away' and Mickie Joe didn't feel like going to see them.

"How about we go on an outing?" Bridie suggested after the lunch. "Might be the last picnic for this year. It'll soon be too chilly."

"Where have you in mind?"

She hesitated. "A surprise?"

"You've no idea, have you?" MJ laughed. "Okay, I'll settle for a surprise. But it better be good."

"Unless you've any brilliant suggestions yourself?" Bridie glanced at him. "No, I thought not."

"Well, that's me sorted then."

She headed to the kitchen and putting on her apron began washing the dishes. She shelled a few eggs she had boiled earlier and set to making a few egg and onion sandwiches. For the last picnic they had gone for a walk up Sliabh Buidhe, the yellow mountain – today she planned to go on a trek through Courtown Woods. If it was warm enough they could have their picnic on the beach. If not, they could sit in the shelter of the sand dunes at the cricket ground.

MJ came into the kitchen and leaning against the door frame watched as she packed the sandwiches into the basket. "Well, Bridie, who are the lucky ones that we'll inflict ourselves on this evening?"

Part of the pleasure of these trips was dropping in to visit friends or relatives for a chat and a cup of tea after their picnic. It was usually Bridie who had the contacts and knew where they'd be most welcome. The people who didn't have access to transport or those where age or infirmity had them confined to home. They were always glad to see them coming in with the news.

"Haven't thought about it yet. Here, pass me over a pot of that apple jelly there. It's on the dresser." She smiled at him. "We'll bring that to the lucky person. We can't go in with our arms hanging. Let's just see where the humour takes us."

They were both aware that in some houses it was better to avoid bringing up politics at all if a falling out was to be avoided. The aftermath of the War of Independence and the divisions between neighbours as a result of the Civil War provided plenty of material for animated discussion in most houses, even though the local skirmishes had long died out, although there'd be a few who'd never let it rest. In those houses it was wiser to stick to discussing general topics and farming prices.

It had taken years to reclaim the neglected fields but he was more or less on top of it now. One by one he had brought them back to usefulness, every corner salvaged from disappearing forever under a thicket of brambles. This autumn was the first year since he bought the place that he didn't have to spend all his spare time at the backbreaking work. It was down to maintenance now. He liked to sit on the granite stone outside the house with his mug of tea and look across the patchwork of fields, proud of his handiwork.

With an hour or so of his time freed up most evenings now after the normal farm chores, he'd spend it in the yard sawing up the branches and trunks of trees he'd retrieved from the last of the thickets and ditches that he'd tamed.

The shed was now full and the overflow pile of logs had grown to a mound in the farmyard. It had happened so gradually as MJ added to it throughout the autumn that he was surprised how large it had become and that was only the overspill. Probably enough to see them through several winters.

Christmas came and went with candles glowing in the windows of every house. Neighbours visited neighbours.

"Come in and sit down and take the weight off your feet. Here, I'll take your coat."

No question was ever asked as to why they had presented themselves at the door, even those who never called in during the year. The good coat and the hat were enough indication that it was a social call. The time of day or evening was the deciding factor as to what refreshments were produced. Whether it was a cup of tea and fruitcake or the bottles of whiskey and port. No-one was in a hurry. This break from the usual routine when only the essential chores were done was considered an unspoken but well-deserved treat.

They sat around the fire, often in the rarely used parlour, and in the short companionable silences between the various topics the visitors seemed content to watch the dancing of the flames reflecting in the ruby and tawny liquid of the glasses before another subject was introduced or the glasses refilled. The chat was interrupted only to feed or milk cattle or to take in more firing.

The callers continued for about a week after Christmas before normal routine was once again re-established. Year after year the season of house visiting was a period of relaxation welcomed by all. A pleasant interlude when all recharged their energies in time for the spring challenges that lay ahead for the farming community.

Chapter 72

1929

Bridie pulled back the heavy dark curtains. Although still early it was bright outside. Not the normal brightening of dawn, but the ghostly grey-white thrown up by an early morning landscape covered in snow, as yet untouched by the rising sun.

MJ had already gone out to the yard. She'd felt him get up earlier as he heaved himself out of the bed. Too early for her, she pretended to be asleep as he took his trousers, shirt and jumper down to the kitchen so that he wouldn't disturb her. She had heard him padding out of the room as she turned over for another few minutes' sleep, rolling into the warmth he'd left behind.

The fire was glowing when she arrived down to the kitchen and his boots were gone. Once she'd set the table and the porridge was almost ready, she put on her coat. She knew he would be just about finished the milking by now. Normally she would simply open the door and call him for his breakfast but the lure of the snow was too much to resist.

Outside she picked up a handful of snow and rolling it into a ball she went towards the barn. He, sensing company, looked up from the milking. Seeing her silhouetted in the doorway he was surprised that she had come out in the snow to call him.

"Out to help me, are you?" He smiled at her.

"Here's your breakfast!" Bridie laughed as she flung the snowball.

He ducked just in time to avoid the missile. "Oh, very funny, aren't we? I'll get you back for that." He made a run at her as she disappeared across the yard. Not quick enough to gather his snowball in time, it hit the kitchen door as she slammed it shut behind her.

The normal post-Christmas work activity had resumed, but it was hampered by the heavy falls of snow that continued throughout most of the days. It covered the countryside with its silent white blanket. Beautiful to look at but a menace to farming. Most of the animals still remaining in the fields had to be brought indoors and farmers spent a lot of their time checking on them. Even with all the precautions MJ had already lost two ewes that had fallen into ditches and got buried in the snow, unable to get up off their backs. Machinery was buried and many vehicles remained only recognisable by their shapes. Drifts of snow totally covered the overflow woodpile in the yard. With no access to it they were reliant on the stocks inside the barn. He was glad now, as the snows showed no signs of abating, that he had managed to get so much of it into dry storage. Even now he could see how the mounds were already beginning to recede.

There was something surreal about this state of 'almost' isolation. The remoteness from the town and the outside world which was forced upon them had local communities drawing closer together – the fact that they could only travel to places within walking distance was, in its own way, a unifying force. Neighbours called more frequently to each other's houses. There was something comforting in this. Bridie loved it, particularly as she'd already begun to miss the Christmas visitors. Those who weren't reliant on the weather to get their work done enjoyed the unexpected lull imposed upon them by nature so soon after the festive season. A rare gift.

With no end in sight after weeks of prolonged snow they took to organising the dinner in a different neighbouring house every couple of days. Bridie and Mickie Joe made it on Monday, the next-door farmers provided it on Wednesday, the seafarers did it on Friday with their catch of the day if they managed to go out in their boat. They went to her mother's house for the Sunday dinner. She'd go over early to do most of the preparations as Maude had slowed up, no longer wanting to take on the job of catering for more than just herself. It was more for the change of scenery that they included her in the rota as it kept cabin fever at bay for everyone and added a bit of interest.

The kitchen was dark when she came down in the morning. She was surprised. The curtains were open and the dawn should have been well in at this stage. It would have been a strange thing to do, but she wondered if MJ had stacked something outside, blocking out the light. As she approached the window, it took only seconds to realise that what she was looking at was snow, packed right up against the glass. The windows were buried under the overnight snowfall.

Opening the door she was met with an almost translucent wall that reached above the top level of the door. As if sensing the gap it began to move slowly like a silent grey-white ghost towards her. Realising the danger, she shoved the door closed quickly, just in time to stop it collapsing into the kitchen. She leaned her full weight against it to force it to close the last quarter-inch. She felt the strain on it as she slid the bolt closed. Reaching up she slid the top one across also in the hope it would take the weight. She had a vision of the door splintering and the avalanche invading the room.

She ran up the stairs to the bedroom. How high did it reach? The house couldn't possibly be buried, or could it? As she reached the door relief flooded her. She could see the leaden sky through the window. Running over she opened it and leaned out. The house was submerged up to the first floor like a ship frozen in a sea of ice.

She worried that MJ hadn't arrived home the previous night. Light flurries of snow danced in the cold evening air as he left to walk to the pub. Neither of them thought much of it because he had worn his hat and was well wrapped up in the thick woolly scarf she'd given him at Christmas. She had knitted it in black and yellow, the colours of the local Gaelic football and hurling teams.

She watched his footprints leave holes in the driveway as he turned back to wave before heading off into the night. When she next looked out, they had disappeared as if he had been a phantom. Back in the kitchen, she banked up the fire and picked up her knitting. She was tired but enjoyed setting herself little challenges. A few rows each night, some with a design, most plain. Tonight's was a diamond pattern. She followed it closely. Concentration was needed to ensure she wasn't a stitch out in any row. Didn't want to end up with a wobbly outline.

She wasn't sure when she'd fallen asleep, hadn't felt herself drift off. No idea for how long before she heard the loose tinkling sound on the floor. She sat up with a start. On her knee was the knitting. The ball of wool had fallen to the floor and the taut stretch on it had pulled half the stitches off the needle. She reached down to pick up the ball and other needle from the floor and began working at it to try and catch the escaping stitches before they unravelled her entire evening's work.

She listened. Not a sound. MJ mustn't be home yet. He'd have woken her had he come in. Would never have left her there, asleep in the armchair for the night. No coat on the back of the door. She went to the window and parted the heavy brocade curtains. Although it was dark the white sheets of snow, falling thickly, were visible but so thick that she couldn't see the outline of the tree she knew was about six feet from the window. With visibility so poor there was no point in putting on boots to walk as far as the road to check if he was coming. Maybe he'd stayed the night with a friend who lived near the pub. That had happened before when the roads were flooded one winter and you'd have needed a boat to get home.

Knowing he'd have taken the sensible option she went to bed. Not entirely happy.

Mickie Joe was missing for a week. He simply went out that evening and never came home. He was last seen leaving the pub, worried that the snow was getting heavier and he had a mile walk in front of him.

Bridie turned into a statue. They managed to get word to the police station as she remained frozen in shock unable to do anything. Her mother kept the fire going but Bridie remained speechless in the armchair. It was happening again.

"Come now, Bridie, and we'll cook a bit of dinner." Maude tried to get her moving.

"I'm not hungry." All Bridie wanted was to be left to her own thoughts.

"Well, I am, so come on now and wash those spuds

there while I'm doing the carrots."

She stood up. It was easier to comply with her mother's demands than have a row.

Ignoring the fact that her daughter was irritated by her interference Maude continued to push in order to keep her occupied. Better annoyed and occupied than idle and distracted with worry.

The locals questioned her for clues as to where he might have gone if he had got caught in the snow storm. They got no new answers, nothing that they hadn't already checked out. Despite all efforts they had no luck in locating him.

As the snows began to thaw the neighbours kept up the search for MJ. The statue in the armchair came to life when the shout was heard from outside.

"*We've found him!*"

Jumping up, her heart rising in her chest she ran to the door, expected to see him in his hat and black and yellow scarf coming up the driveway.

One of the men caught her as she hurtled through the door to greet her husband.

"Hold on, Bridie, hold it a minute."

Two neighbouring farmers were standing by the trailer which had stood, half buried on the north side of the barn. Bridie escaped her captor's hold and ran towards the men, slipping and sliding on the half-melted ice. The thaw had been slow. High piles still remained in the shaded areas while around the house the snow had turned to slush.

She saw the scarf first. Just the tail of it lying in a grey puddle of melted snow. It was attached to something still hidden by a mound. That something, revealed as the men shovelled aside the snow, was the body of Mickie Joe Doyle.

The first thing they uncovered was the heel of his boot, where he had tripped, catching his instep in the towbar of the trailer before cracking his skull on the wall of the barn.

Chapter 73

Apart from the occasional few sentences Bridie rarely spoke much again. Well, not full conversations anyway. Didn't seem interest in engaging with anyone. Apart from the essentials there was no need. She had more than enough to think about. When she did speak it was only when strictly necessary and even then, it came out as little more than a whisper.

"Ah, it must be the shock. But sure she'll come round eventually."

What they didn't realise was that once the initial horror of his accident had passed she just settled into a life of acceptance. She had nothing more to say.

There were three Bridies. It was like her life had conveniently split into three compartments. Looking back, it was as if each section contained a totally different person.

From the distance, the Clare life seemed bitter sweet. Something to be taken out and hugged every so often. The end bit only bearable now when viewed through the frosted glass of time.

As for the 'American' Bridie? That was very different. The key to that box had been lost, deliberately thrown away, never to be opened again. Ever since Mary Jo had gone. It seemed best to leave it like that.

And the 'after America' one. With no big expectations, contentment had been enough and she'd had that by the barrowload. That life had been the least problematic, even now that the worst had happened. It was hard but all the sharp edges had been dulled. None of the gut-wrenching agony of before. She was just thankful she'd had it. This last Bridie – she could live with herself.

She missed him hugely on a day-to-day level. The companionship. His little kindnesses and surprises. His gentle humour. But life itself had deadened the full force of grief she should have felt at his loss.

Her father's words from somewhere in the past about what doesn't kill you making you a stronger person. She'd always thought that a bit of a nonsense. But maybe that's what her life had been about. All the knocks she'd had, maybe they'd been for something after all.

The loneliness was hard but the pain not as sharp. Even the guilt was dulled. The shame that she didn't feel more at his loss. Not something she could admit to anyone. How could she be believed that she had loved him? But she really did. The guilt of not experiencing the devastation. Not a good feeling, but easier than the alternative.

In the months that followed, what they expected to see and did not see, puzzled them. No tears, no shadow settling on her face in a melancholic moment. Instead, when a visitor arrived she acknowledged them with warmth in her eyes and listened to their conversation. Not engaging much verbally, just now and then a gentle nod of her head to show she was with them. Some felt uncomfortable with her silence and only came along with another neighbour so they could talk amongst themselves and include Bridie with an occasional glance or comment in her direction.

"Isn't that so, Bridie?"

"You must remember that, Bridie."

They knew she was content enough with this, and the 'I remember it well' response was simply to satisfy them. That she was at ease simply listening to the chat around her. They knew she required no more of them.

The gaps between social calls from those who felt uncomfortable lengthened until they found themselves not visiting.

"Oh, I haven't called in to Bridie for ages. I feel bad about it. I must make the time to call soon."

Always the same answer to any query about her. But they wouldn't. They meant to but it became too difficult, too much of a duty call and they knew that others did drop in to keep her company in the long evenings. She wasn't relying on them. They eased their conscience with the knowledge that they'd seen her out and about with the chores around the yard and in the village doing her shopping and they'd passed the time of day with her. They were satisfied that she was safe.

The ones who still visited were those who had learned to relax with her in silence when the one-sided conversation was spent. They knew she just needed someone to sit with her and share the calm quietness. The tick of the clock. The click of the knitting needles. The birdsong as they sat with her outside under the apple tree on a summer's afternoon or the patter of the rain on the sitting-room window when the north wind was blowing. Nothing more than that.

These companions were often rewarded when the beauty of her youth sometimes wafted across her face in a faint smile as her mind took her to another time and place. They knew not where. At times when they got up to leave, she would reach out and indicate with a gentle wave of a hand that she would like the company to continue.

"Won't you stay awhile longer?" A quiet request before she would stand up to fill the kettle.

How might she have fared had Joseph lived? Her lovely Joseph. Would they have been the perfect couple? All it took was the smell of clover or a few lilies brought in by a visitor to transport her back to her grandmother's garden in Clare. A few herrings from a neighbour were enough to remind her of Joseph's wind-burnt face. Forever young, it now brought her a peace she thought was gone from her for all time. A life that seemed more a fantasy now that all the pain had gone. Maybe the memory was all it was ever meant to be. Something that she could turn over and over again, only watching the good parts, allowing herself to drift into a doze before she got to the end.

Mickie Joe would never have been in her life had she and Joseph survived. He came at a stage when she was ready for him. Had he happened first he might have seemed dull to the Bridie of that time. A Bridie who was looking for romance and excitement. No, she would not have been mature enough to appreciate his quiet qualities. He would have been wasted on her.

Faces floated into her head as did places. Sometimes just momentary thoughts drifting through. No anchor to fix them long enough so she could look at them in detail. Other times she managed to hold them as if on a silken thread, long enough to give her comfort and keep her entertained as if they were part of a heavenly dream

It was easier now to read her life from this distance. Counting the good things. They stacked up well. There had been times she hadn't been able to see them at all. Sometimes it felt that they had happened to someone else.

h the bad bits had been the difficulty. But
d. Sometimes, just about, in a speed wobble,
side to side out of control, falling down black
uggling to climb out. But she had done it. She
was glad she hadn't given up.

She now knew what her grandmother meant. Mary
Ann's wisdom had gone over her head at the time. "Life is
but a series of obstacles. The challenge is how best we deal
with them." She could still hear her voice.

All those years ago the news of the death of little Mary Jo
from tuberculosis had come at her like a knife. But she could
tell no-one. They all thought the child was long dead, long
before the letter arrived. Just one thread in her web of
deceit. Another knock she would have to bear alone. Even
when the letter came from Seán she had showed it to no-
one. She could show it to no-one. She had simply read it and
replaced it in the envelope. She remembered leaning
forward and poking the edge of the envelope between two
sods of turf as if it were yesterday, holding it there for a
minute as the edges charred. Saving it would not have
brought her daughter back. Holding it there, waiting until
the flame had taken before removing it from the fire, its
orange light licking up the side of the envelope as she
watched the letter disappear bit by bit. The light dying and
the flakes of black dropping onto the hearth.

If there was one other lesson she'd learned, it was that
there's always a price to pay if you don't stick by the rules.
Sometimes it is insignificant, but sometimes it is so enormous
that your brain can't accommodate the sheer magnitude. If
you processed the real cost your heart might explode.

Losing Mary Jo was the one with the biggest cost.
Losing her in life had been worse than losing her in death.
Maybe if she'd stuck by the rules it might have been easier.
She could have talked about it at least when she got the

letter from Seán. Doing things her way had made the obstacles higher. But she had scaled them. Managed to stay alive after each to face the things that followed

She'd never thought to weigh them up before – the good and the bad. She could see it all, the profit and loss columns, clear as day. The ledger now showed very much in her favour. She'd had a good life, made the best of it and had managed to tip the balance.

She often wondered about Mary Ann's Flora. Ever since her deathbed revelation they all wondered. The clues had been too sparse and came too late to piece the story together. The threads of her grandmother's secret had been passed on to weave their way into another generation. Who would have known that Mary Ann had her own private sorrow to deal with? She had been right. How you dealt with the sorrows, how you survived. Maybe that was the point of the whole exercise.

It all made sense now.

Epilogue

Wexford
1978

She died in her bed just short of her hundredth birthday aware in her last hour that she was slipping away in a gentle drift into the next world.

Bridie would never have described herself as lucky. Amongst the last thoughts that floated across the surface of her mind was the Centenarian's Bounty cheque for £50 paid by the President of Ireland. It amused her. The fact that she would be missing it by a few weeks gave her a smile, traces of which were still on her face when they found her.

THE END

Coming Spring 2022

LIVES
REUNITED

Book 3 in the '*LIVES*' Series.

Quiet, gentle Catherine falls for the charming but controlling Thomas who manages to destroy the family in a way that no-one could ever envisage.

Reveal a terrible secret and destroy the family or stay silent? What would you do?

Set in Ireland in Counties Clare and Wexford

Printed in Great Britain
by Amazon